A Ruby Taylor Mystery

ROMANCE RUSTLERS AND
THUNDERBIRD THIEVES

Sharon Dunn

Kregel
Publications

Romance Rustlers and Thunderbird Thieves: A Ruby Taylor Mystery

© 2003 by Sharon Dunn

Published by Kregel Publications, a division of Kregel, Inc., P.O. Box 2607, Grand Rapids, MI 49501.

Library of Congress Cataloging-in-Publication Data
Dunn, Sharon
Romance rustlers and thunderbird thieves: a Ruby Taylor mystery / by Sharon Dunn.
    p. cm.
  1. Women detectives—Fiction. I. Title.
PS3604.U57R66   2002
813'.6—dc21   2002144870

ISBN 0-8254-2496-8

Printed in the United States of America

03 04 05 06 07 / 5 4 3 2 1

To the outsider,
the orphan, the lost one,
the woman with a past:
The Father wants you back.
Welcome home.

Acknowledgments

Michael, thank you for being the best cheerleader and encourager of dreams and for giving me some of my favorite lines.

Jonah, Ariel, and Shannon Michael—you inspire me to do my best, so my children will be impressed with their mama.

To all the supportive people at Christian Center Church, thank you for your prayers, for extending me grace, for giving me a safe place to find healing, and for loving me when I was unlovable.

Nikki, for all your encouragement and support; Susie, for the prayer.

Uncle Bill and Aunt Kathy—this book is the fruit of your witness—thanks for being real.

To the Gathering Place coffee shop and writers group—for the honesty, encouragement, laughter, and good coffee.

To Kathy T.—for, you know . . . everything. My mentor, my hero, my friend.

To all who pray for and attend Mount Hermon Christian Writers conference—what a safe haven you have given me.

To all the wonderful ACRW women and men, thanks for weeping when I wept and rejoicing when I rejoiced.

To Stephen, Janyre, Dennis, and all the great people at Kregel—thanks for believing in me and the redhead with an attitude.

For my sisters and brother—look what God can do—all the pain of our childhood gave birth to my sense of humor and to this book. Thanks for making the journey with me.

To Mom and Dad—wish you could see me now.

ROMANCE RUSTLERS AND THUNDERBIRD THIEVES

Prologue

Ed Lawson didn't know it yet, but he'd just swindled the last woman he was going to swindle because the last woman he'd swindled was going to kill him. Maryanne, the current Mrs. Lawson, loaded six lovely pieces of cylindrical brass into her father's .38 revolver and set it on the dash of the yellow Pinto. The Pinto she had borrowed from her brother because Ed had taken off with her beautiful powder blue '57 Thunderbird, along with every penny Maryanne had managed to save. The creep!

Chapter One

I would later learn the entire tale of the jilted Mrs. Lawson, but the first time I saw Maryanne was in the parking lot of the feed store where I work. As I pulled into the lot and pressed the brakes on my green Valiant, my mother chattered at me from the passenger seat.

"Honestly, Ruby, you should look into Brian's disappearance. Laura and Brian were madly in love. There was no reason for him to leave two weeks before their wedding." She added in a hush-hush tone, "I think he's been kidnapped."

I rolled down the window and allowed the July heat to warm my face and elbow. Summers in Montana are why most people stay here. It gives us something to look forward to during the long, cold winters. Combing my fingers through my tangled red hair, I closed my eyes and basked in the sun's warmth.

I could feel Mom staring at me, waiting for a response. Laura and Brian were supposedly this ideal engaged couple who went to Mom's church. Apparently, they weren't so ideal if Brian had all but left sweet Laura standing at the altar. Experience had made me a real skeptic when it came to romance and men. I didn't know either of these people because I didn't go to church with Mom. Still, she somehow felt I should be involved in their lives.

She continued. "Laura's family, Brian's friends, *everyone* is looking for him. The police are writing it off as a case of cold feet. You have experience with this sort of thing."

"Experience?" I sat up in my seat. "So I typed reports for a private investigator 'cause he typed with two fingers. It was just a job. It helped pay for college. How does that qualify me to moonlight as Nancy Drew?" Actually, most of my experience during that time had been of a romantic nature. Slater Investigations was a father-son operation. I dated the son, Vincent, off and on for two years.

Mom's shoulders slumped. "It's more than I have."

In the silence that followed, I tried to stop myself from reviewing the facts of Brian and Laura's situation—and failed. The police were probably right. My little bit of investigative experience via paperwork told me that the simple, obvious explanation is usually the right one. Most likely, Brian had skipped town to avoid marriage.

I got out of the car, slammed the door, and poked my head through the open window. "Mom, don't be so transparent. The only reason you want me to help is so I'll get to know people from your church, 'cause you think that will make me want to go to your church."

"That's not it. Not this time. Ruby, please, I just want to help Laura and her family."

I felt a little twitch in my heart, just the tiniest of daggers stabbing the surface. Her voice held real angst, even fear. And it took a lot to scare my mom. Maybe she wasn't just trying to find some sneaky way to get me to go to church.

Mom's whole goal in life these days seemed to be to help people, and I wanted to help her. But what could I do? "Got to go get my check. Back in a minute."

I straightened up and headed toward the feed store.

Then I saw Maryanne.

She leaned over her back left tire, which was shredded. After loosening the bolts, she tore the tire off like it was a Cheerio, flung open the trunk, and yanked out a replacement. Her motions were deliberate and mechanical, as if she were tanked up on some wild PMS venom. Even at this distance she was scary to watch.

I went inside the feed store to get my paycheck. The place where I work isn't your standard fuzzy kitten, cute goldfish, can-I-have-that-puppy-in-the-window yuppie pet store, even though it's called Benson's Pet and Feed. Sure we have some small animals, mostly strays and orphans that my boss, Georgia Benson, takes in. But this is a real Montana feed store, and we specialize in serious commercial products for local farms and ranches. Most of our customers are leathery-skinned old ranchers who talk slower than molasses pours and have been in the business for longer than I've been alive.

I like where I work, though my mother thinks I'm wasting my talent because I have a master's degree in literature. The competition for jobs at the local university is fierce. At thirty and after all I have been through emotionally, a part-time job at a feed store suits me just fine.

I picked up my paycheck, spent a few minutes talking with Georgia, and sauntered back outside.

That's when I discovered that Mom was no longer waiting for me in the Valiant. She stood by the Pinto, offering Maryanne a cookie. Honestly, the woman can conjure up homemade cookies out of thin air. Mom held the cookie out at arm's length, like she was feeding a wild animal. Her long, salt-and-pepper hair wafted in the summer breeze. My mom is coming up on sixty, but she dresses like a fan who got lost halfway to Woodstock. On this day, she wore long dangling earrings and a flowing blue cotton dress with embroidery on the bodice.

Despite the attractive, lemon-yellow business suit and stylish hair, Maryanne had a crazed nervousness about her. She looked like a plus-sized Barbie doll having a bad hair day. Mom's new lost cause took the cookie, and I half expected her to shove the whole thing into her mouth at once like some fashionable Cookie Monster, not caring if the crumbs cascaded down over her clothes.

"Ruby." Mom gestured for me to come closer. "This is Maryanne. She went to all that trouble to change her tire, and now her car won't start. We should give her a ride up to Larry's garage. Maybe he can help her out."

Maryanne offered us a grin with lots of teeth in it. All kinds of sirens went off in my head. "Nutcase! Nutcase!" screamed a tiny voice. And believe me, if anyone knows a nutcase when they see one, it's me. I've dated them, lived with them—and been one.

I gave Mom "the look": sort of pointing with my eyes complemented by the subtlest of head shakes. My way of signaling that this woman was not someone we wanted to get to know better.

Mom smiled faintly, totally ignored my warning, and gave Maryanne a reassuring squeeze on her elbow. "We'll figure out something, dear." Not only does my mom take in orphaned kittens, she welcomes abandoned pit bulls.

She can handle both kinds of critters. Mom is a lot tougher than she looks.

When I tell people that my mom served ten years for embezzlement, they laugh at me. "Not *your* mom," they respond. "She's such a wonderful Christian woman." They don't know that she got started on this religious thing when she was in prison.

Mom squeezed into the back seat of the car. Maryanne sat in the passenger seat with her hands neatly folded and jaw clenched so tightly, I could see the strands of muscle in her neck.

Larry's garage was on the other side of town. Eagleton nestles in a valley surrounded by mountains that jut up to a huge arching sky. The town spreads out over about a ten-mile radius. Farmers' fields rest between malls and box stores. Since we had a ways to drive, I figured I'd better attempt a conversation.

"So, did you come to Eagleton to sightsee or visit relatives?"

"No, I came to kill my husband, the creep," she said matter-of-factly, as though she were offering the recipe for pineapple upside-down cake.

If I could have wrenched my head around and raised my eyebrows at Mom without Maryanne noticing, I would have. What we had here was an A-number-one nutbar. I'd tried to tell my mother. But does she listen to me?

"Oh," I responded in a singsongy, pleasant voice. What else could I say?

My mother hummed "Amazing Grace" from the back seat.

Great. I was stuck in a car with June Cleaver and the Black Widow killer. For the rest of the drive, I read the downtown store signs like they were great literature.

As it turned out, Larry couldn't get away from the shop to look at the Pinto for another hour. Mom knows Larry from church. Mom knows everybody from church. The people she knows who don't go to church, she invites to church. She calls this "witnessing." Christians, like engineers and computer programmers, have a language that only makes sense to them.

Don't get me wrong, I like Larry. He found my Valiant, a late sixties model, for only five hundred bucks and helped me get it running. He found Mom's older-model Caddy for cheap, too.

While we stood there in the garage, Mom said something about getting yarn at the craft store. She makes money teaching arts and crafts. She sells a lot of stuff at craft fairs and farmers' markets. Mom discovered two things in prison: crafts and religion.

My plan was to leave Maryanne at the shop. She was Larry's problem now.

"You should take her out for coffee," Mother whispered as she squeezed the tender muscle above my elbow and gave me a meaningful stare. My mother can still make me feel guilty down to my bones.

So I spent the next hour sipping espresso and listening to Maryanne tell me about Eddie Lawson. Only she called him Eddie-Lawson-if-that's-his-real-name. Maryanne cried all over her beautiful yellow suit. Something about those tears struck a chord in me.

The longer I watched the brown streaks from running mascara slowly form abstract patterns on her cheeks, the more her tears seemed to be mine. I felt the same pain in my heart as when Mom had asked me to help find Brian—only this time, the tiny daggers were drawing blood.

"I only knew him three weeks before we got married. I'm almost forty, so I pretty much would have accepted a marriage proposal from a gorilla. He was so nice—at first. I'm a bank teller; I don't make that much money. But he took it all," she sputtered. "And he took the beautiful 1957 Thunderbird my father restored for me."

She took in a shaky breath and gazed at me with big round eyes. Her lower lip quivered.

I reached over and patted her hand. My finger brushed over her wedding ring—a simple silver band. I clenched my teeth. Muscles at the back of my neck knotted. Couldn't good ol' Ed at least have given her a gem and some gold to wear around her finger? Suddenly, I hated Ed Lawson. I didn't even know him, and I hated him.

"I'm really sorry for everything that has happened to you, Maryanne." My sympathy for Maryanne mixed with my own past history with men, my own pain. Now I understood why my first impression of her was that she was nuts. I had done some pretty crazy things in the wake of breakups too, and no one had cleaned out my bank account.

Maryanne managed a faint smile, but her eyes still glistened. "Thank you for understanding."

Boy, did I understand. Deep down, I didn't think it was the money that bothered Maryanne. You can always save up more money. Ed had mocked the whole principle of marriage—that it was forever and that it was for love. This wasn't about money—or the car. No, she wanted to kill him because he'd slaughtered her dreams. She'd given him her heart, and he'd stomped on it and made it all dirty.

That kind of stain never washes out. You just carry all that distrust and cynicism into your next relationship. I've been through more than a few relationships like that, and I've got the footprints on my heart to prove it.

By the time our coffee cups were empty, Maryanne didn't seem so crazy.

There she sat, the jilted bride, wiping her eyes on a napkin with coffee rings on it. Now, I viewed her as less of a crazy woman and more of a soul mate. I had never been married, but I understood her searing pain.

"Maryanne, I'll help you find Ed." My mouth moved mechanically without me having to think about it. *And kill him too,* said that little voice inside my head. This would be my revenge for every man who had ever hurt me. If we could get a jury of twelve women, we'd never be convicted. Well, maybe I wouldn't kill him, just make him pay for what he'd done to Maryanne—and fix him so he could never hurt another woman again.

The news from Larry's shop was that Maryanne's Pinto was going nowhere in a hurry, so Mom and I invited Maryanne to stay with us.

Yes, I'm thirty years old, and I live with my mother. I was sixteen when she went to prison, so I figure she owes me a few years of mothering.

Maryanne and I kept our plans for Ed to ourselves.

Later that evening, Maryanne and I sat in the kitchen, eating reheated casserole and plotting. Through the sliding-glass doors in the kitchen, I could see Mom as she yanked weeds out of her flower garden. The play of the setting sun on her skin made her look like a soft-focus photograph. She worked vigorously, jerking out the weeds that threatened her flowers. When she finished one section, she stood up, massaging her lower back and smiling. Despite all our conflicts, my mother is the kindest person I know. Considering all we've been through, she has a peace in her life that I envy.

"So what makes you think he came to Eagleton?" I asked, turning my eyes away from my mother and gulping down my milk.

"He ran up a bunch of charges on my credit card before I canceled it. All the charges were from around here, and they were from stores that sell women's things."

Either Ed had a fondness for dressing in drag, or he was working on another conquest. His instincts were right in coming to Eagleton. Developers projected that Eagleton, with its ski resorts and nearby wilderness areas and national parks, was going to be the next Aspen. Nobody in Eagleton or all of Montana was happy about this. We're very xenophobic, and the price of real estate is through the roof, thanks to the influx of wealthy people who think this is a quaint little place to buy a second home.

To an operator like Ed Lawson, Eagleton was prime hunting ground. He was probably wooing some unsuspecting, rich single woman as we spoke. What a piece of work this guy was.

"Maybe he lives here. Did you check the phone book?" I suggested.

"I did that just as I got into town, right before my tire blew out," Maryanne responded. "No Ed Lawson listed."

"So maybe the best thing to do would be to track down the car. A '57 T-bird has got to be a hard car to miss."

Mom came in through the sliding-glass door with a bundle of pale orange irises in her hand. "It's such a lovely evening." She plopped the flowers in a vase and set it on the table. "I hope you don't mind, Ruby. I've invited Wesley Burgess over for coffee and cake."

I gathered the dishes together and hauled them to the sink. "Who's Wesley Burgess?"

Mom arranged the flowers. "Wesley is Brian's friend." She stepped back to look at her work. "I told you about Brian. The young man from our church who disappeared."

"Mom." I dropped a bowl in the sink to punctuate my protest. Unfortunately, it was plastic and didn't make the shattering crash I had hoped for. "I told you. These people are not my problem." Why did she do this to me? All of a sudden, I was fifteen again and arguing about staying out an extra hour past curfew.

"I want to help them, and I don't know how." She held an iris so tightly in her hand, the stem bent. "You're smart and capable."

I didn't know if my mom was trying to build my self-image or point out that I hadn't lived up to my potential. Then again, maybe she really just needed the help. She hadn't asked much of me since I'd been here.

With timing that only happens in sitcoms, the doorbell rang.

"That must be Wesley," Mother chimed as she swept past me to answer the door.

I love my mom; I need her. Two years ago, when she found me, I was minutes from a second suicide attempt. She came up the walkway as I opened the door of the car I was planning on driving into a semi. Mom refers to the event as God's divine timing. If that were true, I think God would have had Mom show up a lot sooner—like sometime before the first suicide attempt.

Despite all her religious hang-ups, some days my mom is the only person who keeps me from spiraling back down into depression. Other days, she's the one person who can drive me completely insane.

Maryanne excused herself, saying something about calling her father. Mom opened the door, turned to me as I entered the living room, and smiled. "Ruby, this is Wesley."

I knew Mom wasn't matchmaking. I'm sure she wanted Wesley to marry a "nice Christian girl." Still, my heart beat a little faster when Wesley stepped across the threshold and held out his sweat-free hand for me to shake. He wasn't your standard issue, shirt-and-tie, crew-cut, "can I get you a hymnal, ma'am" Christian.

With his long, curly wheat-blond hair and round glasses, he looked like a cross between Einstein and the lead singer for a heavy metal band. The man had eyelashes that Tammy Faye Baker would envy. And I swear, he batted them at me.

Sometimes in a bus station, library, or at a party, you'll lock eyes with a stranger and feel this wild surge of energy that makes your face hot and your throat constrict. I felt the same thing when I looked at Wesley. I'd sworn off men for the last two years. Partly because Mom made it a rule when I moved in with her, but mostly because a man was the reason for my attempted suicides. Even though my vow of celibacy was not hard to keep, it was nice to know I was still capable of feeling something.

Mind you, I had no intention of acting on those feelings. The abandonment-depression-suicide cycle that seems to come with all my relationships gets old after the first three or four times.

Mom went into the kitchen to get the coffee and cake. I motioned for Wesley to sit on the love seat, and I took a chair opposite him.

After a nanosecond of uncomfortable silence, he said, "So, you might be able to help find Brian? Your mother said you knew something about investigating." His voice had a warm, silky quality.

Where did Mom come up with these things? I only dated a private investigator and typed reports. That hardly made me qualified. I cleared my throat. "Oh, I know a little bit." Come to think of it, I'd dated a surgeon once too. Maybe Mom and I could set up our own little brain-surgery cottage industry right here in the living room.

Wesley continued. "I know a lot of people, including the police, think Brian just skipped town. But they don't know him. We've been friends since we were kids. He loved Laura more than you can imagine."

"Wesley, my professional experience is really—"

He moved forward in his chair. "Laura's family hired a private detective. He hasn't found anything. We've got every family member, every friend asking questions and looking around. Still, we've got nothing."

The tone of pleading in his voice made my chest tight. Now I understood why Mom had begged me to help. These guys were desperate. "I'll do whatever I can. I suppose the first step would be to talk to Laura after you tell me what you know. And then—did Brian have a roommate, or did he live alone?"

Wesley shifted slightly in his chair. "He was living with his parents, trying to save money for a down payment on a house." His voice faded, and he gazed out the window. One hand gripped the other.

I waited a moment before bringing him back. His friend's disappearance was obviously causing him distress. "Wesley, where did he work?"

Mom tiptoed in and put two dessert plates on the coffee table. Wesley continued to stare out the window. Tension showed in his jawline. He opened and closed his hands. Without a word, Mom sneaked back into the kitchen.

He turned back to me as if seeing me for the first time. "We worked together roofing houses." His eyes narrowed, studying me. The stare made me self-conscious. I moved my hand to touch my mouth, wondering if I had food in my teeth.

He picked up the cake and took a bite. "I appreciate you doing this, Ruby. I have to work tomorrow. I can give you Brian's address and Laura's. I'll help any way I can."

I swallowed a bite of Mom's chocolate cake. "It's no problem. I want to help." The unspoken meaning of my response was "I'll do anything for you, Wesley." I had this awful vision of me mending his clothes and making him cookies—anything to insure he would like me. I'd been down this road before. This was how it always started—the overwhelming attraction, and suddenly I was acting like a puppy dog with slippers in my mouth.

Put on the brakes, girl. Put on the brakes. I'd vowed never to fall for a man again. The ending was never happy for me.

A whirl of conflicting emotions fought inside my psyche. Part of me wanted to fall into his arms. And part of me resisted the urge to belt him across the jaw and tell him to leave.

Lucky for him, Mom came back in and proceeded with her "the church is doing this, the church is doing that" chitchat. Over the course of the next hour, I gradually pulled myself back together and began asking a few more questions about Brian, but nothing of any importance turned up.

And I still caught myself sneaking glances at Wesley, relishing the swirl of energy and emotion that physical attraction creates.

Mom gathered up the empty plates and excused herself to the kitchen.

I watched her pitter-patter out of the living room. When I glanced back at Wesley, my heart was going a mile a minute. My safety net, a.k.a. Mom, was gone. Now, what should I say to the six-foot-plus hunk sitting in my living room?

He ran his hands up and down his thighs. "So."

"So?" I said back. Just call me the wordmaster. Shakespeare would be envious.

He studied the artwork Mom had hung on the walls, paintings she'd done herself.

Finally, he stood up and sauntered toward the kitchen. I heard him thank Mom for the cake. He came back into the living room and offered me a smile that made my body feel like wax melting all over the furniture.

I followed him to the door. He was three or four inches taller than me; my level gaze met his chin. I'm five feet, eleven inches, so it's always nice when I'm not staring into a man's bald spot.

Wesley said good-bye and stepped outside. I watched him through the window as he swung a leg over his mountain bike and pedaled away in the gray dusk of summer. It had been ages since I'd felt any kind of spark for anyone.

A thousand wars waged in my head. In the past with each new relationship, I would tell myself that this guy was different. But the pattern was always the same: me making endless sacrifices, compromises, and personality changes, anything for the true sign of total acceptance—a marriage proposal and the promise of for- ever. I don't care how liberated a woman is, how financially in- dependent she is; there is a Cinderella in each of us. We want a man to say he'll love us forever no matter what—and mean it.

I gave myself a little pep talk and some mental slaps in the face. *I will not fall for him. I will not fall for him.*

With a sigh of frustration, I sidled into the kitchen. Mom had the photo album spread out on the table and was giving Maryanne our family history. I've seen her do this before. Mom's dialogue as she turns the pages goes something like this: "Here's when Andrew and I were married. Here's Ruby and her little brother, Jimmy, on their bicycles. Here's me in handcuffs and prison clothes." Usually, after Mom shows them the newspaper clippings of her and Dad's arrest, there's a long silence. And then Mom goes into the spiel about how she "got saved" in prison.

Once, shortly after Mom found me, we went down to Texas to visit one of the only women in the country on death row. Mom had written to her while she was doing her time. When they met, they pressed their hands together through thick glass and wept. The hour-long conversation consisted of them saying, "Isn't Jesus wonderful," and then they would burst into tears again. The whole thing made no sense at all to me. Why would someone drive for days to have a three-word conversation? The woman was executed a few months later.

"Your husband is no longer here?" Maryanne spoke hesitantly and pointed to one of the photographs. I walked to the table and looked over Maryanne's shoulder. The photo was of Jimmy, Dad, and me standing by Grandma's camper on our annual Yellowstone trip. Mom must have taken the picture. Dad kneeled with his arms around both his kids. Jimmy held up a small fish, and I displayed my stuffed bear that I'd gotten in the Old Faithful gift shop. Except for that embezzlement thing, we were the all-American family.

Mom's finger brushed Dad's grinning, two-dimensional face. "He died in prison. I was able to find Ruby through an old foster mother of hers and the university she'd attended in Arizona." Her hand rested on the photo album. "I don't know what happened to Jimmy. He ran away from a foster home, and none of the relatives or social workers could locate him."

Mom's deep breath was almost unnoticeable, but I knew what

it meant: a huge sweeping chasm of pain locked up in a second of silence. As hard as she tried to convince herself, Mom's becoming a Christian hadn't wrapped her life into a nice neat package.

She talked a lot about how sometimes the "healing power of Christ" takes time. I hoped for her sake she was right. The point was that she'd paid for her crimes with the lives of her son and her husband. All she had left was me. In the game show of life, I was a pretty poor consolation prize.

We put away the photo album, and I showed Maryanne the extra bed in Mom's sewing room. Maryanne and I talked as I changed the sheets on the futon couch. She'd brought a small suitcase with her. Apparently she had had the presence of mind to pack before she raced after Ed. She set her gun on the windowsill.

"Is that thing loaded?" I asked. My dad had taught me a little about guns when Jimmy and I were kids. The only time he ever spent with me was teaching us how to shoot.

"I'll take the bullets out if it makes you feel more comfortable." Maryanne straightened a corner of the bedspread. I watched her as she neatly tucked under the edges of the blankets. Despite the gun, there was something vulnerable and helpless about her, like those kids you see standing by themselves on the schoolyard when every other child has someone to play with.

Boy, had she come to the wrong place for help. I have this theory. Every time a tragedy occurs in a person's life—your baby dies or your marriage falls apart—a little piece of your soul gets ripped away. My soul must look like Swiss cheese by now. Maryanne's must be looking pretty ragged too, after all the damage it had sustained during the last few months. Even Mom's soul still carried a lot of scars—painful, irregular voids that her religion had never managed to fill.

I said good night to my new comrade-in-arms, fellow warrior in the war on romance, and trudged down the hall to my room. I fell asleep thinking about Wesley and those blossoming, obnoxious feelings of attraction growing inside me.

Chapter Two

Saturday morning began a little cool but quickly warmed up, becoming a perfect summer day in western Montana. The postcard-blue sky held just enough gently floating clouds to produce endless combinations of light, shadow, and color in all directions across the mountains around Eagleton.

I dawdled around the house for most of the morning, worked a half day at the feed store, and made mental lists of reasons why I should not become involved with Wesley and his friends. Finally, after a late lunch, I lost the argument. I can be such a coward when it comes to internal conflict. I called Brian's mother to let her know I'd be coming, and then I phoned Laura's place to say I would stop by before dinner.

According to Wesley, Brian Fremont's parents lived in a trailer park about five miles outside of town. On the way out, I drove slowly through several residential sections of town looking for Maryanne's Thunderbird. No luck. The search in the downtown business section proved to be just as fruitless. A T-bird is a hard car to miss and a difficult car to hide. I wondered if Ed had thought of that. Maybe it was parked in a garage somewhere or already sold.

Ed was probably working on a new conquest by now. After all, a guy had to earn a living. The thought made me grip the steering wheel even tighter. Maybe Maryanne was wrong too; she could have been the first and only woman Ed had ever married and ripped off, but I doubted it.

I hit the accelerator when I reached the edge of town. Fields, green with alfalfa and rows of potato plants, dotted the landscape. Older houses surrounded by corrals and dilapidated barns punctuated the area between fields. New, glistening metal pole barns were less abundant.

Eagleton is a place of contrast, the old juxtaposed against the new. The population is upward of fifty thousand and growing fast. Most of the people in the farmhouses I passed had been here for generations. They lived year in and year out just getting by. The rest of the population is comprised of new settlers who arrived with money, telecommuted, contemplated opening quaint art galleries, and waved large checks under the noses of the farmers. All the farmers had to do to get the checks was give up land and traditions they'd known for a hundred years.

The road signs indicated that Yellowstone Park was less than ninety miles away. I passed another sign that read "Glacier Trailer Park, 1 mile." I let up on the accelerator.

I suppose Mom and I fell somewhere between those two kinds of people. We weren't farmers, but the house we lived in had belonged to Mom's mother. Mom got the house and a little inheritance when Grandma died.

Yellowstone Park had good memories associated with it. Even with my parents' life of crime and moving around a lot, we came to visit Grandma every summer when she was alive. The annual excursion to the park was one of the few constants in my life.

The Valiant's blinker wasn't functioning, so I stuck my arm out the window and turned right into the trailer court, which ran parallel to the river. A circle of ancient evergreens guarded the twenty-year-old trailers. This was not one of your upscale mobile home estates. Gravel crunched beneath my tires as I slowed down to read the numbers attached to the aluminum siding of the trailers.

It has been my experience that all trailer parks contain pretty much the same thing: a dog or cat that belongs to the whole trailer court, a pickup truck on blocks, and a woman in curlers who comes out on the porch periodically to yell obscenities at her children who are out of earshot on the other side of the trailer court. I'd already spotted the dog and the truck.

As my car rounded the curve, I saw the woman. She was minus the curlers and instead used a frying pan for a prop. Her hair hung around her pale face in the ever-fashionable, I'm-growing-my-perm-out style. Brown, elastic-waist pants and a matching shirt in an orange-and-brown floral pattern adorned her plus-size body.

Resting the frying pan on her hip, she shouted, "Susan and Deedee, you get in this house and clean your room. Do you hear me? Your snack is ready." I looked around. No sign of Susan or Deedee. After a moment, the woman sauntered back inside, shutting the door behind her.

Then I noticed the number on the side of her trailer.

Ah, this was the Fremonts', the trailer I was looking for.

I parked the Valiant and searched for a path through the collection of bikes, empty flower pots, and car parts that surrounded the trailer. Mrs. Fremont opened the door before I had a chance to knock, and she opened her mouth before I had a chance to speak. "You the woman that's gonna find Brian?"

"Yes, I'm Ruby Taylor. I called earlier."

"Well, come on in." She smiled, revealing the most beautiful set of teeth I have ever seen.

Her home stood in sharp contrast to her teeth. Closed, avocado green curtains made the poorly lighted trailer even dimmer. The worn brown upholstery on the recliner and couch exposed the wood and wire skeletons underneath. Little girls' shoes and coats were slung over chairs and strewn across the floor. The air smelled of dust and cooked bacon.

The jars placed on the kitchen windowsill caught my eye. Each of the three jars contained a set of teeth floating in a thick, pinkish liquid.

Mrs. Fremont noticed my stare. "My husband makes false teeth. He brings his work home with him." She smiled, revealing her white, straight dentures. The smile was almost apologetic, as though she'd just confessed that her husband the mortician liked to bring bodies home and prepare them on the kitchen table.

Motioning me to sit in a kitchen chair, she plopped the frying pan on the counter. "Sorry about the mess. I clean other people's houses all day. I don't much feel like cleaning my own when I get home." She turned to face me. Again, the perfect smile. "Can I get you a cup of coffee?"

I shook my head and took a seat at the table. The word "cozy" did not come to mind when I thought of descriptive adjectives for this place. I needed to get down to business. "Do you have any idea where Brian might have gone?"

Mrs. Fremont picked a Barbie doll up off the table and stroked its hair. "He's run off." Still standing, she leaned toward me as if to share a confidence. "I know people think he's so perfect since he started going to church and all, but his father left me shortly after Brian was born. That kind of habit is in your blood. Laura is lucky he did it before they were married."

I glanced up at the teeth in the jars. "But your husband came back."

"Walter is my second husband. The girls, Susan and Deedee, are mine and his. Brian's father hasn't seen him since he was eight months old." Bitterness as thick as syrup flowed from her mouth. "Brian's car is gone. He must be gone too."

I didn't want to get bogged down in the details of her love life. I was here to find out about Brian, and I intended to stay on task. "Can I see Brian's room?"

The trailer shook as we walked down the narrow hallway. I have never liked trailers. Even if you fix them up and put a foundation under them, they still have that paper-thin feel.

Brian's room was an add-on at the back of the trailer, an eight-by-eight plywood box to sleep in. Several posters with references to Jesus decorated the walls. The nightstand by the bed contained a cassette player. His tapes were the same kind Mom listened to, as well as a few that were hand labeled "Preparing for Marriage."

Mrs. Fremont walked over to the closet and slid the half-open door completely to one side. The closet contained one gray suit and three white dress shirts. Brian's mother shook her head at the bare floor of the closet.

"Something wrong?" I prompted.

"Brian had a nice backpack and a sleeping bag. He always kept them here."

"Maybe he took them. When was the last time you saw him?" I picked up the photo on the nightstand: Mrs. Fremont with her hair neatly styled rested her hands on the shoulders of a round-faced man with a handlebar mustache. Two girls, probably three and five years old, sat below their mother and smiled at the invisible camera lens. Where was Brian when this "family" photo was taken?

Mrs. Fremont continued to stare at the bare floor of the closet. "I saw him Wednesday morning. He didn't have his camping gear with him. He said he was taking Laura on a picnic. She's a sweet girl, that Laura. Her parents are a little too goody-goody. It was Friday when Laura called me and wanted to know if I'd seen him."

"So he didn't come home Wednesday or Thursday?"

Mrs. Fremont stood up straight and crossed her arms over her chest. "I wasn't worried. Sometimes he stays in town with that Wes if he has to work a long day roofing." Standing on tiptoe, she ran her hand across the high shelf in the closet. "That was an expensive backpack, too."

Why was she obsessing about how much the camping gear cost? "Maybe he took it with him when he left Wednesday morning."

"I brought some folded clothes in here later that morning. I'm sure it was still in his closet. Besides, he had to work on Thursday."

I heard laughter in the hallway, and two girls, obviously Susan and Deedee, stood in the doorway. They were maybe three years older than in the photo.

"Are you going to find my brother?" The taller girl looked up at me through blond strands of bangs. I didn't want to point out that he was only a half brother, because she didn't see the same distinctions that her mom did.

"I'm going to try, and maybe he'll come home on his own," I offered cheerfully.

The shorter girl spoke up. "I'm going to be a flower girl in his wedding, and Susan is going to be an usher."

Deedee's hair was the same washed-out blond color as her older sister's, except curly, the tight random curls of a home perm. She wore plastic, pink-framed glasses and a necklace made from elbow macaroni. I predicted that in high school she'd probably be one of those girls who never dated, had only one equally unattractive friend, and read romance novels during lunch hour.

I knew because I was one of those girls in high school, except I read poetry. Being a flower girl in Brian's wedding would probably be Deedee's one-and-only shot at being glamorous. I felt a kinship with her, wanted to hug her and protect her from all the pain she would endure.

"The girls are excited about the wedding." Mrs. Fremont pulled on one of Deedee's curls and let it spring back to the child's head. When she looked at her little girl, I saw the glow of genuine affection on her face. I felt ashamed for having been so condescending about the condition of her home. What mattered was that she loved her girls.

Susan grabbed her mother's other hand and swung it back and forth. "I have a beautiful pink dress that Brian picked out for me."

All three of them looked at me in expectation as if I would suddenly jump up and say, "And here's Brian, right here behind Door Number One."

Deedee sucked on her thumb, and Susan swiveled one foot. Mrs. Fremont offered me a faint smile. The edges of her lips curved upward, and she didn't show any of those perfect teeth. My stomach twisted. A man was missing, and his absence had left a hole in these two girls' lives.

I said good-bye and offered some hopeful-but-hollow comment about Brian. I left them there in the plywood room to think about the wedding that wasn't to be.

After I slammed the door of the Valiant, I started the engine and pressed the "reverse" tab on the push-button shift. I pulled out of the trailer court and onto the highway. My mind buzzed. Why was I doing this?

Brian had probably just skipped town to get out of the wedding. Really, that was the most obvious and logical explanation. He realized he didn't love Laura; it happened all the time. I'd already put in a degree of effort. It would be easy to tell Wesley I had tried and then drop the whole thing. Certainly all the friends and professionals they had rooting around would find something.

Yeah, I could just give up, except for Susan and Deedee.

You can usually tell how people feel about you by the way they say your name. When Deedee and Susan spoke about Brian, their words were flooded with nuances of affection. When Mrs. Fremont said Brian's name, she almost spat it out. He served to remind her of a failed marriage. Maybe he looked too much like his father. I suppose she loved Brian, but she seemed more concerned about the dollar value of some lost camping gear than she did about her missing son.

About two miles from town, I was still thinking about Brian when the blue T-bird passed me, going in the opposite direction.

Dust swirled around the Valiant as I pulled it off on a shoulder, cranked the wheel, and pressed the accelerator to the floor. Valiants aren't famous for being chase cars; mine topped out at about sixty-five miles an hour. Two or three cars were in front of me, and none of them was a powder blue Thunderbird.

My heart raced, and I could feel an electrical charge of adrenaline pulsate through my neck, making my head tingle. My hands gripped the big steering wheel.

I was supposed to talk with Laura and her parents in town, yet somehow this just seemed more pressing. I felt detached from Laura and Brian's problems. But chasing the Thunderbird made my blood pressure rise. There is nothing like revenge, albeit vicarious revenge, to motivate a person.

A splash of powder blue darted past my eyes as I ripped by a bowling alley. Again I had to find a shoulder where I could turn around before heading back to where the Thunderbird was parked.

A few minutes later, I pulled into the gravel parking lot and sat behind the wheel, staring at the Thunderbird and wondering what to do next. Maryanne had described Ed as middle-aged with a small pot belly and black hair that he combed straight back. When she told me what he looked like, I had wanted to point out to her that he sounded like a real lady-killer. My sarcasm often gets the best of me. But that time, I restrained myself. I'm sure Maryanne had already had enough lectures about poor judgment. She didn't need another one from me.

While I was waiting, trying to decide if I should go inside and strangle Ed or call Maryanne and tell her to bring the pistol, a woman came out and opened the passenger side of the T-bird. From where I was parked, it was hard to make out any distinct features except for the red hair piled on her head in a modified beehive. Her hair was a shade of red that occurred nowhere in the natural world. Only modern chemistry could produce that metallic, candy-apple color.

The woman pulled a bowling bag and pink shirt out of the car. Good old Ed Lawson, he was a pretty fast worker. I wondered if he'd actually married the redhead or just proposed.

My muscles tensed at the thought. Maybe Ed was inside. I clicked the car door slightly open. This was for Maryanne and every other woman who had ever been dumped or chumped. At the very least, I needed to find out where he was. I'd decide on the next step when I had to.

The redhead sauntered into the bowling alley. I hopped out of my car and followed her.

The bowling alley, except for the lanes, was dimly lit. The redhead joined several other women in pink shirts who were lacing up their shoes. I never understood why bowling alley footgear looked like clown shoes. Couldn't they choose something in a subtle gray or navy?

I stalked around the bowling alley, searching for potential Ed Lawsons. There were no men except for the guy behind the counter handing out shoes. Tiny bits of white fluff by his ears accented his bald head. He had a beak for a nose and dark circles under his eyes. Brown, wrinkled skin hung on his skull like the fur on a shar-pei puppy. Somehow, I didn't think that Ed could change his appearance that much. Ed must have loaned the Bird to his new love, Red.

"You gonna bowl or you gonna stare?" The old man behind the counter had a voice like a campfire, dry and crackly.

I turned and studied the display counter the old man stood behind. There were bowling gloves with price tags on them and candy bars that were so dusty, I suspected they had been there since the Nixon administration.

I looked the old man in the eye. "Yes, I guess I'll get a couple of practice throws in. I'm thinking about joining a league," I lied. "Who do I talk to about getting on a team? Is it one of those ladies out there?" Please, let it be Red.

"That would be Doris. She's not here today. This is just practice."

He slapped a pair of clown shoes on the counter. "What are you, about a size eight?"

"Actually, I'm a size nine." I am almost six-feet tall and have the big feet to match.

The guy's nostrils flared in and out several times before he snatched back the size eights. I could see this was a big inconvenience for him—to actually give me shoes that fit.

With the intensity of a boxer's left jab, he shoved another pair of shoes across the counter.

I managed a customer-service have-a-nice-day smile for the man with no manners and gathered up the shoes.

I could feel my pupils getting smaller as I stepped out into the bright lights of the lanes, size-nine clown shoes in hand. I noticed that the Pink Shirts had their names embroidered on their upper left pockets. If only I could get close enough to read Red's real name. I could ask her the time. No, that wouldn't work. There was a clock on the wall, and I was wearing a watch.

I wasn't actually planning on bowling. In all the fantasies I've had about being a great athlete, bowling has never come up. I was just killing time while I thought of a way to find out Red's name. I pulled off my red-and-turquoise cowboy boots and slipped on the clown shoes. The shoes were huge on me. They must be a men's size nine. I glanced back at the counter. Or maybe Mr. Emily Post thought it would be funny to give me big shoes after I had demanded he give me the right size.

I laced up the shoes and waited for brilliant ideas to descend from the ceiling.

Trying not to draw attention to myself, I grabbed a bowling ball and paced up to the foul line and back, trying to remember some long-buried information about four-step approaches. Red and her friends were two lanes over. What could I do? What, what, what . . .

"Are you going to bowl or wear a hole in my floor?" The old man had snuck up on me. His comment made me jump. This guy would never get a job as a diplomat.

"Sorry, I was just preparing myself mentally," I lied. I would never be mentally ready to bowl. I thought about asking for a different pair of shoes but didn't think it worth the effort.

The man narrowed his eyes at me before returning to his antique candy. The less I had to deal with him, the better.

Any plan I had for remaining inconspicuous went down the drain when I bowled my first frame. Because the shoes were so big, my feet slapped the wooden floor as I picked up speed. I was not a very coordinated person in the first place. Being tall didn't help either. My first two balls rolled down the gutter.

The next frame didn't start out much better. I'd just picked up the ball when I noticed all the pink ladies staring at me. I smiled at them, swung my arm back, stepped forward, and let the ball fly.

My fingers never disconnected from the ball. It swung forward with my whole body attached. I really felt like a clown.

The hardwood floor was surprisingly soft to land on. Only my thirty-year-old knees felt the sting. I slid three or four feet and opened my eyes to a view of my fingers still stuck in the holes of the ball.

I heard the thunder of bowling shoes on wood, and a swirl of pink surrounded me. Mom says that God sets up circumstances that might seem bad at first but that turn out good. My embarrassment melted as I saw an opportunity to find out a little more about Red without her knowing I was on a search-and-destroy mission against Ed Lawson.

A chorus of grandmotherly voices greeted my ears. "Are you OK, dear? Do you need some help up? That was quite a fall."

I glanced around the half circle of women until I saw Red. I reached for her like a toddler stretching out her arms toward her mother. As she pulled me up, I read the name on her shirt, "Smith." Oh great, her name was Smith.

Up close, Smith looked like she was a million years old, or at least sixty. Ed Lawson sure could pick them. She smelled of gum-drops and cigarettes. Bits of gray peeked out between the dyed strands of red. On her shirt collar, a white crystal cat with a black beaded eye stared at me. The crystals caught the intense light of the bowling lanes and sparkled like Christmas bulbs.

"Is she OK, Gladys?" One of the women moved toward us. "I'm a nurse, honey. Is anything broken? Does it hurt anywhere?" Gladys's friend poked my rib cage.

All the aged faces stared at me. A dozen sets of eyeballs on me made me self-conscious. Embarrassment crept back into my emotional database.

"I'm all right, thank you." My cheeks burned. I'm sure they were bright red. On a fair-skinned redhead, this was not a good thing. Pasting on a Miss America smile, I grabbed my cowboy boots and backed away. My knees were killing me. Each step made me wince.

I sensed the heavy stares of the pink ladies as I slapped the bowling shoes on the counter. The old man said nothing, didn't even make eye contact.

Not wanting to spend anymore time as the center of attention, I clutched my boots to my chest and slunk out of the building. I gave myself a D- on my first test as an amateur sleuth: gaining information while remaining inconspicuous. On the other hand, if that had been an audition for Clown College, I think I would have gotten a full-ride scholarship.

Walking barefoot to my car seemed like suitable punishment for being such an idiot. Sharp little stones jabbed at my tender skin.

Mom says I spend too much time calling myself names, beating myself up. I crawled in behind the wheel and took a deep breath. I really had to get a hobby. Needlepoint or ceramics, something that didn't involve trying to fix other people's lives.

I was no good at this detective thing. I'd gotten the name of Ed's conquest, but she was going to remember my face for a long time.

Nancy Drew probably stopped playing detective long before she turned thirty. I would keep my word and talk to Laura, and then I was going to tell Mom and Maryanne and even the gorgeous Wesley to solve their own problems.

I revved the car to life, pulled out on the highway, and headed back to town.

Chapter Three

The Hollimans, Laura's parents, lived on what us poor white folks like to call snob hill. Once I got back into town, I followed the streets through treeless suburbia, past a couple of alfalfa fields, until I turned onto a winding road.

Trees surrounded the avenue, creating a tunnel effect. As the house came into view, I thought about that Puritan belief that said if your life was a mess or you had some kind of financial catastrophe, it must be that God was punishing you for some sin you had committed. And if you prospered, it was because you lived such a good and sinless life. Obviously, life isn't that simple. The formula doesn't explain why missionaries are murdered and inside traders get off with time served and community service.

But the Puritan belief certainly held water when I contrasted the Holliman mansion with the Fremont trailer. I parked my Valiant in the circular driveway, which was paved with cut stones. Centered in the driveway was a bubbling fountain. I turned toward the house and gazed up at the Roman columns and the huge wooden door, very 1940s Hollywood. I wondered if a deformed butler named Igor would answer the door.

I rang the bell and stared down at my khaki pants and white sleeveless sweater. Even if I went home and changed into a ball gown, I'd probably be underdressed. I rang the doorbell a second time.

Figuring the maid or butler must be elderly and suffering some sort of hearing loss, I checked my watch. My excursion into the bowling alley had cost me half an hour. Maybe they didn't have time to wait around for me; by now they'd probably left for a country-club date, or maybe their prize poodle needed to go to the beauty parlor.

A moment later, the door was opened by Mrs. Holliman herself, not the elderly maid or deaf butler. Mom had said that Mrs. Holliman was about her age, but the woman didn't look a day over forty. She wore jeans and a T-shirt with a Bible verse emblazoned on it. A smudge of topsoil marred the perfect image, but she had that same ageless glow that Mom has. Her silver hair was done in a short, wavy bob reminiscent of the Betty Crocker-fifties-housewife era. She held a muddy trowel as she wiped her brow with her forearm.

"You must be Emily's daughter; you look just like her." She stepped back, and a Heinz 57 dog, which had probably never been to the beauty parlor, nudged into the doorway beside her. "Please, come in. Sorry I didn't answer the door right away. I was out back, working in the garden. We'll go in the kitchen. It's much cozier."

Mrs. Holliman walked like she had springs in her shoes and high octane coffee in her veins. The dog followed dutifully behind her. She led me past an open living room done in hunter green, burgundy, and brass. There were an overstuffed leather couch and easy chair; sheer, purely ornamental curtains hanging on brass rods; and neat stacks of virginal *Architectural Digest* magazines decorating the wood and brass coffee table. This living room obviously was for display only; no one actually sat on the couch or read those magazines. They probably had a family room somewhere with wrinkled copies of *Popular Mechanics,* a TV, and a comfortable couch with coffee stains on it. Rich people can afford both a fake and a real living room.

Mrs. Holliman stopped at the base of a spiral staircase and called out. "Laura, Ruby is here; please come down." She gestured to me. "The kitchen is right this way."

In the kitchen, Mrs. Holliman pointed to a stool at the counter. I hopped up on the stool. Her dog, which looked like a cross between a border collie and a German shepherd, settled down in a doggie bed in the corner.

Bundles of drying flowers hung above me. The faint scent of roses and lilacs filled the air. Boots and shoes, from kid size to big-man size, surrounded the back door. Crayon pictures with huge-head/small-body people decorated the refrigerator. Picasso would have been jealous. "Mrs. Holliman—"

"Please, call me Gloria. Now, I have some lemonade or coffee?"

"Lemonade would be fine."

While Gloria poured lemonade and broke ice out of trays, Laura came in, introduced herself with a handshake, and sat on the stool beside me. Her light brown hair was pulled back into a French braid, which fell to the middle of her back. Freckles dotted her cheeks and nose. She hadn't put on makeup, but wore a denim shirt unbuttoned to reveal a white lace T-shirt, a denim skirt, and sandals. Silver hoops dangled in her ears. A delicately structured turquoise and silver bracelet circled her narrow wrist. She was slender, but not I-really-need-to-eat-a-pork-chop, emaciated model thin.

Laura took the lead in the conversation. She asked me several getting-to-know you questions, not in an interrogating sort of way, but because she was genuinely interested in who I was. This all seemed quite normal and chummy except for the fact that her fiancé was missing. I needed to get down to business.

I ventured the cautious question, "You last saw Brian on Wednesday, right?"

Laura's jaw dropped, and she stopped smiling. "Yes, that's right." She stared into her lemonade. The ice clinked against the side of the glass as she swirled it around. Maybe she'd hoped to push down the turmoil of Brian's disappearance with small talk.

As gently as I could, I asked the next question. "Did he have his camping equipment with him, a sleeping bag and a backpack?" The missing camping gear was the only incongruity I'd found so far, the only thing that suggested maybe Brian hadn't gotten cold feet. Then again, he could just as easily have gone camping to get out of the wedding. I didn't want to get hung up on his reason for leaving; I just needed to find the guy.

Gloria stopped bustling around the kitchen and leaned over the counter, touching her daughter's hand.

Laura turned the glass on the counter. "I didn't see anything like that. They weren't in the trunk either because I would have seen them when I pulled the picnic basket out." Tears brimmed in her eyes.

"Do you know of anyone who might have something against Brian? A neighbor? Someone he did work for?" I was really fishing. You don't kidnap somebody because he did a bad job roofing your house. That kind of stuff usually involved a lawsuit.

Laura shook her head. "Everyone liked Brian. He was fair and conscientious." With each sentence, she talked faster, slamming her words together without taking a breath. "He would never leave Wes to finish a job. He would never take off without telling me first. Never." The sharp tap of glass on wood punctuated her words as she tilted the glass back and forth.

I felt a hole forming in my heart in response to her pain. I'm a very guarded person, and I don't let people in easily. But I liked Laura from the moment she wanted to know more about me. I didn't like seeing her hurting like this.

Laura sputtered, mouth tight. Two tears streamed down her cheeks. Her hand, now gripping the glass, trembled.

Gloria scooted the tissue box on the counter closer to her daughter. Judging from the glassiness in her eyes, Gloria would need one of those tissues for herself.

"I'm so sorry." Laura rose to her feet and straightened her skirt. Her words came out in a hoarse whisper. "You'll have to excuse me."

Her footsteps pounded across the tile, then the carpet, and up the stairs.

Gloria held her hand to her mouth and shook her head. She pulled her hand away and rested a tight fist on her chest. "I've raised five children. You always have a special place in your heart for your baby."

"I'm sorry. I didn't mean to—"

"It's all right. Those questions had to be asked if we are going to find Brian. I'm at my wit's end with this. The police say he's not missing because he left a note for his mother. The private detective we hired said every lead is a dead end. We've given him hundreds of dollars, and even he says Brian got cold feet. Everyone who doesn't know him thinks he left because he didn't want to marry Laura. They've never seen those two together." She pulled a picture out of a drawer. "That's their engagement photo. You can keep it if it will help." Her fingers brushed across the photo. "Look how happy they are."

My mind backpedaled. "A note? What did it say?" This was significant. Why hadn't Mrs. Fremont said something? I glanced at the photo: Laura with her arms around a blond man, their faces beaming.

"When I talked to Brian's mother, she told me the note said that he would be back in a couple of days." Gloria massaged her forehead with her fingers. "It's already been a couple of days."

She snatched my empty lemonade glass off the counter. Frustration tainted her every movement as she scrubbed the glasses and stuck them in the drying rack.

She whirled around, dabbed at her eyes, and asked, "Are you hungry, dear? Would you like me to fix you a snack?" Gloria, everybody's mother.

I turned down the food, thanked Gloria for her hospitality, and left. I admit it; I left because I didn't want to see Gloria cry. I was afraid I would start crying too. With all that emotion floating around, I was bound to catch something. I don't like feeling like my emotions are beyond my control. Once, I took the phone off the hook to avoid saying good-bye to a friend who was moving.

The drive down the winding road gave me some time to think. Brian had gone to the picnic with Laura on Wednesday, gone home, written a note to his mother, grabbed his camping gear, and vanished. But if his leaving was planned, why didn't he tell Laura at their picnic? Something must have happened between the picnic and his going to pick up his camping gear. If his car was gone, like Mrs. Fremont had said, it really looked like he had just skipped town.

My old Valiant took curves like a frog rides a bicycle. I was essentially going in a straight line, hoping I wouldn't meet anyone coming up the hill. OK, so I wasn't going to drop the whole thing. Seeing Laura and Gloria all bent out of shape made me want to do something to help them. I was more like my mother than I wanted to admit. I vowed to quit getting on her case about wanting to help everyone.

My mind zigzagged more than my car. Maybe Brian wasn't as perfect as Laura said. I didn't want to push Laura; she was upset enough. Wes might be able to tell me something, and it would be a good excuse to see him. Mentally, I rolled my eyes and shook my finger at myself. *Remember your motto, Ruby. "All men are alike. All men are alike." Say it over and over until you believe it.*

When I got home, Maryanne sat on the porch swing, stringing beads. She had a pile of them in her lap. She held up a necklace of black, white, and blue beads.

"What do you think? Your mother got me started before she left to teach a class. She says it's very therapeutic." Maryanne leaned a little closer to me. "Do you think I need therapy?"

She asked the question, and a train of thoughts ran through my head. *Let's see, your whole life is centered on killing your husband, and you carry around a gun.* I took the last stair up to the porch and answered, "Those are really nice beads." We both had elevators that didn't go all the way to the top. I wasn't any further away from a counseling session than she was.

"Hand painted, your mother said." Maryanne held the beads up to her neck. "Seriously, what do you think?" My mother's unspoken philosophy is "craft your way to inner peace."

I studied the patternless pattern of Maryanne's beads. "Ah, very therapeutic."

Maryanne held the string of beads in front of her and laughed.

"A great artist I'll never be." She seemed calmer now than she had been yesterday. Mom has that effect on people.

I thought that maybe I should simply not tell her about my encounter in the bowling alley. But then my sense of justice reared its ugly head. It just wasn't right for old Ed to get away free and clear. And what if he was out there preparing to marry Gladys Smith and rip her off? It was up to us to stop him.

A confrontation with Ed would help Maryanne put this behind her. I think the counselors call it "closure." Maryanne needed closure, big time—far more therapeutic than stringing beads. I sat down beside her on the porch swing. I'd made up my mind. I would help her find Ed and keep her from killing him.

I told her about the woman named Gladys Smith and the powder blue T-bird that had to be hers. While I talked, Maryanne kept stringing beads, jerking them down the string and slamming them into the other beads with her lips pressed together tight and her forehead wrinkled.

When I finished telling her, she had about the same reaction I had had. "Smith! He's going after some woman named Smith? How many of those do you suppose there are in the phone book? Why couldn't it be someone called Obenbacker or Kronowski?" She swung the string of beads like it was a lasso. "I guess we've got to check out every Smith in town. You know what the woman looks like, and the car is easy enough to spot." Maryanne jumped up. "Maybe we'll get lucky and she's listed under her own name in the phone book." She ran inside.

Any calm Mom had managed to bring to Maryanne, I had chased from the house.

I collapsed in the porch swing, tucked my legs under me, and let the swing glide back and forth. It had been a long day, and it was only five o'clock. The chain and the wood of the swing creaked lazily. My coping mechanism for emotional overload is to sleep. I could feel my eyelids getting heavy. The soft billowiness of sleep fogged my head. My muscles relaxed. . . .

"Find out anything?" A distant voice spoke into my subconscious, soft and booming like waves breaking on the shore.

I could feel myself swimming up out of sleep. Voice recognition yanked me from lullaby-land to reality. My eyes popped open, and I jerked upright. "Oh, Wesley." I hoped I hadn't been drooling or snoring. Nonchalantly, I touched the corner of my mouth, searching for signs of saliva.

Wes had on jeans, a tool belt, and a royal blue T-shirt. His honey-brown hair had that wonderful sun-washed glisten to it, like someone had thrown a handful of glitter on his head.

"The house I'm working on isn't far from here." He pointed the hammer he had in his hand. "Thought I'd come by and see if you'd made any progress."

"Not much. Do you know anything about some camping equipment Brian had? A backpack and sleeping bag? They're missing from his house."

Wes shook his head slowly.

"Laura's pretty upset. I didn't want to press her."

When I told him about the note, a slow smile came over his face. "He's gone up to the cabin. That's got to be where he's at."

"The cabin?"

"It's a Forest Service cabin. We use it for a base camp when we go hunting or rock climbing. He was talking about taking Laura up there for their honeymoon. If the note said a couple of days, maybe something has happened. Maybe he got hurt. We've got to go up there. I can finish up with this job . . ." He looked at me expectantly.

All I heard was the word "we," and a vision of a romantic weekend in the woods floated across the libido part of my brain.

Bad girl. Bad girl.

"I can probably get a few days off from the feed store," I said calmly and cleared my throat.

Maryanne came back out on the porch, holding a phone book. Wes greeted her with a nod as she sat down on the swing beside me.

"Well, we'll plan on that then." He headed toward the sidewalk. "Maybe we shouldn't tell Laura until we know something more definite."

I nodded and watched him stroll out of sight. He walked with his shoulders back, leading with his chin, an easy, confident stride.

"Nice-looking guy," Maryanne commented when he was out of earshot.

I inhaled deeply. "You're telling me."

She flipped the phone book to the white pages. "There must be a hundred Smiths." Maryanne picked up the pencil she'd brought with her. "I don't see any Gladyses or even G. Smith. Of course, it wouldn't be that easy. We can eliminate the ones that have a man's and woman's name listed together." She checked off several names. "Let's start with the first four or five that aren't crossed out."

"We could do five houses a day. But she could be a widow still listing her phone number under her husband's name. If we don't find her by the time we get to the bottom of the list, we'll have to check out the crossed-off ones." I tilted my head back and stared at the sky. A cloud in the shape of Elvis floated by. I'd have to call one of those tabloids and let them know. I could see the headline: "Elvis Spotted in a Small Montana Town."

"We have to start somewhere. Tomorrow is Sunday. Most people will be home." Maryanne continued to cross out names as the swing creaked back and forth.

⌒

The next morning, while Maryanne took a shower, Mom and I performed the routine we do every Sunday. I sat at the kitchen table reading my comics and sipping my coffee. Mom came around the corner, dressed in her lavender suit and smelling like roses and vanilla. She hung her blazer over a chair and held out her hand for me to button the cuffs on her blouse.

"Are you sure you don't want to come to church with me?" she asked as she poured herself a cup of coffee.

I gave her the same answer I always give. "I don't think so, Mom. Maybe next Sunday."

"All right, dear." Like always, because it's part of the routine, she paused and stared at me for a good long time.

I looked up from my paper. I can never catch her lips moving, but I am pretty sure she is praying for me during that pause. My mind shifted gears. I found myself hoping my face looks as good as hers when I'm sixty. She doesn't have the usual shriveling apple skin most older people get. Maybe it's her unclouded blue eyes or natural beauty—Mom's expression always holds a bright, dancing hope.

"Anything interesting in the paper?" she asked.

Usually I read her a comic or tell her about one of the headlines. I never read whole news stories, just the headlines. Today, I told her about a short article describing how buffalo numbers are down in the park and fewer seem to be wandering out of the park. I deduced all this by skimming the article. Then I read her the *B.C.* comic.

She laughed after I finished reading the comic strip. "I wish they still had *Calvin and Hobbes* in the paper. That Calvin is such a mischievous little boy. He reminds me of your brother, Jimmy, when he was little."

Jimmy, my younger brother who has fallen off the face of the earth. Mom is always being asked to give talks at churches about her prison time and her conversion. When she gets to the part where she tells about being reunited with me but not being able to find Jimmy, she pauses and stares out into the audience. I think she keeps waiting, hoping for Jimmy to come screaming down the aisle yelling, "Mom, it's me! I've come home!"

Mom slipped into her blazer and tugged at the cuffs. Her motion was a little too jerky, a little too persistent to assume she was just straightening her sleeves.

I smoothed out the newspaper. "I miss him too, Mom." The newsprint in front of me blurred.

She gazed at me for a moment without saying anything. When she did speak, her voice fluttered like sheets on a clothesline in the wind. "Sometimes it feels like my past will consume my future."

Ice crept into the chambers of my heart. I swallowed hard. Every once in a while, I catch glimpses of the enormous pain Mom battles. Much as I wanted to, I couldn't think of any words that offered comfort.

Mom squared her shoulders and smiled at me. The sparkle returned to her expression, but I still saw darkness behind her eyes. "Thanks for sharing the comics with me." She kissed me on the temple just like she does every Sunday morning. "I guess I'll see you at lunchtime. I love you, honey."

Her heels clicked across the linoleum, and then I heard the door open and shut. I returned to my paper while her Cadillac hummed in the background. Always, she hits the brakes when she gets to the end of the driveway. This day was no different. I heard the shrill squeak and the cranking of the steering wheel. The Caddy is an older 1970s model, so it makes a chug chug sound all the way down the street until it disappears.

I went back to reading my comics. Mom's religion thing is OK for her. It seems to have provided her a degree of solace. It still hurts when I think about the life I lost because of what Mom and Dad did. All those years of staying with men so I could have a place to eat and sleep, the child I gave up for adoption, losing Jimmy.

There is not a day goes by that I don't think about that little baby girl I held for ten hours before I placed her in the arms of her adoptive parents. I see that baby in my dreams sometimes. My life could have been so different. I can't pretend these things didn't happen to me, and I can't whitewash the pain. I have my doubts about God, but I know that I love my mother and hate to see her hurting.

Maryanne walked into the kitchen, combing out her wet hair. She wore jeans and a yellow sweatshirt. "So, what's the plan?"

I unfolded a map of Eagleton that I had on the table. I had marked four streets with blue stars. In the revenge game, you gotta be organized. "We should be able to hit these houses this morning."

Maryanne studied the map. "Maybe it would be easier just to call people and ask, 'Does Gladys Smith live there?'"

"I thought about that. What if Ed answers, and he gets suspicious and leaves town? I think it's better if we find him without him finding us."

Maryanne nodded.

I left a note for Mom, saying to start lunch without us.

Although we were both new at this stakeout thing, we agreed that we'd better have some munchies. On the way to our first Smith house, we stopped and picked up donut holes, espressos, and a big bag of chips. I don't know what makes men bond with each other, but for women it's eating.

Maryanne and I talked about everything while we parked across the street from the first Smith house, a Victorian with bay windows, located in the older part of town. There were no cars in the long driveway, but three were parked on the street by the house. None of them were Thunderbirds. We watched the place for about an hour while Maryanne told me about growing up with two older brothers and no mother.

"If my brothers knew what Ed did to me, they'd kill him before I got a chance to." Maryanne had insisted on bringing her .38 with her. I talked her into putting it into the glove compartment.

"What happened to your mom?" I asked as I shoved the last donut hole into my mouth.

"She left when I was two. Dad never talked about her much. I always thought of my Grandma, Dad's mom, as my mother."

I nodded. The abandonment theme ran through both of our

lives. "I always thought of the university as my parent after I lost mine."

Maryanne narrowed her eyes at me. "What?" She shoved a potato chip in her mouth and offered the bag to me.

I took a handful of chips. The salty barbecue aroma made my mouth water. "When I was eighteen and out of foster care, I entered a new form of institutionalization. I stretched out my degrees. I worked part-time at nothing jobs and went to school part-time. College took care of me. It was a safe place to be." I bit into a chip, and my whole mouth tingled.

Maryanne shook her head. "Guess you had even less of a normal life than me." Genuine sympathy flooded her words.

I shrugged and ate three more chips. It wasn't something I let myself think about for long. "I don't think anything's going to happen at this house. Should we blow this Popsicle stand?" I had already turned the key in the ignition.

The second house was even harder to watch than the first. But not because it was quiet. Shortly after we found an obscure parking place, a woman opened the door. She wore sweats and held a green tricycle. A little boy scrambled past her.

We watched as she pushed her kid up and down the sidewalk. The house was in one of those new developments that had been going up. All the houses on this block were obviously built by the same contractor—pastel green, gray, or pink with only slight variations in design. Spindly little saplings decorated the front yards.

A few minutes later, a barefoot man holding a coffee cup came out and sat on the steps. The woman looked up at her husband, and the little boy smiled and waved at his daddy as he pedaled by.

"Well, this isn't the house we're looking for," I commented. But both of us just sat there, numbly watching the simple acts of a loving family on a beautiful summer morning, torturing ourselves, like when you can't stop picking a scab.

"You know," Maryanne said finally, "that should be me. I'm not getting any younger. And you know what, Ruby?" She turned and looked at me. "I can't figure it out. I'm a nice person. I have a good job. I don't drink or use drugs. I didn't spend foolishly when I had money, before Ed took it. I'm a good cook, and I'd never cheat on a man." She glanced back out at the happy family.

I turned the key in the ignition.

"When is it my turn?" she whispered.

The woman sat on the steps with her husband, and he put his arm around her. This was really hard to watch. As our car rolled by the house, the little boy ran to the open arms of his parents. I could hear their laughter through my open window. I rolled up the window and slammed down the accelerator. "OK, what's the next address, Maryanne?"

She didn't answer. I slowed the car and glanced at her. She turned sideways and rested her face on the glass of the window.

"Maryanne?"

We passed another house where a father was shooting baskets with his son. Maryanne's shoulders shook. I didn't have to see her face to know she was crying. For starters, I got us out of suburbia before we saw one more happy family. I reached the end of the subdivision and pulled out onto a main road.

Her explosion occurred just as I sped up the car. "I hate him. I hate him!" She beat her fists on the dashboard. This was the Maryanne I'd seen the day I met her. Every muscle in her body indicated her rage: tightened jawline, white knuckles, shoulders drawn up toward her red cheeks. Even when she tried to sit on her hands, she couldn't. Instead, she ended up clawing the car seat.

I drove to Hillside Park, which has no playground equipment, so there was less chance of seeing more perfect children with Mom and Dad. After parking the car, I let her continue, because her rage was my rage.

Even if Maryanne did meet another man, a nice guy, she'd be too paranoid to trust him. Whatever horrible things happen to you in a relationship, you take all that garbage with you into the next relationship. After so many bad relationships, even if you do meet the right guy, all you have to offer him is paranoia and insecurity. All that psychobabble about experience, sexual and otherwise, being good for a marriage is way off base.

She stopped suddenly, tilted her head back, and took a deep breath. The roof of my car held her attention while silent tears streamed down her cheeks. Her hands trembled from the power of emotion she had expelled.

Mom tells me the reason God doesn't want people to have sex outside of marriage is so that they don't bring all that emotional garbage with them into the marriage. They start out with each other clean and untainted. Once you've committed yourself to someone, been that intimate, it's really easy to be hurt by that person.

What Mom says makes sense. But the news came a little late for me and Maryanne. We were already tainted. What I would give to undo the past.

I am not very good at comforting people. I wished my mom were here. She's the queen of the comforters, honest.

I crawled out of the car and went around to the passenger side to open the door. Holding Maryanne at the shoulder and elbow, I pulled her out. She was like a rag doll in my arms as I escorted her to the park bench. I put my arm around her and gave her shoulder a squeeze.

Her fingers brushed across her face, wiping the tears away. "I'm sorry." She sniffled.

I shrugged. "Don't worry about it."

We sat for a long time, watching mountain bikers go by on their way up the hill. Most of them were muscular college-age males with dreadlocks or scraggly hair, sporting tie-dyed shirts and baggy shorts.

In the world of prescribed things human beings are supposed to do—go to college, get a job, marry, have children, retire and enjoy the grandchildren—we had missed the plane because we were told the wrong gate number. "I'm sorry, ma'am, no normal life for you; have a nice day."

I felt cheated and ripped off by the world. I had been sold such a false bill of goods: that sex would lead to living together, and living together would lead to marriage. What a lie that was.

Maryanne smoothed her blond hair at the back of her head. Her eyes were red from crying. She crossed her arms over her chest and closed her eyes.

I didn't know what to say to her, my new friend. She'd been sold a lie too. Silly her. She'd assumed marriage was about love and growing old together, not about having access to someone's bank account. We both felt betrayed. Was there anything I could say? If there was, I would have said it to myself long ago.

Hundred-year-old oak trees surrounded the park. Their leaves rustled in the morning breeze. An older man with a dog walked by on the trail in front of us. On the other side of the park, more college students showed up to throw a Frisbee. The day was overcast and chilly. Zipping up the front of my sweat jacket, I shook off the summer cold and stared at the sky. A rain waited behind the clouds. Always, the rain waits.

I sat in the park comforting my friend until the cold rain soaked us through like the despair of our long-dead dreams.

Chapter Four

Maryanne was really quiet later that day. I hate it when heavy unspoken emotions hang in the air like smog. I'd rather have people screaming at me. When Wesley called and said he had finished with the roofing job, I was grateful.

"I think I can locate some hiking gear for you." Even over the phone, his voice had that low, silky quality. "I'll see you at 0500 tomorrow."

"OK." I set the receiver in the cradle, and my thirty-year-old heart went pitter-patter. I have sworn off men for good reasons, but that initial chemical attraction is intoxicating. The intention of the invitation was fuzzy at best.

We're just going to look for Brian, that's all. Yeah, right.

In nonmilitary people time, 0500 is five o'clock in the morning. I was awake and had tanked up on coffee by the time Wesley's Jeep pulled into the driveway. I wore navy shorts and a white T-shirt because that's what L. L. Bean dressed all their hikers in. I didn't know anything about hiking, but I could at least look the part. I opted to leave my favorite foot gear, a pair of red-and-turquoise cowboy boots, at home and wore tennis shoes instead.

After tossing my duffel in with the backpacks, I tried to open the passenger side door.

"Oh . . . ah—that door doesn't work," Wes said, leaning on the hood. "You'll have to get in on my side."

His hand brushed my bare leg as I crawled across the driver's seat, and he tossed a bundle in the back of the Jeep. Little electric blue snakes zinged up my leg and through my whole body. Even if my mind was telling me a relationship was a bad idea, my body was telling me to dive in. I enjoyed the energy of the moment. He slid in behind the steering wheel.

"Well, let's go." He gave me a half smile and turned his head to back out of the driveway.

Could I fall for a man who didn't use his rearview mirror?

We sat in silence as the houses grew fewer and farther apart. He had pulled his hair back and tied it with a piece of leather. I found myself tracing the outline of his ear with my eyes.

Sensing my staring, he turned to me and raised his eyebrows above the rim of his glasses. "Quite a drive. We'll be off the highway in just a little bit."

"Yeah," I said, turning away. My face felt hot. I'd been caught admiring him.

If there is a God, I sure don't understand why he made humans this way. All this chemistry stuff—sweaty palms, beating heart, flushed face—gets in the way of making a purely cold, calculated choice about a mate. If it weren't for chemistry, I wouldn't have such a long string of broken relationships. It has occurred to me that all my relationships were based on that initial attraction and nothing else. No wonder they amounted to nothing more than me having to lug a shredded heart around. Except maybe for Spencer Ashton—there was something more with him. But don't get me started on the Spencer saga.

How do you get beyond all that chemistry and keep yourself from getting hurt so much? According to Mom, the Christian solution is no sex until marriage. Fine for all the virgins out there, but what about me? Guess I missed the train on that one. I don't quite fit the Christian formula for happiness. That's me, always standing outside the equation, looking perplexed.

After about an hour, Wesley slowed down and turned off the highway onto a dirt road. The road narrowed to a trail with waves of dirt. The Jeep squeaked and creaked as we bounced in our seats and the gear slid across the floor. My shoulder slammed against the door, and I could distinguish each spring in the car seat as it poked me in the behind.

"Quite a ride, huh!" Wesley raved. Oh no, he was one of those men who saw rough terrain as some sort of male challenge. He steered with his hands and forearms wrapped around the wheel, his eyes focused straight ahead, chin jutted out in intense concentration.

I fixated on his fingers and hairy forearms, partly because that chemistry thing made me want to study every physical attribute on him and partly because focusing on one thing kept me from getting dizzy. His fingernails were remarkably clean for a man in his profession. I zeroed in on one of the thick dark hairs on his tanned arm just as my head hit the roof of the Jeep.

"Owww!"

"Sorry about that." He didn't even look at me as I rubbed my head. Now I was mad. Mad because my idea of camping was Grandma's trailer at the KOA. Mad because physical attraction made me do stupid things like this. Mad because I was still a slave to my libido. Mad because Wesley didn't just say, "I love you. I love you. Let's run away to someplace air-conditioned with room service."

Eevergreen trees thickened and the road sloped, sort of like the tracks of a roller coaster. My stomach held onto my spine as we defied the laws of physics and the Jeep roared ahead at a nearly ninety-degree angle. The gear and two adult bodies rattled in the Jeep like dried beans in a jar. I couldn't feel my adrenaline-dosed heart beating because all the blood had migrated to my big toes.

Wesley never let off the accelerator. The rougher the terrain, the faster he went over it.

After some trial and error and bruises, I discovered that the best position was to grip the door handle and brace myself by pressing the other hand into the roof of the Jeep. I felt my bones rattle and vibrate as we jerked and lurched down the road, and I use the word "road" loosely.

Finally, the dirt path leveled off and opened up into a circular, flat spot before becoming nonexistent. Tall, stick-like lodgepole pine surrounded our landing pad on three sides. I exhaled loudly and unbuckled my seat belt before resting my head against the back of the seat. Pulling all those Gs made me dizzy.

"I thought we were too back country to see anybody else."

I opened my eyes and discovered the object of Wesley's remark. A newer-model white SUV with the license plates "MAC" had already staked out our territory.

I shrugged. "Getting harder and harder to get away from people since our valley's been discovered by Hollywood and refugee suburban yuppies."

Wesley clicked his door open and leaned into it. "Yeah. Lately, anytime I've gone camping, I've run into a lot of people trying to get away from all the other people."

I stepped out of the vehicle. I looked around while I waited to get my land legs back. The pines blocked out most of the sunlight. They weren't more than six inches in diameter and stood naked except for a flourish of evergreen growth at the top. Wesley had already tossed all the gear on the ground and locked the back of the Jeep by the time I finished my nature study.

"You need to get your things out of the duffel and into this." He unzipped an orange backpack and tossed it in my direction. While I stuffed items into assorted zippered pockets, he placed his backpack on the hood of the Jeep and hoisted the straps over his shoulders. "How much hiking have you done, Ruby?"

"Oh, some," I said as I pinched one of my fingers in a zipper. I soothed the injured digit by sucking on it.

Turning in a half circle, Wes scanned the trees and the trail ahead. "We should make the cabin by dusk. We can head back early tomorrow . . . maybe with Brian."

I lugged the backpack over to the Jeep and hefted it onto the hood. Imitating Wesley, I shrugged the backpack straps over my shoulders.

"Do you need some help?" Wes adjusted my shoulder straps and buckled the myriad of belts and canvas webbing. I felt the warmth of his hand against my stomach as he pulled on the waist strap. His head was so close to mine that his hair brushed my cheek, and I drank in the soapy cleanness of his skin. Momentarily, he gazed at me and took a step back. That brief eye contact was enough to turn my muscles to Jell-O. Pass the smelling salts, please.

"Let's get moving." His head turned in my direction, but he didn't look at me. Guess I wouldn't get any smelling salts.

We stepped into the forest and onto the trail. The trees created a tunnel, causing the light to diminish and the temperature to drop. Bands of sunlight and twirling dust sneaked through the emaciated evergreens now and then. I watched Wesley's backpack bob up and down.

My heart rate increased. His pace was steady and military in style, each step evenly spaced. I was grateful that the coolness of the forest prevented unnecessary sweating. How unfeminine. He might turn around and gaze at me, and I sure didn't want a ball of sweat on the end of my nose.

Like most men, Wesley was hard to read. The only place men were honest about their feelings was in rock songs, and I hadn't noticed a guitar attached to his backpack. What was that whole eyeball dance about? He hadn't said anything to indicate that he had the hots for me. All I had to go on was my perception of those signals he kept sending me. I didn't know if I should trust my instincts. Mom had done that big song and dance about him being a "nice Christian boy." But he was the one who'd suggested we come up here together—overnight.

He turned to me, hands on his hips. "Doing OK?" He unclipped a canteen from his backpack.

"Just . . . fine," I gasped. He wasn't even breathing heavy.

"Good." After taking a gulp, he handed me the canteen. The cool water splashed into my stomach. I should have eaten a bigger breakfast; the coffee was wearing off.

We continued at his furious pace. I watched his backpack bounce, listened to the water slosh back and forth in my stomach, and wondered when I would have my heart attack.

Thick layers of moss and tree debris made the forest floor almost mushy, a soft carpet for my feet. My heartbeat evened out, and I was able to think of things other than my impending death. The silence allowed my mind to wander, perhaps too much.

Here's a little mental exercise I like to perform. If I encounter a frustration in the present, for example, not knowing what Wesley's romantic intentions are, I think of every failure in my life and relive each event in vivid detail until I convince myself I am a total loser. It is a characteristic of chronic depression, so the psychology books tell me. I know this is not healthy, but I don't know how to stop it. While hiking with Wesley, my mind wandered to the whole Spencer Ashton drama.

The forest thinned and opened out onto a sloping meadow. The amber grass grew in clumps that shivered in the cool breeze. At the base of the meadow, an aspen forest sprouted by a stream.

We loped down the hill. The incline was so steep that my legs jerked forward from the ankle up with each step. It was as though the hill pulled me downward. The momentum made me laugh. Wesley turned around and stared at me with a perplexed expression.

"This is fun," I explained.

He continued down the hill at his controlled pace; I let the law of gravity take over. I was sure that this was the equivalent of high impact aerobics and my shins would pay for it later, but I didn't care. About midway down the hill, I passed him and waved as I continued my downward journey. I wanted to hold out my arms and skip, but I thought that would be too much.

When I was ten, I had rolled down a hill like this, laughing, with Jimmy and Mom behind me and Dad sitting stoically at the top of the hill. All my happy memories are tainted by what occurred later in my life. How do I get past this? I wish every day could be like those moments spent rushing down the hill.

I came to a thundering stop beside a stream. The aspen leaves clacked in the wind, and the sun warmed my face. We ate sandwiches and drank water from the canteen before heading up the opposite side of the hill and into another forest. The incline was much more gradual than the decline. Even without the possibility of a romantic interlude, I was kinda enjoying myself—kinda.

Other things in life besides the endless pursuit of relationships and academic and career achievements could offer pleasure. Things like the tiny little yellow flowers that dotted the landscape and the faintly sweet smell of the breeze. Mom tells me that everyone knows there is a God just by looking around at nature. She might be right.

When we came out on the other side of the trees, the sun was low in the sky. The incline of the hill grew steeper. Hard earth replaced the soft mushiness of the forest floor. Rocks caused me to stumble and turn my ankles at unnatural angles. Wesley became a moving silhouette in front of me. The hill transformed into a mountain as we went from walking upright to pulling ourselves up from rock to rock.

Wesley's voice rang out from the ledge above me. "I was hoping we would have more daylight for this last little leg of the hike." His breathing was unsteady. Finally, a bit of nature that challenged his cardiovascular system.

"Sorry, I probably slowed you down." I stood in the fading light of early evening, hands on my hips, dreaming of hot baths and soft beds.

"No, you were the right person to come." While Wesley paused to catch his breath, my little heart did a back flip. He wanted me to come with him. "You know about what's going on with Brian," he explained. Oh, thanks. It was just business. Time for the heart to do a reverse back flip.

In the dimming light, I followed Wesley's lead. Stepping where he stepped. Holding on where he had held. Always he moved with steady confidence as I wobbled along behind him. We came to a tall slab of rock, and I waited while Wesley made his way spiderlike up the cliff. He leaned over the ledge when he reached the top, directing me to the first foothold.

My hand gripped the protrusion of rock above me, and I pulled upward. At the beginning of the day this section of the mountain might have been surmountable, but my muscles were tired, and it was past my bedtime. My hand slipped from the rock as I reached out to find an anchor for my other hand. Fortunately, I left most of the skin from my palm on the rock, so it wouldn't be hard to find my position again.

"Are you OK?"

I rubbed my sore hand and sighed. "I'll live."

"If you can pull yourself up about a foot, I think I can grab you."

I gazed down the mountain and longed for a walk in the park or a cushy couch and a good book. I stuffed my foot into the small crevice and reached for the craggy protrusion with my sore hand. My calf muscle strained to its limit as I hooked my hand on the rock above me and stretched all the muscles in my shoulder and arm. A charge of heat shot through my body. I gritted my teeth and strained so hard, I thought my skull would fall out of my skin.

Wesley grabbed my other arm just above the elbow. The support of his touch gave me incentive. I tightened my grip and pushed with my foot until I was on tiptoe. The warmth of his hand vaporized. I slipped down the wall of rock, scraping my fingernails as I fell.

I stood for a long time, hanging my head and leaning against the rock.

"One more time, Ruby." His voice fell gently on my ears, but I couldn't move. "I can't leave you here," he coaxed.

"Oh, I don't know." I sighed. "A little paint, some wallpaper, I could get used to this place."

He laughed. "Come on, one more time."

Normally in a situation like this I would have given up. But I didn't want to this time, and it had nothing to do with wanting to please Wesley and everything to do with not wanting the mountain to beat me. In the cool of evening, with all my muscles screaming at me, I liked that feeling of fighting to meet a challenge when it felt like I had nothing left to give. Weird.

Once again, I wrapped my shredded hand around the granite protrusion, found my foothold, and strained upward. His hand caught my arm above the elbow. I edged up until my handhold was of no help and I had to let go of it. While I struggled to find another crevice for my hand, his grip was the only thing keeping me suspended. Talk about a trust exercise, not to mention a way to make one arm longer than the other.

I clawed the side of the rock, searching for a place for my hand or foot—anything to boost me over the top. The muscles of the arm he held were stretched to the limit. I swung in anchorless limbo. My heart beat faster as fingertips scraped rock.

"Hang on!"

"I wasn't planning on letting go!" I wasn't quite sure what the big panic was about. At worst it was a five-foot drop to the ledge below.

Finally, my random groping produced a foothold for my left toe. With me pushing from below, Wesley was able to do something other than hang onto me. My fingers found the top of the ledge. His grip around my arm was tight—almost painful. I could hear his heavy, unsteady breathing and feel his face close to mine. Almost home. He gave one final tug and pulled me over the top.

We huddled together on the narrow ledge, listening to each other's raspy, intense breathing and the evening sounds that surrounded us. My shoulder felt like it was on fire. I closed my eyes and leaned against my stone pillow. I'd made it. How heavenly.

I stared out at the sun, a glowing sliver on the horizon. We had only a little gray light left before total darkness.

"You were a real trooper." He patted my hand. "It's a piece of cake from here."

He leaned forward to get up.

I couldn't make my muscles work. "Just a minute."

"I'm not used to covering this ground at dusk, but the cabin can't be far." He pushed himself off the ground.

My heart still hadn't returned to its resting rate. My hands and feet throbbed.

I could hear his feet plodding on the ground as he shouted back at me. "We're not as close as I thought. We won't make the cabin by tonight. We'll have to camp."

I pushed myself to my feet and trudged forward. My internal energy was renewed even if my body wasn't cooperating. The gray sky turned charcoal. Pregnant rain clouds loomed over us, and a chill permeated the air. The ground was still rocky but much flatter. Goose bumps rose on the skin of my bare arms. I had a coat buried somewhere in my backpack, but Wesley wasn't slowing down, and I didn't want to seem wimpy.

After a gradual incline, the land opened up into a clearing beside a lake lit up by moonlight. It was as though we had stepped into a quiet library from a crowded party. The air stilled. The only sounds were the rippling of the waves at the lake's borders and the splashing of fish popping through the surface of the water to catch insects. The perfume of wild mint and pine hung in the air.

Wesley lit a small Coleman lantern and put up the tent.

Mental note: there was only one tent. Not wanting to seem totally useless, I rummaged through the backpacks for edible matter. I couldn't find a stove, so I opted for granola bars and juice.

We sat around the lantern, eating. The food tasted better than any lobster dinner I'd ever had. We spoke little, but an obvious tension hung in the air. I glanced over at the open door of the tent. What exactly had Wesley intended by asking me to come with him?

"Good food." He wiped crumbs off his hands.

"Thanks. I slaved for hours."

He smiled. At least he thought I was funny.

I unsnapped my sleeping bag from the pack and tossed it in the tent. As I backed out of the tent, I felt Wesley's hand on my shoulder. My breath caught in my throat, and the warmth of his hand penetrated my sore muscles. I craned my neck to look at him. The reflection of the flame from the lantern danced on his glasses.

"I'll sleep outside. It wouldn't be proper any other way," he said.

Crouching beside the tent door, I watched him roll his sleeping bag out by the lantern. Proper? What kind of word was that?

Even though I was exhausted, I lay in the tent, listening to the rustling of his sleeping bag. I was angry. The nerve of him turning me down after I sent out all those signals. Other men would not have hesitated, at least that had been the pattern of my life.

At the same time, I felt in some strange way that he was paying me a compliment. I was not accustomed to these kinds of feelings. The old pattern for relationships sure hadn't worked out. Maybe it was time to try something new. The whole thing was very weird. I rolled over and closed my eyes.

At some point in the night, the fog of my dreams lifted enough for me to hear the rain pelting the side of the tent. "Wesley?"

"Yeah," came the faint reply.

"Are you getting wet out there?"

The fog engulfed me again. His reply was indiscernible from the voices in my dreams. "I'm all right."

I drifted back to sleep.

Hours later, the warmth of the sun and smell of clean air greeted me when I unzipped the tent flap. Wesley had already built a fire. His wet sleeping bag was slung over a tree some distance from the flames. He'd changed his shirt to a red-and-blue flannel that was partially unbuttoned. When he saw me, he turned his back to me and buttoned it up.

I hugged the sleeping bag to my stomach. What an unbelievably sweet gesture. His modesty made me like him even more.

"Not more than an hour to the cabin," he said cheerfully, pulling out tent stakes. His honey-colored hair hung in wild kinks around his face, and glints of sunlight caught on his glasses.

I packed and loaded without much help. My muscles didn't ache as much as I thought they would, but I still entertained fantasies about soaking in a hot bath.

We set out for the cabin in standard formation, Wesley in the front, me taking up the rear. His "rejection" of me only made me want him more. As we hiked, the muscles in the back of my neck tensed. This did not make any sense at all. Why didn't he just come out and say he liked me?

I hated trying to read all these mixed signals. He was the one who opted to sleep outside in the rain. In the past, I had interpreted sex as the sign that a man loved me—but those relationships had never lasted. There must be something else.

We trudged through the forest, branches breaking beneath our feet. These evergreens were thicker and fuller than the others we'd come through.

We descended a hill. The cabin came into view, resting at the edge of a glen of trees. Wesley's pace increased. There were no signs of life outside the cabin. Still, Wesley called out his friend's name. "Brian. Brian."

I ran after him.

As Wesley opened the door of the cabin, it dragged on the wood floor.

A table, cupboards, mouse droppings, dust; not much else occupied the room. Wesley opened the cupboards one at a time. "Ah ha." He pulled a jacket and backpack out from one of the cupboards. "This is Brian's," he said triumphantly and continued his search.

The spacious quarters of the living room/kitchen contained one glassless window. As my grand tour took me closer to the second room, where a mattress was visible, an odor that had at first been vague, intensified. Tangy bitterness surged up into my throat, and my nostrils tingled. I tasted bile. The warning systems of my body were trying to tell me something. I wasn't listening. Stepping across the threshold, I surveyed the room. There was one window. A light blue sleeping bag was rolled up and placed in the doorless closet.

The closer I got to the open window, the stronger the smell became.

My eyes watered as the intensity of the stench increased. Like a bimbo in a horror film, I had to know what was outside the window, even though the audience was yelling, "Don't go over there!"

I walked across the wooden floor; my footsteps seemed to echo. A tornado of flies buzzed outside the window. My fingers touched the windowsill, and I leaned out. My stomach turned into a tight knot when I saw the source of the odor.

Chapter Five

I must have run out of the cabin, because I found myself kneeling in the grass. It felt as though all the fluids in my body had been mixed with vinegar and deposited in my throat and nose. The contents of my stomach surged and tightened. I am not the damsel-in-distress, "catch me, m'lord, I think I'm fainting" type, but rancid odors break down my defenses.

"Ruby?" Wesley called from the doorway.

"Over here," I croaked.

He trotted across the field, holding something in his hand. I still hadn't gotten to my feet when he put his hand on my shoulder. "It's all right. It was a buffalo."

"Excuse me, I'm not *that* much of a city girl. Even in its tortured position and with all that blood and brain tissue, I knew it was a buffalo." Like this bit of animal identification was supposed to make the tidal waves in my stomach calm down. It was still a dead buffalo. Or the remains of one. The carcass looked as though someone had placed a bomb in its belly and detonated it. I shivered at the picture that formed in my mind.

"I collected some tissue and fur samples." He shoved his fur sample underneath my nose, and the whole sensory overload experience came back to me.

"No thanks, I've already eaten," I said, pushing his hand away.

"The animal was obviously hauled behind the cabin to hide it. Almost any wild game would be out of season this time of the year. Buffalo are never in season, unless they wander out of the park. I didn't see anything that looked like a bullet hole."

I rose to my feet. "How do you know that animal didn't kill a person? That area was soaked with blood." My legs still wobbled. I can take care of myself in most emergency situations, so I don't know why my body reacted this way. Maybe it was exhaustion.

Wesley glanced at the cabin and then at the fur sample in his hand. "I don't think anything with two legs died. I've got a camera with me. I'm going to take some pictures. I know a park ranger who might be able to help us figure out why it died. I looked through Brian's stuff, checked his coat pockets. There's nothing there that would help us know where he is."

"So why is Brian's stuff in the cabin?" I followed Wesley as he retreated to where we had left our packs outside.

"I don't know." He pulled out the Ziploc bag that had formerly contained granola bars. "Brian would never kill an animal out of season. He sure wouldn't participate in the killing of a buffalo." Wesley dropped the bloody fur into the plastic bag and sealed it.

Mental note: never eat another granola bar again as long as I live.

"Should we take his stuff with us?" I was anxious to leave. The forest seemed much less serene, downright creepy even, since I'd found such awful signs of violent death in its midst.

"No, leave it. It's extra stuff for us to carry, and he might be coming back for it." While I struggled with my backpack, Wesley wandered around the outside of the cabin. "Brian! . . . Brian!" He gazed up at the mountain behind us, cupping his hands around his mouth. "Brian!" His voice faltered the fourth time. "Bri–an."

I had to admire him for the loyalty he showed to his friend, but the most obvious explanation still fit the evidence. Brian had jilted Laura and now was whooping it up, killing forest creatures illegally. It certainly tied everything up into a neat package—except for the shredded buffalo. He might shoot a buffalo, despite what Wesley said, but why blow it up? There must be something else going on here. I hoped for Laura's and Wesley's sakes that there was. Maybe the idea that Brian had been kidnapped wasn't as farfetched as it had seemed a few days before. Except, of course, that I hadn't the faintest idea who would want to do that or how they might have pulled it off. Nancy Drew never had these kinds of problems.

Backpack straps dug into my shoulders, a phenomenon that wasn't noticeable if I was moving, but that wasn't possible.

While Wesley made another search around the perimeter of the cabin and then disappeared inside again, I slipped the pack off and sat on it. What was he hoping to find? Nothing, probably. He just didn't want to leave the last place his friend had been.

My eyelids grew heavy as I rested my chin in my hand. Early morning sun is the best sleeping pill in the world. And I hadn't slept that well in the tent last night—for obvious reasons.

"Maybe we should stay and wait for him, Ruby." I could hear Wesley's feet swishing through the tall grass. "His stuff is here, he must be coming back—or he's hurt." He stopped and stood beside me.

Shading my eyes from the sun, I gazed up at him. "It could be days before he comes back—if he comes back. We found his camping gear. That is evidence that he was here. I think that would be enough to get the police up here to look around."

Wesley crossed his arms and stared out at the forest. I saw anguish in his tightened jaw. This was the closest he'd gotten to finding his friend. It was hard to let go of that one strand of hope.

"I suppose you're right. Police could cover a lot more ground than we could."

Still a bit listless, I stood up and stretched while he picked up my pack and presented the straps for me to slip into. He assisted me with strap adjustment and buckling, which wasn't necessary. After a day of loading and unloading this canvas cargo, I had pretty much figured out the procedure. It was euphoric, though, to have him stand so close to me. As he adjusted my straps, I could feel his breath on my neck. Warmth radiated from his body. With him in such close proximity, I was all atwitter. Oh my, my.

His face was less than *GQ* perfect from years of outdoor work; subtle wrinkles showed around his eyes and across his forehead. He sported a few days growth of dark stubble that contrasted with his light brown hair. Beneath the external features, preoccupation stirred, revealing itself through silence and green eyes looking down as his thoughts traveled inward. I could almost see the gears turning inside his head. I dared not interrupt.

He placed his hands on his hips and looked back at the cabin one more time. "We should go. I'll leave a note for Brian—just in case."

As was established procedure, I followed Wesley, but I found it much easier to keep pace with him. Once I got moving, the fresh air and exercise woke me up. The image of the mangled buffalo haunted my thoughts. We took fewer breaks and talked less than we had the day before.

The landscape did not hold as much interest for me the second time around. With interaction from Wesley at a minimum, and to keep my mind off the smashed buffalo, I thought again of Spencer Ashton. I suppose it was the prospect of a new relationship with Wesley and the frustration of not making any clear progress that sparked the ugly memories from the past.

When I met Spencer, I was completing my master's in literature and working as a teacher's assistant to pay tuition. He was a Ph.D. candidate in history. I was on my way to a Shakespeare seminar when I noticed an amusing cartoon taped to his study carrel, and then I saw him crouched over a thick book. He wasn't particularity good looking—he was even downright gawky, with high cheekbones supporting large, round eyes. But he made me laugh, made me feel smart . . . and pretty—all the important stuff. I moved into his apartment within weeks because this is the standard procedure with modern "love."

I can't tell you how many women who have the much-coveted, high-powered, big-salary jobs allow themselves to be treated like dogs by boyfriends. The irony of modern feminism. I ought to know. I was one of them. I was the golden child of the English department—already published, teaching, and looking toward a Ph.D. After ten years as a professional student, I was envisioning a normal life, marriage, and a real job. At least that's what I thought.

Spencer had one annoying little habit that was my undoing— he really liked his nineteen-year-old female students, *really* liked. Coping involved talking myself out of my suspicions, listening to his justifications (workaholic father, domineering mother, his dog didn't love him, etc.), and staying for a year and a half while he cheated on me again and again.

When Mom found me that day, I was getting into the driver's seat of Spencer's sports car and preparing to find a semi to collide with; I don't know if I was really going to kill myself or if it was my last pitiful effort at revenge for all the hurt he'd caused me. Maybe I just wanted to bust up his precious car to get even.

Earlier that day, a buxom blond had knocked on the door of our apartment. She'd seemed rather surprised to see me. "Oh," she said in a wispy thin voice, "I was looking for Dr. Ashton."

Actually, he wasn't officially a doctor yet. But why quibble where large-breasted women were concerned?

"Who are you?" Her pink lips formed an almost perfect pouty valentine. Central casting in 1940s Hollywood could not have found a better actress to play the other woman.

"I'm the maid," I said, shooting arrows with my eyes and turning slightly so she could see the messy apartment. . . . There had been others, but the pouty blond was the last straw, sort of. If Mom hadn't found me that day, I suppose I would be dead or still tangled up with Spencer until I had no dignity left.

So here I was, two years later, tromping through the woods with Mr. Ambiguous. Throughout the day, dark clouds haunted us with only benign sprinkling. I wasn't up for any kind of Gene Kelly musical number, but light rain was better than blazing sun. The forest opened up into a clearing. Wesley stopped so suddenly that I almost crashed into him.

"What?" I said.

He raised his hand to silence me. He was clearly responding to some sight, sound, or smell that I had not yet detected. I tilted my head and followed the direction of his gaze. Thoughts of man-eating lions and tigers and bears (oh my!) flashed through my mind.

I listened, sorting out sounds. My breathing. His breathing. Trees creaking in the wind. Birds twittering to each other . . . and then a distant whir. Not a natural sound, more mechanical, a consistent steady rhythm—whop, whop, whop. All the other noises diminished as the whir grew louder.

I leaned a little closer to Wesley. A rush of air blew my hair back. The noise increased suddenly, as if someone had turned the stereo volume from two to ten. The machine and the terrible wind it created were upon us. Wesley wrapped his arm around my shoulder and pulled me to the ground.

The helicopter must have come up over the trees that we had just walked through. With tornado force, air swirled around us. The skin on my cheeks vibrated. My lips were pulled back from my teeth. With his hand across my back gripping my waist, Wesley guided me closer to the protection of the trees, both of us crawling through the grass, wounded-soldier style, arms pulling us forward.

The helicopter hovered in the clearing twenty feet from the ground and thirty feet away from us. I looked up through a mass of tangled hair. It was camouflage green, as was the man holding the gun in the open door—a matched set. His rifle moved from a vertical to a horizontal position. He tilted his head to look through his gun sight.

I did not blink once. Without moving my head, I spotted a glowing red bead on my shoulder. The bead traveled across my collarbone and disappeared beneath my chin. All the air left my lungs as though I'd been punched in the stomach. In a moment that stretched out for eons, I drew a protective hand to my neck.

The powerful machine rose straight up as the man lifted his head away from the gun sight, grinned at me, and withdrew the weapon. When he turned his head to profile, I saw that his dark hair was drawn into a sleek ponytail. As the chopper ascended, I caught just a glimpse of a blond head, probably a woman.

We lay for a long time as still as statues, flat against the grass, listening to the chopping whir of the blades and engine fade into the distance.

When all the happy forest sounds returned, Wesley released his death grip on my shoulder, sat up, and wiggled out of his back-pack. I did the same and proceeded to brush the masses of tangled red hair out of my eyes. For one of the few times in my life, I was at a loss for words.

What does one say after a near-death encounter with GI Joe and his glowing red dot? I had an overwhelming urge to request an MRI when I got home, to make sure I still had all my vital organs. If I could have, I would have kissed my esophagus and my lungs, because I had almost lost them.

"What was that all about?" Wesley asked.

Jeepers, I was hoping for something a little more insightful, or at least a little sympathy for me and my near-death experience.

My bodily responses didn't make a whole lot of sense. I nearly fainted from the sight of dead animal remains, but I was Miss Cool Cucumber when it came to nearly losing my life. Strange, my heart wasn't even beating real fast. For the moment, the pul-sating pain in my back held my attention. Both of us had lain with the full weight of the packs on our backs.

After some time spent taking body-function inventory (Throat, check. Heart, check. Pancreas, check. Brains, negative.), I responded to his question. "Military exercises?" I suggested, and the idea wasn't totally off the wall. Eastern Montana housed some of the biggest missile silos in the country. We were a ways from silos, but the military could be doing secret army things in the remote woods.

Wesley shook his head. "I was in the marines for three years. Even with all that camouflage, there was something real unmilitary about the whole thing. The weapon didn't look like anything military issue. And they don't let guys in the military have ponytails. The helicopter looked like a Huey."

"A Huey?"

"They're military, used in Vietnam, but they sell them to civilians now." He narrowed his gaze and fell silent as he stared out into the expanse of clearing. "Do you suppose it has anything to do with what we saw at that cabin?"

"I don't know; I'm out of brilliant ideas, Wesley." All of the sudden, the trauma of what had just happened to me flooded my emotional system. It was as though my fear response had shut down so I could deal with the situation. Now that I was safe, anxiety raged through my body. I held my trembling hand in front of me while my heart thudded in my chest. My breathing was shallow. I massaged my forehead and temples and tried to think happy thoughts. No use. Every happy thing I could think of ended up getting blasted away by a shotgun.

"I'm sorry I put you through this whole thing, Ruby." Wesley's fingers brushed my cheek lightly, removing a strand of knotted red hair. After two days without a shower, I probably looked like quite the little glamourmoose. Heavy on the moose. I didn't care anymore; I just wanted to go home. He grasped my trembling hands. "You're shaking like a leaf. Are you going to be OK?"

He cradled my small hands in his. The warmth and the roughness of his calloused skin calmed me. Finally, I was able to take a deep breath.

The rest of the hike was uneventful. Under a canopy of darkness, we stepped into the clearing where the Jeep was parked. A billion stars twinkled above us in the clear night sky. Our Jeep was the only vehicle in the clearing. We didn't so much load our gear as toss it in the back of the vehicle.

Once we were over the rough part of the road, I dozed, turning sideways and resting my head against the back of the seat. My eyes were closed and my muscles relaxed, but my mind raced. For an egghead accustomed to only reading about adventure, the past two days had provided heart-attack level excitement.

I woke up when I felt the Jeep turning and the road beneath us getting smoother. I craned my neck to look outside. "Hey, we're going the wrong way."

Wesley had that tunnel-vision look in his eyes. "I know someone who might be able to tell us something about what we saw."

"I want to go home." I sounded like a whiny five-year-old. "It's late."

"It's not that far out of our way." He was too determined, and I was too tired to argue. I put my head back on the seat cushion and closed my eyes.

I didn't wake up until my body felt the Jeep slowing down. Glare from street lamps burned through my eyelids. We'd entered a small town, complete with darkened tourist shops and overpriced cafés. Garden Spot, a Yellowstone Park entryway, although I couldn't be sure because my internal compass had been confused by sleep. I hadn't been here since my early teens, but it looked like Garden Spot.

Wesley turned off a side street and parked in front of a square little house with green siding.

We got out of the car and headed up the walkway. A house light guided us up the path. Flower pots with blooming something or other (Mom would know what they were) populated the porch.

After Wesley rapped on the door, we waited in silence. I drew my coat tighter to my chest and crossed my arms. It was chilly this time of the night . . . make that morning. Presently, a light went on and a female voice called out, "Who is it?"

Wesley leaned closer to the door. "Rachel, it's me."

The door swung open almost immediately. A pair of female arms engulfed Wesley. "What a surprise." She gestured for him to enter.

"Sorry to bother you this late." Without acknowledging me, Wesley stepped across the threshold. I scurried in like a bad little puppy, hoping the door wouldn't hit me on the behind.

Rachel leaned over to turn on a floor lamp. Her long brown hair fell forward in that attractive, sensual way I have never mastered. "Actually, I just went to bed a little bit ago. I'm working on a report for the state."

I noticed the park-ranger uniform hung over the back of a kitchen chair. The house was done in early seventies earth tones, gold shag carpet and green couch, yellow-and-brown wallpaper in the kitchen. A recliner was covered with a much cheerier, floral-print throw, and the tablecloth was equally bright. Still, there was no disguising the decade of bad taste. Except for the Jesus poster and a few wildlife pictures, the walls were bare. This was probably a rental.

Rachel straightened and tossed her long mane of silky hair over her shoulders. If this woman had been sleeping, I couldn't tell. Her skin, bare of makeup, was unblemished, and those dark brown eyes sparkled. Women who look that good at that hour of the day should be shot.

When it was combed and under control, my own fine hair had the texture and color of an Irish setter who frequently sticks his head out the car window while it moves at high speeds. After two days without a shower, and a style job by Helicopters-Are-Us, I had a lot in common with the shag carpet. Yes, I was jealous of Rachel and her good looks for no good reason. But emotions are rarely logical.

"Come on in. I'll make you a cup of tea." She was already opening cupboards and pulling out chairs. Wesley followed her into the kitchen. Patting my stomach, I glanced down at my body to make sure I hadn't become invisible. I was certainly starting to feel that way.

"Oh, Rachel, this is Ruby," Wesley said in what sounded like an afterthought.

I stepped forward. The invisibility spray must have worn off. Rachel nodded at me and took another mug out of the cupboard. "Don't go to any trouble, Rach," Wesley added. "I just need to ask you a few questions." He pulled the Ziploc bag out of his pocket along with a canister of film.

"Can you find out what killed this buffalo?"

Rachel took the bag and held it up to the light. "You found a dead buffalo?" While she boiled water, Wesley recapped finding Brian's stuff in the cabin and the close encounter with the helicopter. He ended by asking, "Brian's camp gear is enough to send search and rescue out to look for him, don't you think?"

Rachel poured the steaming water over the tea bags in each cup. "Poor Laura." She set a cup in front of each of us and pulled a sugar container off the counter. "That cabin's not far from the park border. I'm tied up with a project, but I can probably find another ranger to swing by and have a look, and I'll give search and rescue a call. I'll get the film developed and let you know."

Wesley and Rachel made small talk for a while about a Bible study and fellowship group they had been in together in Eagleton.

With half the tea still in our cups, we said good-bye and climbed back into the Jeep.

Wesley shifted into reverse. "Well, that was helpful."

Don't ask me why, but I was fuming. So that I didn't have to admit to being too childish, I attributed my bad mood to exhaustion. "It was a very little bit of help for a lot of extra time."

Except for the people exiting the bars, Main Street was deserted. "Is something bothering you?"

As we neared the edge of town, a group of men stood below a flashing neon sign that read "Oasis." Some had their hands in their pockets; others held beers. Oasis—I think a state law mandates that every small town has to have a bar by that name.

Wesley had asked me one of those loaded questions. A million responses ran through my head before I finally said no and crossed my arms.

He accelerated when we hit the highway. I spent the rest of the journey staring out the window. About twenty minutes from home, I asked, "Known Rachel long?"

"Oh, two or three years."

Without comment, I returned to counting the yellow lines that zipped by on the highway.

The sky had changed from black to gray by the time we pulled into Mom's driveway.

Wesley pressed the brakes and planted his hands on the steering wheel. "Well, thanks for everything, Ruby." He hesitated. "Could you tell Laura what we found? I'm not very good at dealing with emotions. I'm afraid she's gonna fall apart."

"Yeah, sure," I said, trying to push the door open.

"The door is jammed. You'll have to crawl out my way." He had already opened his door and stepped out. "Thanks," he added, "I couldn't do this without you." His hand touched my shoulder as I crawled out.

My anger flared. So that's what I was, the faithful little companion and helper. I turned and glared at him. The street lamp backlit his face and hair. Man, he was handsome. No wonder Rachel had endless hugs for him. "Well, it's a little hard to compete with someone who has perfect hair and a biblical name," I said. The second I said it, I knew I wasn't making any sense.

Wesley's wrinkled forehead confirmed my self-diagnosis. "What are you talking about?"

Wanting to hide my embarrassment at my enigmatic blathering, I turned and headed toward the house. I was halfway up the stairs to the porch when I said, "Oh, never mind."

As I opened the door, he stuck his head out the window and shouted. "Thank you, Ruby. I'll call in a few days."

I waved good-bye without turning around. Why was he so clueless? Couldn't he see I was nuts about him, even though I hadn't said or done anything to indicate my feelings? What I needed in a man was a mind reader.

Mom and Maryanne were still asleep when I came through the

door. My bed felt wonderful. I plopped down on top of it without bothering to pull back the covers. The sun had just begun to glare through my skylight. Pulling a pillow over my head, I rolled on my side and waited for the fog of deep sleep to envelop me. The last thought in my mind as consciousness faded was that I had to tell Laura what we had found in the cabin. But for now, I could sleep and hope the events of the last forty-eight hours wouldn't erupt from my subconscious.

Chapter Six

I was still groggy when the alarm went off, and I trudged into the kitchen for breakfast. A note on the refrigerator told me that Mom had taken Maryanne with her while she taught a class. It looked like Mom had adopted Maryanne. Guess I had a new sister.

I read some Flannery O'Connor while I munched on a bagel and cream cheese. Even after Flannery, I couldn't clear my head. I longed to go back to bed, but it was my turn to open the store. I had already taken two days off. Georgia was pretty flexible about work, but not *that* flexible.

It wasn't just physical exhaustion that made me long for my down comforter and soft mattress. The strong net of depression cocooned around my mind and body. I couldn't pinpoint the specific reason for the downward cycle; there usually wasn't one.

As I dressed for work, energy drained out of me. I needed to find strength: I had to work six hours at the feed store—and I needed to tell Laura what we had found.

I drove to work with the window rolled down, not because I liked to feel the breeze but because sometimes the handle gets jammed. My Valiant is like that. Usually a good swift kick to the door unjams the handle. The bit of wind on my face kind of woke me up. If I downed a couple cups of coffee at work, I would be able to fake coherency. I had put off calling Laura with the exhaustion plea. But I was running out of excuses.

As soon as I turned the key and opened the door to Benson's Pet and Feed, a demanding yowl greeted me.

"Good morning."

A female Siamese rubbed against my leg and meowed at me again.

"I'll get your food. Just be patient, Your Majesty."

Your Majesty is the official guard cat for Benson's Pet and Feed store. She came here three years ago as a pampered purebred, but she was so ornery that no one would buy her. She was sweet as molasses to Georgia and me, but anytime a prospective buyer picked her up, she was all claws and teeth. She had a similar reaction to any male Siamese we tried to breed her to. Cats don't usually pick out people to bond to so much as they choose places, and Her Majesty had picked the feed store. She owned this place and was nice enough to let me work for her.

I liked her. I wished I had Her Majesty's audacity and independent spirit.

After I fed the little queen, I put on a pot of coffee and hauled bags of feed to empty shelves. *Call Laura, call Laura,* my internal voice nagged. I heard the tinkle of bells as the doors swung open and knew who it was without turning around.

"Morning, Leland. Coffee's on." Without looking, I knew what Leland was wearing: plaid shirt in a green or blue pattern, Levi jeans with a round crease in the back pocket made from the smokeless tobacco can, and a greasy baseball cap with a farm equipment name on it. Georgia, a rancher's widow, had sort of made the store a hangout for retired, failed, and getting'-by farmers.

Leland stirred his coffee slowly, lingering at the counter. "Rain will be good for the hay. Spring calves will fatten up nice." The only spring calves left in Leland's life ran in his dreams. I hoped those herds were big and healthy. The old man glanced up and down the counter. "Any donuts?"

I heaved a twenty-five-pound bag of goat feed onto a shelf. "I didn't notice any. Georgia's got some muffins in the refrigerator, next to the calf vaccine."

Leland helped himself—to the muffins, not the vaccine.

By one, with only two more hours left on my shift, I knew it was time to let Laura in on our discovery. I called Laura's house, and her mom gave me her work number. When I phoned Laura and told her I needed to talk to her about our hike, her voice got that hopeful pitch to it that I could detect even over the phone. I cut the conversation short, telling her I'd see her in a few hours, and asked her the location of the dress shop where she worked.

After work, I found a parking space a few blocks from the shop. Downtown Eagleton is mostly antique stores and art galleries catering to the tourist crowd, with a few upscale clothing shops and restaurants thrown in.

In one of those visual flashes that vaporizes quickly, I saw a beehive redhead disappear into a gift shop. Was I seeing things or was that the elusive Mrs. Smith from the bowling alley, Ed Lawson's latest pursuit? I glanced up and down the street but saw no sign of the blue T-bird.

Still, I stepped inside the gift shop and wandered around. The place seemed to deal mostly in glass bowls and vases of different colors. Shelves and shelves of blue, green, and red glass were lighted in such a way that the glass on display glowed. The lighting in the rest of the shop was subdued. A myriad of tiny glowing gold teardrops, reflections from the cut glass, danced on the dark walls. Metal wind chimes tingled in the background.

As I wandered around the tall shelves, I counted six customers, but none of them sported a modified beehive. Maybe I hadn't seen her at all.

It occurred to me that the bowling alley was the closest I was going to get to the T-bird and Ed Lawson. I kicked myself for not staying there that day and following the T-bird.

I waited around for a while, but no one came out of the back room.

I was about to leave when a tiny crystal cat in a glass display case of jewelry caught my attention. As with the other displays, tiny lights were set to make the jewelry more dazzling than it actually was. Black unseeing eyes stared out at me. Where had I seen that cat before? I kept seeing it against a background of pink. Pink? Oh well, it would come to me. Probably tomorrow morning when I was slurping coffee and munching cereal.

I left the shop with the vision of that crystal cat seared into my head and nagging at my subconscious. It took a few minutes for my eyes to adjust to the bright light outside.

The front window of Laura's shop displayed a wedding dress and several satiny looking formals in royal blue. Once inside, I was greeted by a tall, thin woman wearing a businesslike navy blue dress. The dress had huge, square shoulder pads. She wore her glasses on a chain around her neck. Her gray hair was pulled back into a tight bun with no soft wispies framing her face. Drawn-in eyebrows arched over narrow-slit eyes, and I wondered if she stuck toothpicks under her toenails to maintain that look of permanent surprise.

"May I help you?" She enunciated each vowel and consonant perfectly.

"I'm looking for Laura."

"Oh." The woman rubbed the chain of her glasses and used the other hand to point toward the back of the shop with a long finger that had about a quarter inch of clear polish on its nail. "She's in the back room doing alterations."

I found Laura sticking pins into the side seam of a long black dress that was turned inside out and worn by a dress dummy. Her long brown hair was still French braided. She wore jeans and a blouse and just a hint of color on her cheeks and eyes.

"Hi." She looked up at me smiling. She really thought I had good news for her.

The power of her emotion made me want to bolt for the door. I planted my feet and held onto the door frame.

"Have you had lunch yet? I've got half a sandwich left." She pointed to a Styrofoam container resting on a cushioned footstool.

I helped myself to the ham on Swiss and sat down in a chair beside a sewing machine. The room could not have been more than twelve-feet square. In addition to the sewing machine, there were shelves on three walls stacked with boxes bearing labels like "thread, silk, blue" and "sequins." Three glaring fluorescents hung from the ceiling, providing the only light in the windowless room.

"Pretty dress," I commented between bites. I was eating more to procrastinate than because I was hungry. Small talk and food was easier than the news I had to give her. After our first emotional meeting, I wasn't optimistic about the results of this one.

Laura grabbed the hem of the dress and touched the silky fabric. "It is beautiful. I've got a woman who wants me to take it in for her because she lost weight. Usually, I'm doing the opposite." With the soft rustle of fabric, she let the skirt of the dress fall. "Ruby, whatever the news is, I can take it."

Am I that transparent? I hate people who can read my mind. "We found some of Brian's things in a Forest Service cabin—a sleeping bag, backpack, and jacket." I had already opted to leave out the info about the bloody buffalo.

"Did you bring them back? Where are they?" She stopped pinning and held her hands together in a tight knot.

I put the sandwich down. "We left them there in case Brian came back for them."

"I want to go up there." She was ready to grab a coat and race out the door.

"I don't think that would be the most productive thing to do right now. At least not until after search and rescue have looked, and Wes has a ranger friend who said she would help us. If they don't find anything, it might make sense for us to go up there." Besides, I was still recovering from the first hike. "I need you to tell me about the last time you saw Brian."

Laura's shoulders drooped, and she bit her lower lip. "I suppose you're right. It probably wouldn't do any good for the three of us to try and cover the whole forest on foot." She set the food container on the floor and seated herself on the footstool.

"I think that if we can figure out why he went up there, we have a better chance of finding him. Tell me what you remember about the last time you saw him."

Staring straight ahead as though viewing a video in front of her, she spoke. "We went on a picnic in the park that day. We put a 'to do' list together for the wedding and divided up tasks."

I rested my elbows on my knees and leaned closer to her. "Did he seem upset that day?" I was fishing. Right now, the only line I had in the water was trying to figure out what made Brian go up to that cabin. "Did he have plans to go camping? Are you sure he didn't have the camping stuff with him?"

She shook her head. "The picnic basket was in the trunk of the car. I would have seen the gear."

Asking the question again helped me put together a sequence of events. He must have gone back to his trailer after he was with Laura. But why?

"Nothing unusual happened?" I continued.

"No, it was a nice afternoon. Wait. . . ."

She brought her hands to her mouth and stared at the carpet as though she were looking through it. "There was a woman who came up to us and started talking to Brian." She touched her fingers to her forehead. "I forgot all about her until just now."

"Who was she?" I spoke in a whisper, not wanting to disrupt the flow of the memory.

"I didn't know her, but from what I picked up as they talked, she knew Brian when they were in high school and for a while after."

"Did they seem friendly?"

"Yes, there was nothing unusual about the conversation. The weird thing was that she came up to us pushing this baby stroller, but there was no baby in it. And I didn't see a kid playing anywhere around the park. I didn't think anything of it at the time, but Brian kept staring at that baby carriage."

"Was he upset after talking to the woman?"

"Kind of, but he just said that we'd better get going because he had things to do."

Maybe the whole event meant nothing. But so far it was the only thing I had to make me feel like I was moving forward. "If I could get hold of Brian's old high school yearbooks, do you think you would recognize this woman?"

Laura shrugged. "It's worth a try. Do you think she has something to do with Brian being gone?"

My turn to shrug. I threw in a head shake for good measure. "I don't know. I'll have to figure out what else happened that day." I stood up to go.

"You want to see my wedding dress." It wasn't so much a question as a suggestion. Laura was already opening a closet. She pulled out an array of sparkle and satin. "I still have a couple of rows of sequins to do." Holding the neckline up to her chin, she stretched one of the sleeves out and did a half twirl. "I know, you probably think it's stupid to work on it now."

"No, I don't think it's stupid."

"I believe he's coming back, Ruby. Brian wouldn't do this to me unless he had a very good reason or he was taken against his will."

The best response I had to her intensity was silence. I picked up the empty food container and tossed it in the garbage.

"I get home at about six." She opened the closet door and carefully placed the wedding dress inside. "If you can get the yearbooks, I'll help you look through them."

I told her to assume that was the plan unless she heard otherwise.

On my way out the door of the shop, a shimmering blue dress caught my eye. The dress was stuffed back in a corner on the discount rack. Prom season was over. I touched the skirt of the dress with my fingertips. Two layers of sheer fabric covered light blue silk and a mesh underskirt, similar to the dress Cinderella wore in the animated version of that story. I'd never gone to the prom.

Odd how the sight of such a dress can bring back a fourteen-year-old bitterness.

My parents had been arrested around prom time. I suppose I could have worn a nice formal to the court hearings.

"Are you interested in that dress?" Eyebrow Woman had stalked up behind me. The way she asked the question suggested that the dress was too good for me.

I pulled my fingers away from the dress like a child caught with a hand in the cookie jar.

She looked down at me from the bottoms of her eyeballs. The woman must have been more than six feet tall.

"Sorry, this is a little too down market for all those Hell's Angels rallies I've got to attend. Thanks ever so."

The woman's mouth fell open.

With my chin in the air, I strutted out of the shop. Ah, life's little thrills.

Getting hold of Brian's yearbooks involved having to go out to trailer court heaven again. When I arrived, Brian's mom wasn't in attendance, but his false-teeth-making stepdad and the two girls, Susan and Deedee, were home.

Mr. Fremont sat at the table in a T-shirt and dress slacks, sipping a soda. The newspaper was spread out over the table. "I think Brian may have some stuff out in the storage shed," he offered without looking up from his reading. "Susan, Deedee, go help the woman."

The two girls rose obediently from their position in front of the television set.

I stood my ground as the girls headed for the door. "Mr. Fremont, I don't suppose your wife figured out when Brian came back for that camping gear? Did she ask any of the neighbors if they saw him come by?"

He raised a bushy eyebrow at me. "Both of us work all day, most days. Deedee and Susan stay with my sister. We don't know none of the neighbors."

Well, guess that settled that. It had become important to me to sort out the sequence of events that led to Brian's disappearance. Mr. Fremont wasn't helping.

Mr. Fremont rolled his soda can in his open palms. "Wish that kid would get home soon. I got a hundred dollar towing bill for his car the other day. "

"His car?" This was news even if Mr. Fremont didn't think so.

"They said they found it at the city park. It had been there a couple of days, so it was considered to be an abandoned vehicle." He crushed the soda can with one hand, probably one of those barroom tricks he'd used to impress Mrs. Fremont when they were dating. "The car's in his mother's name. He sold his to pay for that wedding."

So it was the money that was bothering him, not the loss of his stepson.

I felt a tiny, cold hand press against my palm. "I'll show you where the shed is."

Deedee dragged me out the door with her older sister taking up the lead. The storage shed was one of those metal do-it-yourself jobs in pea green. Deedee bounced up and down and swung on my arm while Susan hauled broken bikes and boxes out of the shed.

"Do you like Barbie dolls?" Deedee asked.

I looked for her eyes through the mass of tight blond curls. She was kind of angelic underneath all that badly styled hair. "Oh, they're OK," I offered. "They sure have lots of cool clothes."

"Yeah," Deedee agreed, shaking her head and contemplating the deep truth an all-knowing adult had just given her.

Susan emerged with a box cryptically marked "Brian" in black ink. With her treasure in her hands, she beamed. "I found it for you."

I reached out and touched her head lightly. "You did! Nice work."

Proud of her accomplishment, Susan supported the box with both arms and her stomach. Her jaw tightened, and her cheeks reddened from the exertion. I took the box off her hands and walked toward my car with the two girls following behind me.

After I put the box in the back seat, I noticed the girls standing at attention, waiting to be dismissed. "Thank you both so much." There was something poignant about the amount of attention they were giving me, a virtual stranger.

Susan leaned on the car door when I opened it to sit behind the wheel. "Will you find Brian?"

I touched the white fingers that rested on the rim of my door. "I'm trying, Susan. I really am."

Deedee stuck a finger in her mouth and then pointed with it across the trailer court. "My aunt lives right over there." Already halfway into the car, I craned my neck around to see where she was pointing. "I saw Brian come and get his camping stuff."

This news was enough to make me get out of the car and close the door.

Susan poked her sister in the shoulder. "You did not." She looked at me. "Deedee makes up stories."

Deedee stomped her foot. "I'm not making it up. You and Aunt

Beverly were inside watching *Wheel of Fortune*. I yelled at him, but he didn't hear me."

I got down on my knees and looked Deedee in the eyes. "Was he with Laura?"

"No, he was with a lady who had hair my color, and it wasn't his car, either. It was a fancy white truck-car."

"A truck-car?" I asked. Deedee nodded, indicating that everyone knew what a truck-car was. I am not prone to be affectionate, but I hugged Deedee and Susan both.

The blond woman had to be the same one Brian and Laura had seen in the park. If his own car was left in the park, this was looking more and more like a kidnapping. I wasn't chasing my tail; this was a genuine lead. Now to figure out who the blond woman was.

As I backed out of the driveway, the two girls waved at me. I watched Susan grab her little sister's hand and hold it. They walked toward the trailer to return to their game shows. Brian was significant in the lives of so many people. Even though I had never met him, he mattered to me because he mattered to so many people. Those little girls really loved their big brother.

Laura deserved to wear that wedding dress.

I had to find him.

Chapter Seven

When I brought the box of Brian's stuff into the kitchen, I found Maryanne baking bread. I plopped the box on the kitchen table.

The sugary moistness of cinnamon rolls perfumed the kitchen and dining room. Several pans of something in various stages of rising were hidden under flour cloths on the counter.

"Where's Mom?" I asked as I tore open the box. Dust and a bitter smell similar to wet leather clouded the air.

Maryanne opened the oven and poked at something. "She had an evening class to teach."

I lifted a pair of worn football cleats and a trophy off the top of the box, definitely not clues for figuring out who the blond was. No need to haul them over to Laura's house.

"Have a good day helping Mom with her classes?" I asked.

Maryanne's cheeks were rosy from peering into the oven. She pulled a strand of blond hair off her forehead. "She's a really great teacher. Your mother has a very calming effect on people." Maryanne was wearing a pink satin blouse that looked new.

The pink triggered something in my head. The crystal cat I'd seen in the glass shop was the same one I'd seen pinned to Gladys Smith's pink bowling shirt. There had to be a connection. I needed to go back to that glass shop.

Maryanne glanced at the pile of stuff on the table. "What's in the box?" She seemed so content. I decided not to talk to her about the glass shop just yet.

"Brian's life," I responded. A framed photograph caught my

eye. A younger version of Brian dressed in a tux, his arm around an attractive brunette in a flowing yellow dress, looked up at me. Her thin wrist was decorated with a huge corsage. Prom night. The girl had brown hair, but maybe our blond was out of a bottle. I put the photo back in the box. The prom photo made me remember the blue Cinderella dress I had seen in Laura's shop. "Maryanne, did you go to the prom when you were in high school?"

She lifted a steaming pan out of the oven and flipped it upside down. Humid, sweet perfume with just a hint of cinnamon enticed me to the counter. Placing her hands on her hips, Maryanne stepped back from her creation. "I never went; I was a cheerleader and everything. You'd think I would have gone at least once. My father was picky about the boys I went out with." She snorted. "Lot a good it did, huh?"

I tried to picture a slimmer, younger Maryanne in a cheerleading outfit sporting a perky smile; no matter how hard I tried, the image remained distant and blurred.

Without my prompting her, she placed a steamy cinnamon roll on a plate and handed it to me. My drooling must have given me away. I propped myself up on the counter and tore off a strand of bread, savoring the luxury of gooey warmth and caramel before continuing. "I never went either. Just another one of those normal things I missed out on."

Maryanne leaned against the counter and crossed her arms over her chest. "I remember one year I had the dress and everything, a little pink thing with white polka dots. Even had a boy Daddy approved of." She stared out the window where the memory floated by. "And then that Saturday, my grandmother died."

"You're not very lucky, are you?" I teased, trying to lighten the moment.

Maryanne swatted me with the dishtowel she had hung over her shoulder. "You don't have a lot of room to talk."

"Good cinnamon rolls," I commented through a mouthful.

"Thank you. I like baking. I'm a good cook." I watched her jaw tighten as she tossed a dirty spoon in the sink with a little too much vigor. "I would have made someone a real good wife—and one heck of a prom date."

Mom had done a good job at calming Maryanne down, but all her bitterness lay just beneath the surface.

I patted her on the shoulder as I hopped off the counter. "Just think of all those pimpled teenage boys who missed out on our company." Gathering the half-sorted box in my arms, I headed toward the door. "I'm supposed to be at Laura's right now. Thanks for the cinnamon roll." I was lying a little bit. I wasn't late yet. It was Maryanne's rising anger that made me want to leave.

I heard her voice behind me as I turned the doorknob. "Maybe you and I can get back to our plan; we still have some houses to stake out. Maybe you were right and Gladys is a widow. We could look at some of the houses listed under a man's name."

I pressed my back against the door to open it. The weight of the box pulled at my arm muscles.

She twisted the dishtowel and waited for me to answer. She'd drawn her hair back with a clip, which made her round brown eyes even rounder and more puppy dog like.

Did she still really want to kill him, or had tracking him down become her own self-prescribed "letting go" therapy? Neil Sedaka was right; breaking up is hard to do, especially when there is a .38 pistol and a blue T-bird involved.

"Yeah, OK," I offered noncommittally and swung open the door. I wanted to help Maryanne. I considered her a friend. More than anything, I wanted to make all her pain and rage disappear. But if I didn't know how to get rid of my own bitterness, how could I help someone else?

The evening sun waned as I drove up to Laura's house. Her mother, dressed in slacks and a short-sleeved sweater, greeted me at the door. "Laura's upstairs. First door on the right. We're just having an empty-nesters Bible study. Have you had supper yet, dear?"

I leaned against the wall; the box was heavy. "Oh, sort of."

She patted me on the shoulder. "I'll bring up some stew."

Laura sat on a floral bedspread, reading. I tapped on the open door.

She set the book down. "You're early."

"I couldn't wait."

"Put the box on the bed. I have a surprise for you. Wait right here." She left the room. I heard her feet padding down the stairs.

Her floral bedspread matched the curtain, which matched the pillows on the chair, which complimented the rose shade of the rug. I often wondered how people managed to coordinate their rooms like this. I had a hard time getting my socks to match. While I waited for Laura, I perused her bookshelf, partly because I was killing time and partly because I'm a snoop. If she didn't come back in a few minutes, I'd peek in the medicine cabinet in her adjoining bathroom.

You can learn a lot about people based on the books they own, whether they've read them or not. Laura had the usual Christian books I'd seen on my mother's shelf. In addition, she had some coffee-table books on design and color, and picture books on Monet, Degas, and Picasso.

Laura returned holding the blue Cinderella dress I had seen in the shop. "Recognize this?" She beamed.

"Yes, but how did you—"

"I'd come out to ask Octavia something. I heard you talking with her."

"Octavia? Is that her name?" Grabbing the hem of the dress, I let the layers rustle through my hands. The top layer of transparent fabric shimmered in the dim light of Laura's room.

"It's yours to keep, Ruby." She held the dress, still on the hanger, up to my shoulders.

"But I—"

"Octavia might act like she owns the shop, but actually, my grandmother holds the papers." Resting her hands on my shoulders, she turned me toward the full-length mirror. I didn't look half bad. 'Course, this lighting was a little subdued. I leaned a little closer to the mirror, searching for flaws.

"I don't really have any place to wear this."

Laura plunked down on the bed beside the box of Brian's stuff. "You'll think of something."

I pivoted away from the mirror, partly to look at Laura and partly so I could hear the dress make that wonderful swishing, rustling sound. A plan began to form in my mind. "I don't suppose you have a pink dress with white polka dots, about a size fourteen? It's for a friend." Neither Maryanne nor I had gone to the prom; maybe I could do something to rectify that.

"We've got tons of stuff in storage. I'll have a look and bring it over if I find something," Laura offered as she opened the box. "You can hang that on the coat rack over there." She pulled out several yearbooks.

I hung up the dress and sat down on the bed beside her.

For the most part, the box contained athletic awards, yearbooks, a few letters, and lots of photos, framed and unframed. I tackled the written material while Laura searched the yearbooks for the blond. I caught Laura shaking her head as she flipped through the pages.

I looked up from a letter Brian had received from the Social Security Administration. He'd spent some time trying to locate his biological father. "What did you find?"

"Oh, it's nothing important." She slammed the yearbook shut. "Brian is six years older than me; I never knew him in high school. We've been through all this premarital counseling, so I know that he's not . . . that he had sex with other women before he became a Christian. But they were just these anonymous nobodies out there." She opened the yearbook again. "Now I get to see their faces and read what they wrote to him."

"If I knew what the blond woman looked like, I wouldn't make you go through all this. I could find her on my own," I said.

She touched my hand lightly. "I know. I'm just struggling with a little doubt, that's all." She slammed a yearbook shut and with an audible sigh grabbed another.

"Back to work." I tried to sound hopeful and positive. But the letters weren't helpful. Some of them were from Wesley when he was in the marines, a few from women and old sports cronies who had left the state and wanted to keep in touch, and the rest dealt with Brian's futile search for his real father.

I spent a little too much time staring at the letters Wesley had written, memorizing the curve of his letters, the slant of his words. That guy did have an affect on me. Throughout the day, my thoughts had returned to him.

Somewhere between finishing the stew Mrs. Holliman brought up and the summer sky turning dark, we hit pay dirt.

Laura switched on her bedside lamp. "This is her," she said, staring down at a framed photo.

I leaned over her shoulder as she held the picture up to the light. Judging from the grayness of the exposure, the photo was taken outside in wintertime. Brian and the women on either side of him were wearing ski gear. One of the women, a slender brunette, waved ski poles with her free arm. The other, our mysterious blond, saluted the camera with a beer glass. Out-of-focus people in various states of party revelry surrounded them, and above their heads was a red neon sign that said "Lenny's."

I took the photo, slid it out of the frame, and turned it over. Blank. Just as soon as things looked like they were going to be easy, they got harder. We still had no name. "You're sure this is her?"

Laura nodded. "I'm pretty sure that's the girl we saw in the park that day. I have a good memory for faces."

The gears in my head started turning. I had a clue to work with. "Wesley might know who she is. Or Brian's mother might know. We have the name of this bar. Have you heard of it?"

Laura shook her head. "I'm not from the bar crowd. But I could check the phone book." She was already halfway to the door.

Still studying the picture, I followed her into the hallway. Laura disappeared into what I assumed was another bedroom. Mentally,

I compared this Brian to the prom picture and to the more current ones I had seen. I guessed that this photo was post high school by maybe two or three years. That would make him about twenty or so.

Laura returned holding an open phone book. "I can't find any 'Lenny's' in here."

I was already on my way back to the room. I needed to look at the other photos to make sure of my calculations. "How long ago did you meet Brian?"

"About three years ago. We've only been dating for a year and half. Why?" She followed me into the room.

I pulled out the prom photo and the engagement picture Laura's mom had given me when we first met. This woman was from Brian's past. I needed to sort the sequence of events that led to his disappearance. "So that would make him about twenty-six when you met him?"

"Yes. He'd only been a Christian for about a year."

I grabbed my dress off the coat rack and held the picture with the other hand. "You get a good night's sleep. I'll call you tomorrow if I find out anything."

"I'll help you. Just let me know what I can do." I left her standing by her bed.

She'd have enough work to do tonight battling the doubts she was having about Brian's character. Beautiful, perfect Laura. There was a part of me that wanted to set her on a shelf behind glass with a big "do not touch" sign.

Cool summer air rippled over my face as I rolled down the window of my Valiant. My mind was racing too fast for me to go home and sleep. Instinct told me the blond was important to the bigger picture. The bank clock read ten o'clock as I pulled out onto Main Street.

What next? We needed a name to go with the face. If Brian had known this girl in high school, maybe Wesley would know who she was.

I stopped at a phone booth and called Wesley. He picked up on the first ring and answered cheerfully and coherently. He must be one of those night owls, or worse, someone who could function quite well on four hours of sleep. I told him what we had found, and he gave me directions to his house.

As always where Wesley was concerned, my motivations were mixed between the truly noble and the simply selfish. Yes, I wanted to track down the blond for Laura's sake, but I was also looking forward to being in the same room as Wesley.

It was dark when I pulled up to his house. The yard, which looked like it had been recently leveled with topsoil, was void of vegetation. The warm glow of incandescent lighting shone through the large windows. I knocked on the door and watched through the window as Wesley emerged from the kitchen with two large mugs in his hands. He placed the mugs on a coffee table before opening the door.

Shoving his hands in his pockets, he stepped aside. "Come on in." He was wearing jeans and an oversized plaid shirt in shades of blue and turquoise with the top two buttons undone. He was barefoot.

Everything about Wesley's living room said "I like wood." The hardwood floor supported a couch, coffee table, and big chair, all made in that rustic, hand-peeled pine style, like the kind they have at dude ranches. The aroma of cedar filled the air. Wooden beams stretched the length of the ceiling.

I am always amazed at men's ability to resist the urge to collect knickknacks and doodads. There was nothing on Wesley's shelf except a few books, CDs, and a CD player.

Wesley placed a warm mug in my hand and retreated to a drafting table covered with blueprints.

Sipping my tea, I wandered over and peered at his drawings. "What are you working on?"

Color tinted his cheeks. He rolled and then unrolled the papers. "Oh, it's nothing. Just building my dream house."

"Did you build this place?" I glanced around at the clean sparseness of his house. "It's nice."

He dropped his head and smiled shyly. "I remodeled the inside. But it's not the same thing as building a house from the ground up. . . . You said something about a photograph?"

"Oh, yeah." I returned to the coffee table, where I had set the photo.

Wesley took the picture and leaned back in the chair by the architect's table. I stood for a while holding my tea and then made myself comfortable on the big chair close to Wesley, sinking into its soft leather cushion.

Wesley studied the photograph for a long time. His finger touched each figure, pausing, probably going through a mental list of possibilities. I sipped my tea, waited, glanced around at the bare walls, and waited.

"I don't know her, the blond. The other girl looks kind of familiar . . . but I can't quite place her."

I set my empty mug on the coffee table and leaned toward Wesley. "Laura thought she was someone Brian knew in high school before you left for the marines."

Wesley ran his hands through his ruffled hair. "We were kind of wild then. We knew a lot of girls."

Wesley's comment clicked on my anger switch. I'd spent the evening rummaging through a pile of "jock stuff," including an endless stream of pumped-up men with their arms around "a lot of girls." Girls whose names they couldn't even remember now.

"Well, if you don't know her, you don't know her." I snatched the photo out of his hand.

I must have given him a paper cut, because he drew his finger up protectively to his chest. Served him right.

"I recognize the bar they're at, if that helps," he offered timidly. "It's not called Lenny's anymore. It's called The Arena."

"Wine, women, and song. That's pretty much what your life is about, isn't it?" I plopped back down in the chair and glared at the photo.

"That's what my life was," he whispered. "I've changed. Christ has changed me."

"So, you're honestly going to tell me that you haven't slept with a woman since your magical conversion moment?" This is my biggest sticking point with Christians. They talk about how they are born again and brand new, but they still seem to bring all their bad habits with them, while making all kinds of announcements about their transformation.

Wesley sat down on the floor close to my chair, facing me. It was an odd place to sit, like a puppy or a child. He rested his forehead in his open palm. "You caught me. I've stumbled. I've messed up in the four years I've been a Christian."

This honesty was hard to know how to take. I had expected him to be more defensive—to deny the bad things he had done.

"You know, I could very well be one of those women you used and threw away."

He looked straight at me. "I know." I thought I saw tears glisten in the corner of his eyes. "That night up in the woods, I wanted to. I had even made plans around it. . . . But I knew it was wrong."

"So you're saying you are attracted to me, but—"

His hand rested on the arm of the chair, barely touching my fingers. "But I gotta learn how to treat women with a little more dignity and respect before I become involved again. The only way I learned how to relate to women was through sex, and that's wrong."

I stared at him for a long time, trying to read what was in his face. Did he mean what he said, or was this just some kind of big brush off? Instead of the cliché "let's just be friends," his way of letting me down easy was to say he needed to live like a monk. I tested the waters. "So what you're really saying is that you don't want any kind of a romantic relationship with me because I'm not in the club."

My ambiguity caused him to sit up straighter. "What?"

"I'm not a good little Christian girl. That's what you are holding out for, right?"

He grabbed my hand and squeezed it. "No, Ruby. That's not what I meant. All women, regardless of where their faith is at, deserve to be treated like ladies. Isn't that what the fourth chapter of John is all about?"

I had no idea what the fourth chapter of John was all about. "That isn't what Brian did. Judging from the contents of his 'memoirs,' he used a whole string of women and then chose innocent and perfect Laura for his bride."

Wesley grabbed me at the elbow and pulled his face close to mine. For the first time since I'd known him, I saw anger in his eyes. "Don't ever say that about Brian." He loosened his grip. "If you could have known him before. When I came home from the marines, Brian had been saved only a few months. He was a different man. Brian did everything he could to make amends with the women he had hurt." He let go of my elbow, stood up, and turned his back to me.

"I didn't mean to say that about Brian. I'm sorry."

He didn't respond. I was still a little overwhelmed by his reaction. I picked up the photo and headed toward the door. Rejected and confused, woman exits stage left. But I couldn't leave without clarification, my little way of making sure the knife was driven in real deep. "We have an understanding then. Nothing between you and me?" I closed my eyes, not wanting to hear the answer.

"I think that's the way it needs to be," he whispered. His hand touched mine; I pulled away.

"I'll still help find Brian." I could feel emotion rising. My throat constricted. "Regardless of what you think of me, I care about Laura and those little sisters of Brian's."

"Ruby, it's not you. It's me. I . . ." Again he touched me, this time on the forearm.

Again I jerked away. "Oh, shut up. You can wrap it in whatever spiritual package you want. The point is you don't want—" I stomped toward the door.

"Ruby, you don't understand."

I opened the door and stepped outside. "Thanks for letting me down easy."

His voice hit my back as I headed down the dark sidewalk. "The

Arena bar is in kind of a rough part of town. I could go with you if you wanted."

What was up with this guy? He was having a harder time dropping this than I was. "I think I can handle myself. I don't need your help anymore."

I left him standing in the doorway. The light from his house flooded across the threshold and created a halo around his head, an angel wrestling with some of the same demons I knew intimately.

I still couldn't go home. I was even more stirred up than I had been before going to Wesley's. So I drove through the flashing neon of downtown and out onto a frontage road.

If the thing in the woods wasn't rejection, this definitely was. He didn't want me. The hurt cut deep.

The thought struck me that I could just keep driving. I could run away. I'd done it before when things got too tangled. But for the first time in my life, there was so much holding me here. My mother for one thing, and the promises I'd made to Laura, and Wesley, and Brian's little sisters. Just because someone says "no way" to involvement doesn't mean all my feelings just dissolved.

After Spencer Ashton and my suicide attempt, I'd become emotionally dead. I'd vowed I would never be in another relationship. Meeting Wesley had brought that part of me back to life. I had just allowed myself to admit I cared for him, and then he'd gone and stabbed that knife in me.

There was no traffic. I drove with the window down and the breeze hitting my face. The Valiant didn't have a radio, so I was left to bebop to the maddening melody of my own thoughts. On bass guitar—the puzzle that is the disappearance of Brian. On lead guitar—that heartbreaker Wesley. Pounding out a steady rhythm on drums was all the little bits of truth my mother shared with me. And featuring the haunting and soulful lyrical styling of Ruby's past.

I drove until the road turned to gravel and my eyelids were heavy. I pulled off by a large chain-link fence; nothing else was visible in the darkness. I could feel that tightness in my throat that is always a prelude to tears.

I crawled into the back seat and fell asleep, using the blue prom dress for a blanket.

Chapter Eight

Five or six hours later, the warmth of the sun shining through the window woke me. The driver's side door opened with a screech as I stepped outside, stretched, and sat on the hood of my car.

I'd parked by the city dump. Through the twelve-foot-high chain-link fence, I watched magpies pick at the raked-over dirt, pulling out bits and pieces of edible debris. At first glance this place wouldn't appear to be the city dump. City ordinances are big on cleanliness and environmental friendliness, so all the trash is buried almost as soon as it's dumped.

But all the garbage was just below the thin covering of dirt. The magpies knew how to find it.

The morning sun felt wonderful on my face. Despite the deep pain I felt over Wesley, I'd slept better than I had in months. It seems kind of nuts, but I'm less likely to have insomnia sleeping in an odd place than in a feather bed with a down comforter. We moved around a lot when I was a kid, and sometimes the move was in the middle of the night. I suppose that just comes with the territory when your parents are embezzlers.

Mom called it "playing pretend." We slept in bus stations, the car, hotel rooms for two or three weeks before settling down into middle-class America, where Dad could prepare to set himself up in another unsuspecting corporation. Sometimes we'd change our appearance—cut or die hair and perhaps gain or lose weight. When I was eight or nine years old, it all seemed like some wild game.

I sat through their trial. When it was all over, they got time for four counts of embezzlement in the millions of dollars. Although judging from the number of times we'd moved, I'm sure there was more embezzlement that they didn't get caught for. Later, Mom admitted her guilt, but Dad never did. He gave some wild justification about getting even with evil corporate America for the working man, like some kind of demented Jimmy Stewart. Mom was real quiet while he ranted.

In retrospect, I think that Dad was just an adrenaline junkie. He liked to race motorcycles, ski the most treacherous mountains, and drive a hundred miles an hour at night. I think Mom helped him because she loved him. Love gets you into so much trouble, makes you do things your good sense tells you not to do.

Fourteen years later, there is still a lot to sort out. Most of it will probably never make sense. Life doesn't wrap itself up into a nice, neat little package like in a sitcom or a short story. Well, maybe a short story by Flannery O'Connor. At least Flannery knew that life was ambiguous and rarely had a laugh track attached to it. The Brian puzzle seemed easier to work on than my life. What were the pieces? On a Wednesday, two and a half weeks before his wedding, Brian has a picnic with Laura. They meet the blond woman with an empty baby carriage in the park. Brian takes Laura home, hooks back up with the blond woman, and drives out to the trailer park to get his camping gear, leaving his own car at the park. If he wasn't being forced or coerced in some way, he would have taken his car to get the gear and met the blond woman later. Deedee says she saw Brian drive up in a white "car-truck," probably some off-road vehicle or an SUV. By Friday, Mom had drafted me to find Brian. A week after he disappears, Wesley and I find his camping gear in the cabin.

A few loose ends troubled me: Was Brian's disappearance connected to the GI Joe we saw in the helicopter? The white car-truck nags at my subconscious. Have I seen it somewhere before? The whole empty baby carriage is very haunting. What does it mean?

Still sitting on the hood, I rested my chin on my knee and watched the magpies in their feeding frenzy, dive-bombing each other for a morsel of rotting food. In the distance, over the hill, I could hear the rumbling roar of a bulldozer. This was probably the back side of the dump since I didn't see any fee collector's shack, entry gate, or signs indicating weights and amounts to be paid. Ironic that in the twentieth century, we must pay money to throw our garbage away, hide it from view.

I liked it here. The next time I needed to clear my head, sort things out, I'd come back. Boy, did I have a lot to sort out. Pretending that what Wesley had said to me hadn't hurt, wasn't working.

As a coping mechanism, the pain of rejection congealed into anger. Then I relived all the mistakes of the past with men. When I looked down at my hands, they were balled into fists. Feeling tension through my whole body, I uncurled my hands. Little half circles from my fingernails pressing into my palms reminded me that the line between affection and rage was very thin.

I dubbed the dump "my thinking place." The only drawback was the faint odor of refuse. But it was quiet; no one would bother me here.

I slipped behind the steering wheel, backed up, and headed for home. By the time the gravel became pavement, I could feel the net of depression descending on me again. The anger over Wesley dissipated, and all I felt was sadness.

Depression is like living permanently in a pit with muddy walls and overcast skies. The occasional cloudless moment is just so much teasing. Endless streams of counselors have told me that I am clinically depressed, but none of their solutions have worked. I wish there were a drug-free way out of this pit.

When I pulled into the driveway, I saw Maryanne and Mom in the garden at the side of the house, a Norman Rockwell painting for the nineties. Mom hunched over a patch of tomatoes, yanking thistles out at their roots and tossing them outside the garden boundaries. A French braid of salt-and-pepper hair descended ornately down her back. Soft gray curls surrounded her face. Her cheeks were rosy. A heaping bucket of carrots and zucchini rested beside her.

Maryanne sat cross-legged in the strawberry patch. The clear plastic bowl in her lap revealed only a bottom layer of strawberries. "Hey, Ruby." She yanked a strawberry from the vine and popped it in her mouth. I recognized the velour turquoise jogging suit Maryanne was wearing as one of my mother's.

Massaging the small of her back, Mom stood up. "Missed you last night, honey."

"Sorry, I should have called." I knew she wasn't worried about me. I had the habit of disappearing for a day now and then. She was pretty accepting of my need to get away and think.

Mom picked up her bucket and walked toward me. Her hand rested on my shoulder. "I was praying this morning, and I had a word from the Lord for you."

Mentally, I rolled my eyes. I hated it when she said that, because it was never just one word. Usually it was a whole sermon. Wrapping her arm around my shoulder, she led me toward the sliding-glass door. "Psalm 40, Ruby. Psalm 40."

After I opened the door for her, she patted me on the back. I watched her set the bucket on the counter and remove vegetables for washing. Her Bible sat open on the kitchen table.

I went to the bathroom to wash my face. When I returned, the Bible was still sitting open on the table, taunting me. Mom didn't say a word; she just kept shoving dirty carrots underneath the faucet and pulling them up shiny and orange.

I plopped down and glanced at the Bible.

"Psalm 40," she commented as she opened the refrigerator, stuffed the carrots on a shelf, and shut the door. She left the kitchen without another word. What can I say? The woman was good.

I turned a few pages until I found Psalm 40: "I waited patiently for the Lord; he turned to me and heard my cry. He lifted me out of the slimy pit, out of the mud and mire; he set my feet on a rock and gave me a firm place to stand."

Out of the slimy pit? I sat back in the chair. Did I hear *Twilight Zone* music playing? I decided to chalk it up to coincidence that just this morning I had called my depression a pit and then Mom had pointed out this specific passage. The alternative was too scary to think about. Maybe I'd have to look up John 4, Wesley's chapter, and see what coincidental messages I found there.

Maryanne came into the kitchen holding a pink dress covered in a plastic bag. Even through the plastic, I thought I saw the hint of white polka dots.

"What's this all about?" she asked. "Your friend Laura brought it by a few minutes before you showed up."

"You and I have got a prom date tonight at a classy little place called The Arena." I shut Mom's Bible, still trying not to think about the "coincidence." I needed to go to The Arena anyway, to try and track down the blond. Why not kill two birds with one stone?

Maryanne wrinkled her forehead. "What are you talking about?"

I stood up and patted Maryanne on the shoulder. "Just clear your calendar for after dinner tonight."

She smiled hesitantly at me. "I'm trusting you on this one."

"I'm redeeming you from all the disappointment you suffered in high school." I added as I headed toward my room, "Remember, you said you never had a date to the prom. We'll get started after I get home from work."

I spent the rest of the afternoon at the feed store, helping Georgia unload and shelve shipments of dog and ferret food and thinking a lot about slimy pits. Then I took a walk to the glass shop downtown, where I thought I had seen the red-headed beehive lady.

The dim lighting and tinkling wind chimes had an entrancing quality as I stepped across the threshold. Except for the middle-aged man behind the counter, I was the only one in the shop. I held up several vases and placed them carefully back on the shelf. Everything was out of my price range. Then I spotted a small crystal angel. She was about four inches high, and her hands stretched heavenward. Most importantly, I could afford her. I brought the angel to the front of the store and set it on the counter.

Without any verbal exchange, the clerk pressed the buttons on the register, took the ten-dollar bill I laid on the counter, wrapped the figurine in tissue paper, placed it in a brown paper bag, and handed me the bag and my change.

"This is a nice shop," I said.

"I don't own the place, but I'll pass the compliment on to Gladys."

My ears pricked up. "Gladys? That wouldn't be Gladys Smith, would it?"

The guy took two steps back from the counter. Even in the dim light, I could see that his face had drained of color. "Why are you asking?" His attempt at casualness was betrayed by the quiver in his voice.

I shrugged. "Just asking." I maintained a surface calm, but underneath, my heart was screaming, "Yippee!" Ed's T-bird-driving honey owned this place. There must have been some communication to employees about people asking questions about her. I wasn't sure what that meant. I headed toward the door. "You've got nice stuff here. Maybe I'll come back."

Maybe I *would* return. Next time with Maryanne. But on the drive home, my confidence waned. I wanted to prevent any violence from taking place, even against Ed. Maybe the best thing to do was not let Maryanne know what I'd found out. I could just keep the information to myself and hope Maryanne went back to her little town and resumed a normal, albeit lonely, life instead of spending the next two decades in prison. Or maybe I could convince Maryanne to be reunited with Ed minus the .38? She could have a good shouting match with him, and that would be it. We needed to get the T-bird back. She at least deserved that. But I had to talk her out of that gun.

When I got home, a dinner of stir-fried, garden-fresh vegetables and chicken was already simmering in the wok. The strawberries were cut and resting peacefully in the fridge, awaiting their debut atop a pound cake.

The three of us sat down at the dinner table, Mom said grace, and we dug in. In between bites, I clued Mom and Maryanne in on my search for the blond and my reason for wanting to go to The Arena.

"Wesley said it's kind of a tough bar, but I figure its nothing two thirty-something women in prom dresses can't handle." I shoved a big chunk of carrot and snow peas into my mouth.

Maryanne giggled. "Sounds like fun, like playing dress up. Growing up with two brothers and no mother didn't give me much of a chance to do that sort of thing."

Mom pushed her plate aside, laced her fingers together, and rested her elbows on the table. "Sometimes I worry about you going off the deep end." She tried to make it sound like a joke, but there was something in her tone. She shook her head and smiled as she carried her plate to the sink. "Prom dresses to a sports bar?"

A little burst of anger struck the strings of my heart. She was the reason I'd never gotten to wear a prom dress in the first place. I wanted to point that out to her. But I resisted the urge.

I did that a lot where Mom was concerned. From the time we were reunited, we had never had a blown-out angry fight about anything. Part of the reason for that was the contrast between the nervous, on-edge Mom I knew before prison and the serene Mom I had now. Getting mad at calm people seems unethical. And yet, every once in a while, a bubble of rage would erupt from the smooth reservoir of my emotions, and I'd have to clench my fists tight to keep from belting her across the chops.

I cleared the table and set to the task of getting dressed up. Since Mom was the one with the full-length mirror and all the makeup, I borrowed her room. I slipped into the dress and cinched the zipper up halfway. The hemline hit me at the ankle, and the dress swirled around me in billowing softness. The fabric sparkled as I danced in front of the mirror. If a clear field of snow could be warmed up and woven into fabric, this is what it would feel like.

I caught a glimpse of my face in the mirror and stopped midtwirl. My skin was freckled and ruddy. I had the white lashes typical of a redhead. Like I said before, my hair was the color and texture of an Irish setter's on a bad hair day. I gave up years ago trying to keep it untangled.

I sat down at Mom's vanity and leaned close to the mirror. Was I pretty? Was I pretty to anyone? Where did "pretty" come from? Did it well up inside a person until it burst out and everyone could see? Or did an outsider, usually a man, have to confirm that indeed you were pretty before it became true?

Pulling my hair into a pseudo-bun with my fingers, I turned my head from side to side. What did you do with hair like this? Declare it a Superfund site? Sighing heavily, I let the hair fall and brushed it over my face. Maybe there was a bald Irish setter somewhere who was in the market for a wig.

I felt Mom's open palm gather the hair out of my face. She must have been standing in the doorway watching me. "I think a French braid would work with all these different lengths you have." She separated the strands, tugging gently on my hair. There is something hypnotic about someone combing or braiding my hair, like being enveloped in a cloud. I closed my eyes and concentrated on nothing. My mind cleared as Mom's hand brushed my temples and then gathered the wisps of hair at my neck.

"All finished," she commented after a period of time that could not be measured. The warmth of her hands resting on my shoulders soaked through my skin to the bone. Contentment.

Mom pulled an escaped strand of hair off my forehead and tucked it back in the braid. "I used to braid your hair all the time when you were little. What do you think?"

I tilted my head and looked at the two of us in the mirror. Mom pressed her cheek close to mine and rested her hand on my shoulder. Her blue eyes glowed with joy. The wrinkles, the crow's feet, the small white scar on her chin. They all just made her more beautiful. Mother and daughter, together in a room but eons apart. How many miry pits had my mother climbed out of in her life? A single tear trickled down my freckled cheek and fell on her hand.

She kissed my cheek where the tear had traveled. "My beautiful little girl." Arms enclosed around me, and she held me, her little girl. Her sixteen-year-old little girl, left to survive on her own. But Mom was here now, holding me. The miles between us shortened; some of the anger subsided.

I cannot put to words the degree shift that took place in my soul. But the hug meant more to me than all the Bible verses she'd quoted and all the sermons she'd come home and repreached to me. I soaked in the long, peaceful moment and tucked it away for safekeeping.

"What do you think?" Maryanne stood in the doorway, a vision in pink and polka dots. She'd pulled her shoulder-length blond hair up on her head.

Mom released me from the hug as Maryanne twirled.

"You clean up nice," I said. "Let's go redeem ourselves from not going to the prom." I wrapped my arm around her shoulder and steered her toward the door.

Strange things were afoot in my life, things I could not explain. Perhaps it was this sense that things were going to change for me, or maybe it was just another way of dealing with the Wesley problem, but when Maryanne and I crawled into the Valiant, everything suddenly struck us as being funny. I'm sure it had something to do with the fact that we were two grown women dressed in formals and headed to a tough bar.

We made jokes about the names of the shops we passed. The sight of a man tangled in his dog's leash while the dog bounced around him made us laugh. We pulled up to The Arena, and I discovered that my dress had been closed in the door and had dragged on the ground the whole time we were driving. I moaned at the sight of the dirty, tattered hem. My initial frustration dissolved into humor. We couldn't contain ourselves. Our giggles became guffaws as I gathered my muddy skirt around me and stuck my chin in the air with mock dignity.

Maryanne laughed so hard that she stumbled in her high heels. I caught her by the arm just as she was about to go down on the sidewalk. The whole event was cause for more laughter as we entered the solemn interior of The Arena sports bar.

Holding her hand over her mouth, Maryanne tried to contain her sputtering. I oriented myself and held my hand on my stomach, which ached from laughing so hard.

We stood in sharp contrast to the other bar patrons, who looked like they were a week away from their last shower and light years from the winning football season that made them frequent a bar for old high school sports heroes.

Two men sat at a corner table slumped protectively over their beers, unable to hide potbellies and bald spots. A younger man throttled a pinball machine. A fourth twirled a bottle cap in his fingers, watching the big-screen TV and yelling at the unresponsive players on the baseball field. I guessed it must not be The Arena's big money night.

Various items of sports paraphernalia—skis, tennis rackets, and jerseys—decorated the walls. Behind the bar were shelves of trophies and framed photos. The bartender busied himself wiping down the already clean bar, and polishing glasses. An Arnold Schwarzenegger wannabe, he wore a pink polo shirt and sported spiked hair with an oily glisten to it. I always wondered if people who had the time to build up those kinds of muscles had real jobs. Now I knew.

We were still giggling and exchanging knowing grins as we made our way through the murky dimness to the bar. The other patrons offered only passing glances. Apparently women in prom dresses came in here all the time.

"What can I get for you?" The muscles in the bartender's neck rippled when he talked.

"I'll have a 7-Up," I said, rifling through my purse in search of the blond woman's photo.

"Me too," said Maryanne as she climbed on a stool.

Bartender boy hesitated, offering us a raised eyebrow.

"And put a human hair in it," I growled in my best tough-guy, John Wayne voice.

My remark sent Maryanne into a tizzy. She laughed so hard, she slipped off her stool. Holding onto the railing of the bar for support, she sputtered one final guffaw and wiped a tear from her eye.

With bushy eyebrows furrowed, the bartender stared at us. "Maybe you've already had enough."

He had quite a range of emotion in those eyebrows. He must do exercises for them too. A marketing idea for a video shot through my brain: *Bartender Boy's Amazing Eyebrow Workout.* There could be money in that.

"You want ice in those?"

We both nodded. By the time he set the drinks on the bar, we'd gathered ourselves into a serene moment, and I had the presence of mind to slide the photo across the bar. "Do you know any of the people in this picture?"

He held the photo up to the light. "That was taken quite a few years ago, when they had the outdoor tables. I didn't work here then." He shouted at the man watching the baseball game. "Hey, Marvin!"

Still holding his beer, Marvin lumbered to his feet, taking several backward glances at the game. "Whatcha need?"

The bartender slid the picture across the bar. "Know any of these people?"

I could hear the force of Marvin's breath. Air rattled through his lungs and nose as he inhaled and exhaled. He smelled like aftershave and cigarettes. A smile formed on his lips and filled up his eyes as he stared at the photo. "Oh, yeah. That's little Meagan Hahn." He pointed to the dark-haired woman. "I coached her for two seasons. The girl could do lay-ups like Michael Jordan. Hahn's not her name anymore. I heard she got married."

"What about the blond?" I hated to pull the man from his memories.

"She was always palling around with Meagan." He lifted his head, his glassy eyes staring far into the past. "Sarah? Shannon? Something. She didn't play ball."

I said thank you, and Marvin shuffled back to his baseball game. I wrote the name Meagan Hahn on a piece of paper and shoved it in my purse. We finished our 7-Ups and were out the door, leaving the patrons of The Arena to reminisce over last-minute touchdowns and big victories.

The maiden name of the blond woman's friend wasn't much to go on, but it was more than we'd come in with. This town was small enough that a trip to the courthouse or the library would result in an engagement announcement or marriage license. I hoped she still lived around here.

There must have been something in the air, because the minute we stepped outside, we started laughing. As we drove through downtown, Maryanne rested her head on the dashboard.

"Oh dear. Oh dear. I haven't laughed like this in ages," she said.

She sat up. I laughed again, relishing the healing properties of having a really good friend.

We drove by the glass shop that Gladys owned. The darkened windows stared at me like raccoon's eyes. I glanced nervously at Maryanne as she leaned back in her chair and gazed up at the ceiling of the car. I had a secret I was keeping from my friend.

"I like this car," she said, touching the dashboard. "I like older cars."

Were visions of T-birds dancing in her head?

I decided to keep the secret to myself until I knew more and had a little more control over the outcome.

Chapter Nine

Maryanne and I were still giggling when I turned the corner onto Mom's quiet street. I stopped laughing. Wesley's Jeep was parked outside our house. Muscles at the back of my neck tensed. That guy had some nerve. Wasn't last night the big kiss off? And now he's parked by my mother's house. I hate a tease.

"Something wrong?" Maryanne's question interrupted my righteous rage. She must have noticed my knuckles turning white and my mouth foaming as I gnashed my teeth. Just kidding. There was no foam.

"It's a long story," I said. I shoved the car door open and tromped up the sidewalk. The screen door swung wide and hit the side of the house. I scanned the empty living room, my anger forming a tightly focused bead like the laser scope on a rifle. The target entered my cross hairs as I turned the corner into the kitchen. It sat at the table sipping tea with my mother. Herbal, no doubt.

Mom looked up at me. "Ruby, you're home," she chirped.

It turned and smiled at me. Mentally, I heard a click-click as I racked back my weapon of rage and chambered an emotional bullet.

"I was worried about you," he said in a sugary sweet voice. His eyes traveled from my feet to my head. "You look nice." The comment was almost a question.

I pulled the trigger. "What are you doing here? I thought we agreed not to see each other." I felt the bullet melting in midair. I had managed to costume my deep hurt with anger, but the disguise fell away quickly. "What kind of cruel man are you? Get out of this house." My vision blurred from the tears that welled up. "Get out, I said."

The last thing I saw before I ran out of the room was Wesley's confused look as he raised his eyebrows at my mother.

I ran to my room and lay on my bed, and stared at the grayness of the night through my skylight. Clouds drifted by. I willed myself not to cry and concentrated on the shapes and outline of the clouds. This was ridiculous. I was thirty years old and acting like I was thirteen. I'd done everything but slam the bedroom door.

The power of my emotion frightened me. I hadn't felt—hadn't allowed myself to feel—that kind of intensity in . . . years. Maybe not since my breakup with Spencer. I was OK as long as I remained an emotional zombie. That was not possible with Wesley in the room.

I heard muffled voices in the kitchen and the ding of the microwave. Then laughter. A man's laughter. The nerve. I hated him. Scratch that, I didn't hate him. I cared for him. That was the problem. I didn't want to feel these feelings.

I recalled junior high dances, dressing up, spraying on my mother's perfume. I talked on the phone for an hour with my best friend as we debated whether she should wear her glasses or not. And then standing by the bleachers in the gym, giggling with my friend. It was laughter designed to hide the pain of a three-hour rejection. I remember the longing as I watched other kids walk to the center of the gym. Someone please dance with me—just one dance. It occurred to me that I'd spent the last fifteen years waiting to be asked to dance.

I heard a door closing and a car pulling away. The house grew silent, and I pulled my comforter up around me.

Mother's slippered footsteps pitter-pattered down the hallway and across my wooden floor. She set a steaming mug on my nightstand. "I brought you some cocoa." She made herself comfortable on the edge of the bed. "We thought you needed some time alone."

I sat up. "I hope the two of you had a good laugh over me." I was still embarrassed by my emotional explosion.

She pulled a strand of hair out of my eyes. "We weren't laughing at you, Ruby." Her words were gentle. "And you were right," she added.

I reached for the cocoa. "What do you mean?" I inhaled the steam. My nasal passages were clogged from crying. I relished the warm feeling of the mug in my hand. This is what mothers were about. The cocoa they made had magical healing properties.

"If the two of you agreed to cut off any romance before it began, then it was cruel of him to come over here."

I sipped the rich chocolate, allowing it to soak into my tongue. "I don't know why he has to play these games."

"Because he likes you, Ruby; he's having a hard time letting go, but he knows it's not healthy for either one of you."

"Yeah, after all, I'm not in the club."

"The club?" My mother straightened the covers.

"The good little Christian girl club."

"Wesley has hardly been a good little Christian boy. We had quite a talk before you showed up. He was very honest. He's battling his own temptations, as far as sexual sin is concerned."

"Yeah, but he turned me down. In the middle of the big forest when I was the only woman around. What an insult." At least when you slept with a guy, moved in with him, you could fool yourself into believing for a while that you weren't being used.

Mom leaned over and picked up a pair of jeans that lay on the floor. "I wouldn't take that as an insult. I think that was the hardest thing he ever did." She folded the jeans and smoothed them over with her hands. "Sex isn't love, Ruby. Which do you want?"

"I guess I'm just tired of you Christians talking about being good and doing right, and then not doing it." The comment was intended as a jab mostly because I was angry and my mom was the nearest target. Sex or love, which did I want? I'd settled for sex all those years. Why? Because I didn't think I was worthy of love?

Her response was calm. "Ever hear of grace?"

"Who's she?" I sipped my cocoa.

Mom laughed. "I'll explain it to you sometime. It's a concept, not a person." She put the jeans on the end of the bed. I didn't want to point out to her that they were dirty after all that work she'd done. She rose from the bed and kissed me on the forehead. "Sweet dreams, angel."

"Mom?" My voice stopped her in the doorway.

"Yes, sweetie."

"I'm not special to anyone. I think that's my big problem."

She took her hand away from the light switch she was about to shut off. "You're special to me."

"No, I mean to a man. I was never special to Dad. All his time was taken up keeping the world safe from corporate America or whatever it was he was doing. Any time he had left over was for Jimmy."

She stood in the doorway for a long time. "I'm sorry," she whispered.

I knew her apology wasn't just for this moment but for her part in the life she'd set up for me and Jimmy.

"There were a lot of men before you found me. But it was only sexual. Once the attraction died away or a crisis hit, they were gone."

She didn't answer for a long time. The light spilling in from the hallway allowed me to see her silhouette. "I didn't know that there were lots of men . . . guess I just thought it was that one fellow you were living with." Her head rested against the door frame.

Was that despair I heard in her voice . . . or shock? I had spared Mom the gory details of my life before she found me. "I don't want that anymore. I don't want endless relationships. I want something more. I want to be special to someone . . . forever."

"Oh Ruby, you are special to someone. He loves you with a much deeper love than romantic love, and he has more to offer you. John 4 says so." She turned off the light and shut the door.

Jesus. He was Mom's solution for everything. John 4 was the same chapter Wesley had mentioned. I'd have to read it sometime. I pulled back the covers and crawled into bed.

That night as I slept, I dreamed. I was lying in a grassy field when a brushing sensation against my bare foot woke me. I startled awake and stared into the onyx eyes of a buffalo as his tongue moistened the base of my foot. A muffled heartbeat that was not my heartbeat but the life of the forest drummed in my ears.

There was a kindness in the buffalo's face that told me not to be afraid. Not too far from me, an elk raised and lowered his head and stomped the ground with his front hooves. He turned in my direction, and the eyes looking at me were not elk eyes. They were the same eyes that had stared at me from the myriad of photos Laura and I had sorted through. Brian's eyes.

The elk exhaled, and steam rose from his nostrils. The whop-

whop of a helicopter and roar of a truck engine replaced the heartbeat.

I ran barefoot with the clomping of elk hooves beside me as the helicopter and the white vehicle pursued us. We ran, our breath rising as steam in the morning air, and the helicopter noise pressing intensely on my ears.

I stopped and looked down at my bleeding feet. There was silence. The elk, the helicopter, and the truck were gone. I watched as a trickle of blood from my feet traveled across the ground into a placid lake. An empty baby carriage floated by. I scanned the expanse of the lake, which was full of empty, broken strollers.

It was this image that woke me from my sleep. I struggled for breath as my senses oriented me in the dark. I felt the bed beneath me, made out the outline of my dresser and bookcase. I was safe. I took in a deep breath and waited for my heartbeat to return to normal. I sat in the dark for a long time, unable to shake the image of the empty baby carriages.

A misty dew of sweat formed on my forehead, and my hands trembled.

My subconscious had spoken to me in riddles, making connections that might or might not have been valid. One thing was clear to me; the truck/car that Deedee spoke of seeing Brian and the blond leave in was the same white sport-utility vehicle that was parked at the trailhead when Wesley and I hiked to the cabin. It just had to be. I knew there were plenty of white SUVs around, but they just had to be one and the same.

My digital clock glowed 2 A.M. I turned on the light and slipped out of my prom dress. The photo of Brian, Meagan, and the unnamed blond sat on my dresser. The blond was the key. I hoped the former Meagan Hahn could tell me who she was.

I crawled back between my covers and slept soundly. No more dreams.

The next morning, I called Laura while I sipped my morning cup of coffee. My career as a professional student made me quite proficient at research, but I thought maybe an extra set of eyes would make the work go faster. Since Wesley was no longer my assistant, it made sense to call Laura.

She picked up the phone on the first ring. "Hello." Her voice sounded a million miles away.

I was temporarily distracted as I watched Mom and Maryanne skip out the door on their way to garage sales and to sell crafts and garden veggies at the farmer's market. They were dressed in matching pantsuits with fake jewels around the neck, one of Mom's favorite crafts projects. Mom wore pink and Maryanne sported navy. Twins. They waved good-bye at the door. Maryanne did all the stuff with Mom that I refused to do. Part of me was happy they had so much in common, and part of me was jealous. But no part of me wanted to wear that pantsuit.

"Hey, Laura?" I said holding the receiver close to my mouth.

"Ruby, hi." Her voice was faint.

"Is everything OK?"

"Do you know what today is?"

"Saturday, garage-sale day, farmer's market," I said.

She laughed noncommittally. "I wish that's all it was. Today was supposed to be my wedding day." I felt my heart drop into my shoes. "I remembered to cancel everything except the flowers. I'm sitting here surrounded by four hundred dollars worth of pink and burgundy roses."

Give me the award for queen of the inconsiderate. "Oh Laura, I'm so sorry."

"It's not your fault." I heard her sniffle. "I can't return them. Do you want to help me take them up to the retirement home and give them out? That way I'd be turning a bad thing into something positive."

I wish I could learn to think like her. I said I'd be glad to help out.

"I called the police this morning. They haven't been able to find a trace of him. They said when someone has been missing this long, they've either skipped the country or are dead," she said.

"Brian's not dead, Laura. I feel it in my gut." I didn't tell her about the dream because I doubted that that held much validity over years of police experience. I told her about finding out the brunette's maiden name, and she agreed to go to the library with me after she'd picked me up and we'd dropped off the flowers.

For a small town, the library had well-referenced files of local newspapers. It didn't take us long to find an engagement announcement. Meagan Hahn was now Meagan Struthers. A trip to the phonebook revealed that she and her husband had settled in his hometown, Sparkling Gulch, which was about forty miles west of Eagleton.

Laura asserted that she wanted to go with me, and she offered to drive. Her eyes were red from crying, and I wasn't about to make her cry again. Whatever Laura wanted to do today, we would do.

Sparkling Gulch was one of those former turn-of-the-century gold rush towns that now prospered because of a new kind of gold, tourism. Places like this hibernated through the winter and boomed in the summer. As we entered the town limits, I noticed the traditional museum and specialty shops as well as a few historic brick structures now renovated into upscale clothing boutiques and art galleries.

Our Mrs. Struthers lived not far off Main Street, which is where everybody who resided in town lived. A stable population of one thousand doesn't exactly call for suburbs. As we pulled up to the house, an athletic-looking man in his early thirties came around the side of the house, carrying one child in a backpack and holding an older boy by the hand.

Laura was the first to get out of the car. I scrambled up behind her as she introduced herself. "Hi, we're old high school friends of Meagan's from Eagleton. Is she around?"

I gave Laura one of my best furrowed-brow, sidelong glances. We hadn't talked about taking on some kind of persona. But it made sense in case Meagan had some reason to protect her blond friend. Laura was good at this.

"Meagan's working down at the soda fountain today. I'm Jim, her husband." He narrowed his eyes at us. "Thought I knew all of Meagan's old friends. What did you say your name was?"

Laura looked at me. "Actually . . . " I cleared my throat. "Laura was a few years behind Meagan, but I was on the basketball team with her. Good ol' Meg could do a layup like Michael Jordan."

Jim shifted his eyes back and forth between us. The little boy yanked on his hand. "Come on, Daddy. Let's go to the park."

"Look, I'm on kid duty today." The child pulled Jim toward the sidewalk. "Like I said, she's down at the soda fountain."

The soda fountain was one of two restaurants in town. The other place, a bar and supper club, was closed until two o'clock. It was about ten-thirty when we entered, so the lunch crowd hadn't shown up yet. We were the only patrons besides a booth full of high school girls who were crooning over a fan magazine and throwing ice-cream toppings at each other.

"Very retro." I looked up at the fan on the ceiling and the row of pink vinyl counter stools. We both took a seat at the counter.

Meagan emerged from the back room with a tray full of clean ice-cream sundae glasses.

"What can I get for you ladies?" she said as she stacked the glasses. Her hair was shorter, but Meagan didn't look much older than she did in the photograph. Even after two children, she had the svelte, toned body of an athlete. Her arms and legs were tanned. She wore shorts, a floral T-shirt, and a white apron.

"I'll have a vanilla shake," Laura said. I was still looking over the menu when Laura elbowed me.

"Me too." It occurred to me that I hadn't had any breakfast, and a milk shake wasn't the best thing to put into an empty stomach. I read the breakfast specials that were written on construction paper with a marker and posted above the grill. While Meagan mixed our shakes, Laura pulled the photo out of my purse and put it on the counter.

Meagan put the shakes down in front of us. "Anything else?"

I was about to ask for waffles with strawberries when Laura pointed to the blond in the photo. "Can you tell me what this woman's name is?"

Meagan glanced at the photo. Her customer-service smile disappeared, and the color drained from her face. "Where did you get that?"

Laura leaned across the counter as Meagan took two steps back. "Please, I need to know her name," Laura said, a note of anguish in her voice.

Two things occurred to me. One, I was not going to get any breakfast, and two, maybe we should have thought of a lie to tell Meagan to extort information from her, 'cause the girl looked like she was about to utilize some of her athletic ability and either beat us up or run away.

"Are you guys police or something?" She wrung her hands.

I thought Laura was going to climb over the counter. "This man is my fiancé. He's missing, and this woman might know where he is." Laura pointed to Brian and then to the blond. "This is you in the picture, isn't it Meagan?"

"I . . . um, I . . . don't know. I haven't seen her."

The bells on the screen door tinkled and a patron entered. Just when I thought Meagan's skin couldn't get any whiter, her face turned bloodless and her eyes grew wide. She began to shake her head and wave her arms at the person who had just entered.

I swung around on my stool and looked into the living eyes of the blond from the picture. Holy coincidence, Robin, it's our suspect! The blond bolted out the door. I grabbed the photo, and we rushed out after her.

Chapter Ten

The wooden sidewalks were just beginning to fill up with tourists when we dashed outside. The blond was less than a block ahead of us, in clear sight. Her long, honey yellow hair was easy to see as she raced across the street and disappeared into an alley.

Laura ran ahead of me. Already I was breathing heavily, but my legs, motivated beyond their physical ability, pounded the pavement of the street. I'd been chasing this woman for too long; I wasn't about to lose her now. Gravel crunched beneath my feet as we entered the alley, which opened up into a huge unpaved parking lot. I didn't have to see the white SUV to know why the blond had run this way.

Out of breath, Laura stopped and turned to look at me.

"The car! Go get the car!" I commanded. "I'll watch and see which way she goes."

Laura shot back down the alley and disappeared. I ran to the high end of the parking lot and waited for the sound of an engine starting up. From where I stood, I could see the roofs of four white vehicles. No engines roared to life. I scanned the silent lot three or four times. Maybe she could see me. Was she waiting for me to leave before she took off?

I ruled out one of the vehicles—too low to the ground. Except for Main Street parking, this had to be the only lot in town. A couple with a girl of about ten entered from a side street and walked to the center of the lot. They offered me only a brief questioning stare as I waved at them. Maybe I'd been wrong. Maybe she'd gone right through the lot. I craned my neck to look at the trees and hill behind me. She could be hiding there.

An engine cranked to life and then a second one started up. I snapped my head around and scanned the lot. The couple's red BMW pulled out of a spot. As I honed in on the white roofs, I could hear a second engine humming. A battered blue pickup screeched out of a space in the far corner of the lot, zigzagged past the red BMW, and zoomed out onto the street. I had just enough time to see a blond head and to mentally kick myself. She'd probably been sneaking up to the truck the whole time I was watching white roofs.

Laura pulled up and slowed down long enough for me to grab the handle of the back door and fall onto the back seat. I was nose to nose with a pile of *Bride* magazines. I sat up, gripping the headrest of the driver's seat and swaying slightly from the power of the G-forces as Laura jerked the steering wheel into a sharp right.

"Blue pick-up. Heading toward I-90," I offered.

"I saw her." Laura's eyes focused on her unseen target ahead. She drove with sharp, deliberate movements on the curving two-lane. Roaring up to a blue Volkswagen van, she snaked around it on a double yellow line. As we raced by gas stations and rest stops, I checked for the blue truck.

The two-lane opened up into the interstate. Laura hit the gas, and the needle topped out at one hundred. My stomach grabbed my spine. Her little sports car whizzed around the slower vehicles and careened back into the right lane. Traffic thickened, but none of the vehicles were the blue pickup.

"Maybe she turned off somewhere?" I theorized.

Laura's arms slackened at the wheel. "I think she just got too far ahead of us."

"She didn't have that big a lead on us. I say we backtrack."

As we drove back to Sparkling Gulch, we spotted plenty of dirt roads the blue truck could have turned onto. Laura pulled into a truck stop just outside of town. Turning off the key, she tilted her head against the headrest. "What a way to spend your wedding day, huh?"

I leaned forward. "You and I are pretty good at this cops-and-robbers thing. I say we go back to Meagan's house and interrogate some evidence out of her."

Laura laughed. "She's not going to tell us anything. She thinks she's being righteous by protecting her friend. But we could go watch the house. Maybe the blond will come back."

It was close to noon when we pulled back into town, and my stomach was growling. Since eating at the soda fountain was out and the supper club didn't open for another two hours, we stopped at a convenience store and picked up some microwave burritos, which are almost like food.

The neighborhood didn't provide many places to hide, unless we chose one of the hedges that grew in the surrounding yards. Even that wouldn't give us full camouflage, and how do you explain to a homeowner why you are crouching in his greenery? We drove around, munching chips and burritos, until I noticed a tower in the park next to Meagan's neighborhood.

Laura pulled some binoculars out of a camera bag in her trunk, and we took turns climbing to the top of the tower and watching the house. While Laura tried to keep kids out of the tower by pushing them on the swings, I spied on the house, waiting for the blue pickup to pull into the drive. The truck had to belong to Meagan and Jim. The blond would have to bring it back sooner or later.

"What are you lookin' at?" I pulled the binoculars from my eyes and glanced down to see a girl of about seven. Her hair was carrot red, and freckles garnished her cheeks. She smiled in a way that made her green eyes dance. She must have slipped past Laura's patrol.

"Nice hair," I commented, hoping to change the subject.

"Mama says it's the way God made me. I love Jesus. Do you love Jesus?"

I peered through the binoculars just in time to see the garage door open. "You people are everywhere, aren't you?" My heart rate increased as the white SUV pulled out of the garage with Jim at the wheel. I glanced back at the little girl. "Do kids at school give you a hard time about your hair? They used to tease me all the time."

The little girl leaned against the windowsill of the tower. "Doesn't matter what they say. God thinks I'm beautiful." She smiled up at me, green eyes sparkling. "Your hair is pretty too." She touched it lightly.

I wish I had had her self-confidence when I was seven. I glanced down at the white SUV. It turned the corner and disappeared.

"There's my mom. I have to go." The girl bolted across the floor and down the ladder of the tower. I watched below me as she ran into the arms of her mother and they walked across the park, holding hands. Mom tells me that God sometimes speaks through people. I don't know if that's true or not. Had God sent a little red-headed girl to tell me that he, God, thought I was beautiful? Sometimes I get to wondering. Mom might be right.

Laura and I waited until late in the day, when Jim returned and parked the SUV on the street by the house. We watched as he pulled his lawnmower out of the garage. Meagan trimmed hedges while he cut grass, and the children ran through the sprinkler.

My upbringing has made me a pessimist. Despite this apparent picture of domestic bliss, no family is that happy. Meagan was probably embezzling from the soda fountain. And on top of that, she was protecting someone who might have kidnapped Brian.

Toward dusk, the family went inside and, except for the glow of the TV set, all the lights went out. Laura and I sat on the floor of the tower, strategizing.

"I bet there is all kinds of information in that SUV." We stared out the window of the tower. The gray veil of night decreased our visibility, but the white SUV glowed like a beacon.

"Assuming the vehicle belongs to the blond, her name would be on the registration," Laura said.

"Time for some breaking and entering, I guess." I pulled myself off the floor and headed toward the two-by-four framed opening for the ladder that led down to the park. I stopped halfway down the ladder and called up to my fellow conspirator. "Hey, Laura." She came to the opening and stared down at me. The haziness of evening made her face look like it was in soft focus. "You don't have to come with me if you don't want to. I know this stuff is legally questionable."

She leaned toward me, perching on her knees. "I'll go with. I need to find Brian."

The street where the white vehicle was parked was abandoned and nearly dark. Most everybody in Beaver Cleaver land had put the kids to bed and settled down to an evening of laughless sitcoms.

Laura and I walked like normal people until we were about half a block from the car, and then for some inexplicable reason, we fell into a Three Stooges routine minus one stooge. A man walking his dog approached, and we both dove for a hedge, falling on top of each other.

"Evening, ladies," said the man as he walked by the hedge.

I shrugged at Laura, and we both pulled ourselves up off the ground.

"Our guilty consciences are showing," I theorized.

"We're not stealing anything," Laura explained. "We're just looking for information."

We approached the car from the sidewalk side, crouching to avoid being seen by Meagan and Jim as they watched TV. Jim rose up off the couch and glanced out the window on his way to the kitchen. I flattened myself against the sidewalk. Concrete was cold at night. Laura pressed against the dark tire of the white SUV.

"Is he gone yet?" I whispered.

Laura lifted her head slowly. "Wait 'til he sits back down."

I'm a fairly creative person, but what explanation would I come up with if someone came by and found me lying with my cheek pressed against the sidewalk?

"OK, he's sitting down." Laura pulled herself up and scrambled around to the back of the vehicle.

"What are you doing?" I scream-whispered at her as I inched along the sidewalk in a crouch.

"I'm memorizing the license plate number. It might come in handy." This girl was definitely the sharpest knife in the drawer. I was going to have to keep her around. "Washington plates and it says 'Mac.'" She came around to the side of the vehicle and tried the back door. Locked. So was the passenger side front.

I didn't need to go around to the other side to know we'd have the same kind of luck there. I bit my fingernail and looked at Laura, who did the most amazing thing. She pulled some kind of hair-holding device off her head and jimmied the lock with it. Good girl Laura knew how to open locked cars. I *definitely* had to keep this lady around.

"You'll have to explain to me sometime where you learned how to do that," I said as I crawled into the front seat. I unlocked the back door for Laura, and she slipped silently inside. The dim interior lights made the registration hard to find among the glove compartment papers. It was even harder to read.

"Hey, look at these." Flopping her hand over the top of the seat, she handed me a pile of photographs.

More interested in finding the blond's name, I shuffled through them quickly. All of them were of a blond child that more distinctly became a boy as the child aged in the pictures. The last picture was of a boy about eight years old, wearing overalls, standing in a meadow dotted with yellow flowers.

"Looks like somebody's kid." I handed them back to her.

I finally found the registration. Holding it up to the street lamp, I read the name, "Serena MacDonald." Bingo! My reverie was interrupted by a tapping at the window. I could just make out the police officer behind Jim's angry face.

We stepped out of the vehicle. Meagan stood, hands on her hips, backlit by the porch light. "Make sure they didn't take anything, Jim," she commanded.

I set the registration back on the seat and burned the name "Serena MacDonald" into my brain.

Jim, dressed in a bathrobe and slippers, turned to his wife. "Do you really think we need to file charges, honey?"

While the officer patted us down, Meagan read her husband the riot act. "They broke into her—our—car, Jim. They may plan on hitting a few more."

Oh, Meagan, Meagan, you know that's not why we're here, I thought. The lies just got more and more elaborate for her, all in the name of protecting her friend.

The officer didn't even handcuff us. Instead, he escorted us the two blocks to the city jail and invited us in. City jail consisted of a single desk and a counter. I could finally get a good look at the officer. He was an older man with gray temples. I suspected somebody somewhere called him Grandpa. "Do you ladies want a latte or a mocha? We just got our new espresso machine."

I leaned over and whispered in Laura's ear. "If this is what a life of crime leads to, I should have signed up a lot sooner."

"Aren't you going to throw us in a cell or something?" Laura asked as she took a steaming cup of cappuccino.

"Honestly, you ladies don't look like dangerous felons to me. After eighteen years as a cop in Chicago, old Maury O'Reilly knows a violent offender when he sees one. So why don't you just tell me what you were doing in that car?"

In *Reader's Digest* form, I related the story of our search for the blond, Serena MacDonald.

"That's a real sad story. Sorry I can't help you ladies."

Like most cops, he knew more than he was saying. Probably felt protective of Meagan and her family and the community he'd been hired to serve.

Without benefit of a court or lawyer, Maury cut us a deal. Maury said that Meagan would probably cool off by morning and not want to push for breaking-and-entering charges if we agreed to stay out of town and not bother her anymore. Since it was late, he said we could spend the night in an unlocked jail cell.

Jail wasn't bad, especially with the door left open.

Maury told us there was one other patron, a drunk woman, in the unlocked jail cell. This was starting to feel like we were in Mayberry. I hoped her name wasn't Otis.

There were two sets of bunks in the single cell. Maury left the light on for us and said goodnight. The cell's other occupant, a woman of about forty, sat up from the upper bunk, where she had been snoring. Laura and I settled on the lower bunk opposite her.

Pulling her straight brown hair out of her face, the woman yawned and stretched her arms toward the ceiling. Her multicolored skirt draped to her ankles. She wore a tie-dyed shirt and a necklace with a huge crystal dangling from it. Except for the Birkenstock shoes, I would have guessed she was a welfare case or a starving student. She was probably only playing at poor.

"Hey, when did you guys come in here?" Her speech was the slow drawl of someone who had been drinking. "I heard you out talking with Maury." She attempted to lean back casually by planting her arms behind her. Her rubbery arms waffled, setting her off balance. She caught herself before her upper body fell completely back. Instead, she settled for leaning forward and resting her elbows on her thighs.

Uncertain how we should respond to this level of inebriation, Laura and I sat like obedient schoolgirls and listened.

"Don't worry about old Maury. He tries to take care of this town and keep . . ." She paused as though the remainder of the sentence had been stolen from her. Her glassy eyes stared at the brick wall as if profound truths were written on it. "He keeps this place pretty peaceful."

She swung off the bed like an animated rag doll. Both Laura and I nearly leaped up to help her.

Holding up her hand with a stop motion, she assured us, "I'm all right." She found a wall to hold her up and continued. "I think I know the girl you were asking about. Got a picture of her?"

I pulled the photo out of my purse.

She studied the photo. "Yeah, I've seen her around. She's come into my shop, I don't know, a couple of times. I own an eco-boutique."

"An eco-boutique?" I had to ask.

Watching this woman was like watching a dubbed foreign film. All her gestures were delayed, not quite matching up with the words. "You know, natural fiber stuff, hemp products, little chocolates with endangered species on them." Her voice crescendoed up into the high pitches. I feared that soon only dogs would be able to hear her talking, and they would start baying outside the window. "I used to sell furs in New York. No market for that anymore."

The woman flopped down on the lower bunk opposite us. "She stays with Meagan. A couple of times, three guys have come with her."

Laura rifled through her purse and pulled out a more recent picture of Brian. "Was she ever with this man?"

The boutique woman took the picture and let the other photo drop to the cement floor. She opened and closed her eyes several times, trying to focus. "No, I would have remembered someone that handsome. These guys were scruffy looking, like a good shave was two weeks behind them. One of them is just a kid and one of them is an older guy with a ponytail."

"What about the third guy?" Laura pressed. "It could be Brian. He may not have had a chance to shave."

Without warning, the boutique woman flopped back on the bed and pulled the pillow up to her stomach. Within minutes, her loud garbled snore filled the tiny cell.

"I don't think you are going to get any more out of her, Laura."

Still alert from the coffee and the excitement of the day, Laura and I were nowhere near ready to go to sleep. We flipped for bunks. I got the bottom.

We sang a couple choruses of "Swing Low, Sweet Chariot" and "Nobody Knows the Trouble I've Seen," but the songs lacked luster without a harmonica.

"So, Laura," I said, staring at the springs of the upper bunk as I lay back on my cot. "You gonna explain to me where you learned to pick locks?" Since we were in "the joint," "the big house," "doing time" together, it seemed like a good time to share secrets.

The upper bunk squeaked as Laura sat up. "When I was in high school, I went through what I guess you would call a crisis of faith. It just looked like everyone else was having a better time than I was. So I rebelled. Started hanging out with some people who, among other things, knew how to pick locks."

"Really." I propped up my elbow and rested my head in my palm. "I'm having a hard time picturing you doing anything bad."

"It didn't last long. I missed my Savior. How about you? Ever have a crisis of faith?"

Laura must have been assuming that I held the same religious beliefs as my mother. "A crisis of faith? Oh, a few."

"Is that why you don't go to church with your mother?"

Ah, so she did know. I wondered if my name had ever come up in any of her prayer circles. "Something like that," I said. "I'm getting tired. That coffee is starting to wear off." I rolled over and faced the wall.

I heard Laura yawn. "Not that church attendance is a sign of spiritual health or anything. It's more about the condition of the heart." Her words faded out.

I lay staring at the wall for some time. The condition of the heart, my black heart. Is that the color God saw when he looked at my heart? I was glad she hadn't told me to read John 4. That would have been just too freaky.

It had been a good day in more ways than one. I had a name to go on now, Serena MacDonald. She had actually been here in this town. I wasn't sure what those pictures in her car meant, if anything. My mind flashed to the empty baby carriage in the park. Serena had approached Brian and Laura, pushing an empty baby carriage. What did it mean?

I'd spent the whole day solving other people's problems. Not once had my mind begun to sink into depression. Not once had I thought about the past. This was good.

Baby carriages? Pictures of a child? Serena coming and going from Meagan's. Never with Brian. Something kept Brian from being able to come home or contact Laura. "Laura?" I spoke into the darkness, my mind racing.

"Yeah," came the sleepy reply.

"Did Brian ever mention Serena by name or talk about a woman he'd had an extensive relationship with?"

Laura roused herself from sleep. "No. I think I would have remembered that. He just said that there had been other women in the past and that they didn't mean anything to him." Her voice was tinged with anxiety.

I didn't want to push her. Other women in the past . . . and perhaps a child.

Laura's voice came from a million miles away, as though she were speaking from some vast emotional desert. "Brian hasn't run away with her. He loves me."

I wanted to believe that was true.

⤻

The next morning, we left town without stopping for breakfast. Keeping our word to Officer O'Reilly would not be easy. Meagan probably held all kinds of secrets that would make finding Serena a lot easier.

"Those were Washington plates on her car. Notice that?" Laura asked as she turned the wheel into a tight curve.

Well, take away my junior detective badge. I'd forgotten about that already. "Yeah, I noticed that too."

"So my guess is she just moved here or is visiting. Maybe she stayed at one of the hotels in town."

We'd been looking for the name of the blond so long that I hadn't thought far enough ahead to decide what we would do with the information when we got it. "I suppose we could check the hotels. But I'm not sure how that would help us."

"She may have given a home address or something in the registration," Laura continued. "Or maybe the hotel workers remember something about her. Maybe they saw her with Brian."

My mind was on a different track. One that I didn't want to share with Laura. What if Brian and Serena had had a child together? Maybe she'd had the baby in Eagleton. Certainly there would be a record of the birth. Would a man leave his fiancée to try and work things out with an old flame just because they'd had a child together?

It didn't make sense. There had to be some reason why Brian didn't try to contact Laura. Even if he didn't want to experience her rage and hurt, wouldn't he at least tell his best friend, Wesley? Either he could not contact anyone because he was being held against his will . . . or he was dead. No, I couldn't let my mind go there.

It was mid-Sunday morning when Laura dropped me off at Mom's house. We still hadn't come up with a clear plan on what to do next. *We* hadn't come up with a plan, but I had. Monday morning before work, I was going down to the courthouse to check birth records.

Mom was still at church. Maryanne's room was empty as well. When I went to the refrigerator door for breakfast possibilities, I saw the note pinned underneath a magnet. In Mom's neat handwriting it said, "Ruby, Wesley called. Strictly business, he said."

He did, did he? Part of me wanted to ignore the note, forcing him to call me back. The other part of me was already at the phone dialing the memorized number. He picked up on the third ring.

"Why aren't you at church?" I blurted out.

"Hi, Ruby." Wesley laughed, making me feel even more childish. "I go to late service. I spend the morning praying."

What a devout little scoundrel, I thought. "Mom said you called."

"I did. Now, before you get upset with me, this is official business only."

I closed my eyes, marinating in the gravelly liquid base tones of his voice. "Official business only." More than anything, I wished he was standing in the room with me. I wanted to feel his warmth and smell the soapy freshness of his skin when he was close. "Well, hurry up. I don't have all day." This was hard. Never in my life had I resisted desire. More than anything, I wanted to revel in the dizzy intoxication that physical attraction produces.

"I talked to Rachel."

All my good feelings vaporized. "How is good old Ranger Rachel."

"She sent somebody to look at that cabin and the buffalo carcass."

"And—"

"No sign of Brian or his stuff," he said.

"I'm sorry," I said. "Maybe we should have waited for him to come back to the cabin."

"It's not your fault, Ruby. Do you want to hear the weird part? Rachel said all the buffalo's legs were broken, like he'd been dropped from a great height."

"Ah, the infamous buffalo-dropping tournaments."

He chuckled. "I miss your sense of humor."

"Not to be confused with annual hamster-juggling competitions." I was on a roll now. "Or the now-famous porcupine-bowling tournaments."

Wesley was laughing so hard, he couldn't respond. Finally, he cleared his throat. "Ah, that puts some strange pictures in my head."

"So who would want to drop a buffalo from a great height, and why?" It felt good to make him laugh.

"I don't know, but that helicopter we saw must have something to do with it."

"Poachers who like to torture their prey before they shoot it?" I speculated.

"Maybe. But there were no bullet holes in the buffalo."

My mind shifted gears; I had news for him, too. "Did Brian ever mention dating a Serena MacDonald?"

"He may have. I went into the marines right after high school. That could have been when he met her. I wasn't a great letter writer. Or maybe she was part of a group we hung with in high school."

"I know. There were a lot of girls, and you don't remember their names." Romance was funny. Why was it that if I couldn't have his affection, I'd settle for irritating him, jabbing him where it hurt?

"Let's not get started on that again, Ruby."

Right, this was strictly business. "Did he ever mention having a kid?"

"A kid?" I had to hold the receiver away from my ear. "Ruby, that's a little bigger deal than just another girlfriend. I'm sure he would have said something to me about it."

"Not if he was ashamed of having a child out of wedlock. You did say he was a Christian when you got back from the marines."

"He still would have told me." Even over the phone I could feel Wesley's angst levels rising. "Brian did everything he could to make amends with his past."

"Maybe having a child was so big, it was the one thing he couldn't deal with."

Wesley sighed. "Still, he would have told me."

He'd kept the secret from Laura. Why would he tell Wesley? They both had a blind spot where Brian was concerned. No point in pushing. "So why did you come over the other night?"

"I was worried about you going to that bar by yourself. And you seemed really hurt after—"

"I'll be fine." *Give me a couple hundred years. I'll get over you, Wesley dear.* "Let's just work on finding Brian."

I listened to the static on the phone before he answered. "That sounds like a good idea."

We said good-bye, and I hung up. I clicked the phone back onto its cradle on the wall. If Brian had had a kid, there was maybe only one person he would have told, his pastor. I wondered if pastors had to keep confessions a secret like priests did.

I had this vision of buffalo falling out of the sky. One thing was for sure. Sooner or later, I was going to end up back at that Forest Service cabin. The answers to Brian's whereabouts were in that forest somewhere, and in Serena MacDonald's past. If it wasn't a child that connected them, what was it?

Chapter Eleven

The courthouse birth records didn't show Serena MacDonald having given birth in the last nine years. She could have had the baby anywhere between here and Washington. I had no way of knowing.

I sat on the courthouse steps and watched children play in a park across the street. Three dark-haired children took turns on the only unbroken swing while their mother sat at a picnic table, flipping through a magazine.

Pieces in this puzzle just were not fitting. Empty baby carriage. Pictures of a child. Like not being able to remember someone's name, a thought hung at the periphery of my consciousness. What was I overlooking?

Obviously, Serena would not be pushing an eight-year-old child around in a baby carriage. Was the carriage intended as some kind of signal to Brian? A way of saying, "I have our child"? Why not just bring the kid up to him? Maybe she had told him the little boy was in the Forest Service cabin, and that was why he went with her.

I watched as the mother herded her children together, including the stray one who had wandered over to the slide. With one child on her hip and two trailing behind, the mother hoisted a large bag over her shoulder and walked toward a car. The short distance was covered at a snail's pace because she had to keep adjusting the child and the bag and turning around and commanding the two older children to keep moving. Trash and rocks they found on the ground seemed to hold endless fascination for them. She loaded and buck-led three children in their car seats and drove off.

The playground was empty. The swing made an "eek eek" noise as it wound down from the force of children swinging in it. Play-grounds without children are creepy, almost haunting.

A strange anxiety rose up in me. I felt the clamp in my chest tightening as my eyes scanned the vacant steps of the slide. I watched the paralyzed merry-go-round, willing it to move, visu-alizing children pushing it and laughing, their small heads close together, their silky hair shining as they ran. I shivered.

When I looked at those empty swings, a sense of panic flooded through me as though I must run from house to house screaming, "Red alert, red alert. Empty playground. Send out your children!"

There is something not right about an empty playground, like a birthday cake with no frosting, candles, or decorations.

So far, my morning had been highly unproductive. I was about ready to give up on the baby theory altogether. But I had one more place to go before I caught an afternoon shift at the feed store. If anyone would know about Brian fathering a child out of wedlock, it had to be his pastor.

I called Mom's church. The secretary said that it was Pastor Carpenter's day off, but she gave me his home phone number when I said it was urgent. I dialed the number. He picked up on the fifth ring.

"Pastor Carpenter? This is Ruby Taylor. Emily's daughter?"

"Yes, I know who you are." His voice had a cheerful ring to it.

Of course he knew who I was. Mom was probably constantly asking for prayer for her "unsaved" daughter. I know how these people talk when they think no "unsaved" people are around.

Although I didn't mind being prayed for, I resented the label. What does that mean anyway, "unsaved"?

"I need to talk to you about Brian Fremont—about his past, about any children he might have fathered before . . . I just need to talk to you."

Silence filled the line for a long moment. "Ruby, if Brian had shared that sort of information with me, it would be confidential."

How did I know he would say that? "It might be the difference between finding him and not finding him." I waited. He didn't say anything. I heard a deep sigh on the other end of the line.

"Pastor, please."

"I need time to pray about this. And I need to talk to you in person. Why don't you meet me at the church in half an hour?"

The few times I'd been to my mom's church, I'd hated it. Today was no different. Even though it was Monday and I didn't have to deal with the throngs of terminally cheerful Christians, I still got this feeling of "badness" and unworthiness every time I stepped across the threshold. The church had no high ceilings or stained glass, but I could feel a shift in reality as I walked through the entrance and into the church part of the building. The pews were empty, and no one stood at the podium. Still, I had the feeling that this place was holy—and I was not. We didn't fit, this church and I. What did you have to do to feel worthy, to sit on one of those benches?

The pastor's office was at the other end of the building. The only way to get to it was to walk past the empty benches and the streams of light coming in through the windows. I did a nutty thing when I got to the front of the church. I sat down and stared at the vacant stage.

"Hi, God," I said. "It's me."

Not that I was expecting an answer or anything. It just felt good to sit there in the sacred silence. I know there is a God. I'm just not sure what I'm supposed to do about it. Call it a breakthrough moment. It passed without much fanfare.

While I was sitting contemplating deep things, a short man with thinning light brown, wavy hair emerged from the office. He always looked smaller than he did behind the podium. "Ruby, thank you for coming over. I didn't want to address this over the phone." He spoke in flat tones and looked directly at me, eyes probing.

"Pastor Carpenter." What a name for a preacher. Other than the phone call, this was the first time I'd spoken to him directly. "Thank you for talking to me on such short notice."

He held one hand in the palm of the other and stared at me. It felt like the guy was reading me under my skin. What did he see? "I've been thinking about what you asked me over the phone," he said slowly. "We better go into my office."

I followed dutifully. He shut the door and positioned himself behind his desk.

I sat down in a chair with a worn fabric cushion. Bits of foam peeked through the frayed blue fabric, and it squeaked slightly when I moved. Pastor brought his hands up to his chin. His light gray sweatshirt had frayed cuffs and grass stains on it. Earlier, I had noticed oil and grass stains on his worn jeans. He'd pulled himself away from his yard work to talk to me. That made me feel—well, important.

He seemed reluctant to begin, so I spoke. "I know I'm asking you to tell me something very personal about Brian."

He thumbed through the pages of the Bible that was sitting on his desk. "But it could help you find Brian?"

"Yes."

After closing his Bible, he leaned forward, resting his elbows on the desk. His eyes were clear brown, no gray or green specks. Despite all the hypocrisy I saw in my mother's church, I liked her pastor.

"Ruby, I want to find Brian as much as you do. But I cannot reveal anything told to me in confidence in a counseling session."

I sat back in my chair. I had to admire the guy for his ethics. But it didn't help me any. Pastor Carpenter was my last lead. "Well, could you just signal to me when I ask you a question? Raise your eyebrows for yes and twitch your nose for no?"

Pastor Carpenter laughed. "I'm sorry, Ruby."

"Did he ever mention someone named Serena MacDonald?" I persisted. Something in his eyes sparked. I was right. He stood up, turned his back to me, and ran his hands through his hair. I felt myself leaning forward, willing him to tell me more.

"I can't break a confidence." He kept his back to me when he spoke.

I had to be right. Brian and Serena had had a child together. I remembered Brian's mom saying that Brian's father had left when he was a baby. Brian probably didn't want to repeat the same pattern. He would have done anything to see his son again. That had to be it. And Brian hadn't told Laura. . . .

I stared at Pastor Carpenter's back, feeling the ire envelop me.

"Why didn't you make him tell Laura? It wouldn't be a minor issue in their marriage if Serena showed up on the doorstep with the kid." I swallowed hard to try and push the anger back down in my throat. "Isn't that what Christianity is all about? Coming clean with all your dirty little secrets?" I was upset, because if anybody was getting slighted in this whole deal, it was Laura.

He turned back and looked at me. His usually serene forehead wrinkled, eyes drawn into a squint. "Please, Ruby, I appreciate your loyalty to Laura. But you must not persist in this. I cannot break a confidence."

I hung my head and stared at my hands. "I'm sorry. I'm not mad at you. I'll go." I thanked him and excused myself. As I stood at the threshold of the door, I asked, "Don't you think Laura should know—especially now?"

"If it were true, would it help anything to let her know?"

What kind of answer was that? I walked toward the entrance of the church. Obviously, the man was taught by Jesus, the original answer-a-question-with-a-question guy. I was 90 percent sure that Serena and Brian had had a child, a boy. But the child hadn't been born in Eagleton.

Two days passed. I worked full days at the feed store and tried not to let my mind wander. Information hung on my heart like a lead weight. I was the holder of two explosive secrets, and I had to decide whether to light the fuse or not. I knew about the redhead in the glass shop who could lead me to Maryanne's Ed Lawson. Maryanne could load up her pistol and have her revenge. Of course, I would visit her in prison. Or I could tell her about the glass shop and make sure she didn't leave the house with the gun. As angry as Maryanne was, she might just kill him with her bare hands.

And then there was this thing about Brian's child. If Brian was dead somewhere, Laura need never know about the child. She could continue to see Brian as her perfect prince.

What was this need I had to protect Laura from harsh reality? Most likely, only Serena and Pastor Carpenter knew about the baby. And I was pretty sure one of them would never talk.

But if Brian was alive, how would telling Laura help anything?

I was at an impasse. So I did what I always do when life gets difficult—crawled into bed and went fetal. But even sleep was not suitable therapy. All my dreams, regardless of where they started, ended with buffalo falling out of the sky.

I had to do something, even if it was wrong. After working long shifts, I had a few free days. So I called good old Ranger Rachel and asked if I could talk with her and if she could take me back up to the Forest Service cabin. With the kind of perkiness she exuded, she was not my idea of the perfect hiking buddy. I preferred the bespectacled male kind with kinky, honey brown hair. Although I had no evidence for it, I somehow felt like Rachel was a romantic rival for Wesley's attention. I know, I know, Wesley and I were not even thinking of being an item, but who says emotions make sense? This was business, and Rachel would work for that.

When I called her, she said that she was not staying in town but at a ranger site just outside of town. She gave me directions, and I agreed to meet her there later that afternoon. She told me that she had plenty of backpacking gear I could borrow.

Mom caught me in my bedroom as I was throwing a toothbrush and a change of clothes in a duffel. "Going away?"

"Only temporarily. Rachel, a friend of Wesley's, is going to answer questions for me and take me back up to the Forest Service cabin where we found Brian's stuff."

She sat on the end of my bed while I debated over taking a

faded red T-shirt or the newer one. I never said I had variety in my wardrobe.

"I have a dear friend in Garden Spot I haven't seen in months. Rachel lives by there, doesn't she?"

I tossed the faded T-shirt into the duffel. This wasn't a fashion show after all. "Yes, she's staying close to Garden Spot. Would you like to go with me?" The woman is so subtle. An ice-cream headache kind of subtle.

"I'd love that. We can take my Cadillac."

"I'd love that." The thought of driving the Valiant any distance was scary. We'd be alone in a car driving for at least two hours. Was she trying to set up one of those long talks for us?

Mom packed a lunch and an overnight bag. She left a note on the fridge for Maryanne, who had gone for a walk. We pulled out of the driveway in less than half an hour. Mom drove, and I read my Flannery O'Connor. I don't know what it is about Flannery, but I keep going back to her. She's got lots of religious types in her stories, but nobody comes off as a saint.

The miles on the curving road clipped by. Mom sang along to the hymns on the radio, and I buried myself in a story about an old woman whose selfish choices get her and her whole family killed.

I didn't look up from my book until Mom let up on the accelerator.

"Shall we stop and eat?" She hit the blinker and turned into a rest stop.

I had totally lost track of how far we had gone. Reading has a way of doing that to me. I could always escape personal turmoil by falling into a story. It was a habit from childhood. And for some reason I didn't want to have a deep talk with Mom—I feared it. Would she chastise me for sleeping with all those men, waggle a self-righteous finger at me?

Mom clicked open her door and grabbed the cooler from the middle of the seat. "Are you coming?"

I closed my book. Mom and I hadn't said twenty words to each other since we'd left Eagleton. We ate lunch without saying much. When we got back into the car, I returned to Flannery at lightning speed.

I looked up from my book just as we entered the heavily forested area outside of Garden Spot and the entrance to the park. "Wait a second. We've got to turn off onto a dirt road before we get to town."

The plan was to have Mom drop me off before she went into town to see her friend. She'd pick me up in two days, after Rachel and I had hiked into the Forest Service cabin. I pulled a piece of paper out of my jacket pocket and read out loud. "OK, look for the fishing access sign and then take a right."

The Caddy slowed as Mom pulled off onto a dirt road. "My gas is low. How far did you say it was?"

I leaned over to check her gauges. Mom is kind of a worrywart. "Just a couple of miles. You have enough to get back into town."

In the minutes that followed, a heavy silence settled over the car. Ahead of us, evergreens created a dense, darkening tunnel. I rechecked the directions I had written down and looked up ahead for any sign of a clearing and the cabin.

"Are you sure we're on the right road?"

"Yes, Mom."

She focused her eyes straight ahead. I saw beads of sweat glistening on her forehead. Her hands tightly gripped the steering wheel. This image of my mother transported me back twenty years. The car was different and her dark, elaborately braided hair had no gray in it. But the look of controlled panic was the same, the same tight lips and locked elbows.

Three days earlier, we'd put Dad on a plane to Canada, and then the three of us—me, Mom, and Jimmy—made our exodus from suburbia. I didn't know it at the time, but Dad had some kind of secret bank account in Canada where he kept some of the embezzled money. We drove like crazy out of Arizona. We were supposed to meet Dad in a place called Balboa Park in San Diego. Mom got lost. We ended up pulled over on a shoulder of the freeway, Mom slumped over the steering wheel, crying. I was ten; I didn't understand what was going on.

Now I saw the same expression forming on my mother's face. If we were lost, I hoped she wasn't going to lean over the steering wheel and cry. The trees thinned, and I saw a clearing. The cabin had to be just around the corner. Mom's thumb tapped the steering wheel, and she wetted her lips.

We rounded the corner only to see another empty grassy field. "It can't be much farther now," I said without much confidence. I looked at my notes again. "This was the only road that had the fishing access sign."

"We'd better turn around, Ruby." Mom glanced at the gas gauge. "I should have filled the tank at that last gas station."

"It has to be here. I'm sure Rachel has extra gas for vehicles. She made it sound like it was just off the road." I was mad at myself for not writing down more accurate directions.

This time it wasn't Dad that had gotten Mom lost, it was me.

Because emotions are rarely linear or logical, I was suddenly angry at my dead father.

"We know what is behind us. I say we turn around, go to town, and fuel up. Does Rachel have a cell phone?" Mom was in problem-solving mode now.

"A cell phone wouldn't work out here because of all the mountains and trees, Mom!"

"Don't snap at me, young lady. I was just trying to get us out of this pickle."

I hung my head like a repentant ten-year-old. It was unusual for my mom to raise her voice at all. We drove on in silence. I pressed my hands into tight fists. The anger I felt toward my father boiled inside me.

"There's a place up ahead where we can turn around." Mom pulled the car off the side of the road. Cranking the steering wheel, she lurched forward and then backed up and repeated the same action.

I peered out my window. The road was elevated about three feet above the grassy ground, with sharp banks off of either side. "It's awful narrow here, Mom." A mixture of dirt and gravel had probably been hauled in to make this section of the road, because the existing dirt was too gumbo to work with.

"This Caddy can handle it just—"

The back wheels slipped off the edge of the road. Mom's response was to press the accelerator hard. The back wheels spun, spraying dirt that created a dust cloud behind us. The big engine chug-a-lugged and made the grinding sounds of mechanical exertion.

We did not move.

We were stranded, just like we had been in San Diego twenty

years ago. I waited for Mom to rest her head on the steering wheel and cry. Instead, she looked at me and smiled. "At least we didn't run out of gas."

I waited for her to scream that this was all my fault. But she opened the car door and said, "Maybe we can set something behind the wheels to get more traction." Something had changed in the last twenty years. My mom's responses in a crisis were different.

We both walked around to the back of the car. The tires were embedded in dirt. Mom's exercise in futility had created deep trenches for both back tires. I know two things about cars: how to check the oil and how to put gas in. My vast mechanical repertoire wasn't going to help us with this problem.

Mom opened the trunk of the Caddy, and we peered inside. There was a bag of yarn, an umbrella, some undecorated wreaths, and old Christmas ornaments. Oh great, we could do some craft projects while we starved to death in the woods. We both shook our heads in unison and closed the trunk.

"How long did we drive on this road?" Mom asked as she reached inside the back seat to grab her jacket and the water jug from our lunch.

"Not more than twenty minutes." I looked up. To add insult to injury, the sky had darkened, warning of impending rain. The tops of the trees wavered as the storm front descended. The intensity of the wind increased, causing my untucked T-shirt to flap in the breeze. I popped the trunk open, pulled out the umbrella, and pressed the button to open it just as the first drop hit my nose. I continued to push the button as another drop hit my forehead.

"This thing is broken," I said through clenched teeth.

Mom zipped up her windbreaker. "You just have to fool with it a little bit, dear." She handed me an old sweatshirt she must have found in the back seat. "No need to get so angry."

I grabbed my jean jacket out of my duffel. Nothing else I'd brought would be useful.

No need to get so angry? Of course there was a need to get angry. I pulled the sweatshirt over my head and then put on the jean jacket. My arms had begun to get goose-pimply from the cold. The muscles in the back of my neck tightened as I stared down the long road. This was not going to be a fun walk. Mentally, I kicked myself. How could I have gotten the directions wrong?

The umbrella popped open with a loud burst, and Mom laughed. "Well, amen to that."

I wrinkled up my forehead at her. What was she laughing about? Sometimes my mother acted crazier than a pet coon. I kept thinking about the old woman in Flannery's story. The family had been dragged off into the woods and shot.

The trees creaked in the wind. I doubted there were armed gunmen around here.

Mom gestured for me to come stand under the umbrella. "Praise God for this rain. The farmers can use it."

I shivered, holding my arms across my body. Now I was sure that my mother was a couple slices short of a loaf. "Mom, there is nothing to be cheerful about here."

"God decided to make it rain, and his timing is exquisite." She winked at me and made a clicking sound with her tongue. This was going to be a very long walk. "Do you have any warmer clothes in your overnight bag, Ruby?"

"No, just an extra T-shirt and underwear." I glanced down at Mom's low-heeled pumps.

"Only another pair of sandals." She straightened the jacket of her navy pantsuit. Wind pushed back her long, beaded earrings.

By now, the drops were hitting me four or five at a time. "Maybe we should just wait in the car."

"It might be days before someone comes along on this road. It's not that far back to the highway. This rain will let up in a few minutes." She gestured for me to come stand under the umbrella. "Let us make our pilgrimage."

With a shrug, I joined her. Rain drizzled steadily as we entered the semiprotection of a grove of trees. At least the wind wasn't hitting us so hard. Mom's umbrella proved to be close to useless, because it kept collapsing.

"I think if we hold it at the base here, it will work." She demonstrated. Her hand had to be completely vertical, held above her head, clasping the top of the umbrella stem.

"That's going to make you tired real quick, Mom."

She let the umbrella fall to her side. One of Mom's braids had come undone, and the wet hair matted against her cheek. Her eyes were dark with running makeup. Our shoes had taken on the extra weight of wet gumbo.

We trudged forward in the steadily increasing rain. Ten minutes ago, it would have made sense to turn around and head back to the car. But ten minutes ago, we thought we had a working umbrella. I have no memory for topography. With each turn in the road, I expected to hear cars rushing by on a paved road. Maybe we had driven farther than I thought.

I shivered as a trickle of water ran down my back. Except for the little spot above my chest where I'd been crossing my arms, I was soaking wet. Rain dripped off my nose and ran in little streams down my cheeks. A chill had permeated my skin and was on its way to my bones. That kind of chill takes days and many hot baths to get rid of. This was no fun.

I walked a few paces ahead of my mother. Don't ask me why, but every time I get upset, I remember every other thing in the world that makes me angry: my father, the endless stream of jerk boyfriends, teachers who gave me bad grades, store clerks who were rude to me.

Mom's words broke through my anger-fest. "It can't be that much farther." Her voice quivered with the infestation of freezing cold. When I turned to look at her, she smiled.

My mom, the ever hopeful one. Her attempt at cheerfulness was irritating. We could be in the middle of a nuclear blast, and she would comment on the pretty lights and warmth of the mushroom cloud.

"Mom, take a reality pill. Sometimes there is nothing to be cheerful about." I pointed my finger at her. "I don't want to hear the word 'blessing' come out of your mouth."

"I was just trying—"

"Don't, Mom." I sliced the air with my arms, thereby sacrificing the only dry spot on my body. "Sometimes there is no reason to be happy. There is no silver lining, and life is a pile of crap. So would you please get over this 'I'm happy no matter what because God loves me' kick." Having made my point, exaggerated gestures and all, I whirled around and marched forward.

"What are you really mad about, Ruby?" She had to shout to be heard above the rain.

I yelled over my shoulder, "I think you know what I'm 'really' mad about." This was the first time I'd yelled at my mother since we'd found each other again. I stopped and turned so I could make eye contact with her. "I'm talking about being robbed of the possibility of a normal life because of what you and Dad did. I'm depressed all the time. I don't have kids. I don't have a husband. I don't have a real job. Some days I can barely function." I didn't want to wait for her reaction. I was afraid of it. Whether it was anger or sorrow, it would be way too much emotion for me to deal with.

"It's not all about you, Ruby. Can't you see how self-centered you are?"

"Oh please, Mother." I turned and took one step forward when I felt the sensation of a foot on my rear end.

I stopped, stunned. Had my mother, the senior citizen, the sweet churchgoing lady, just kicked me in the rump? I rubbed the point of impact. Even with all that fatty tissue, it had hurt. I stared at her, shaking my head in disbelief.

She strode forward and put her face close to mine. "You're not the only person in the world who has felt pain. I have to pray about regrets over the past every day of my life. Do you think it's easy seeing you like this? Don't you think I hurt too?"

"You caused it. I was a child, I had no choice." I was still reeling from the sensation of being kicked in the rear by my mother. The only thing that hurt more was her saying I was self-centered. "I deserved a normal life. I wanted to be married. I want to have kids."

"You can't blame me for everything. If that's what you wanted, you shouldn't have slept around so much." Her hand went to her mouth as though that would keep more cruel words from spilling out. "I am so sorry. I shouldn't have said . . ."

Her words froze my soul, cut deep. So that was what she thought of me. I opened my mouth to speak. Nothing came out. What she said was so out of character for her. But I guess in a moment of crisis, the truth rises to the surface. My own mother thought I was a slut. Her words kept zinging around and ricocheting off the walls of my brain. I was paralyzed, unable to respond.

"I didn't mean . . . I am so sorry. . . . I . . ." She touched my arm; I pulled away. "Please forgive me." Even in the rain, I could tell she was near tears from the quivering in her voice. "Please forgive me."

I shook my head, still uncertain how to respond. Is that what I am, self-centered? I took a step back. "We're going to get hypothermia if we don't keep moving." What a cliché tactic. If you don't know what to say, resort to talking about the weather. "Rain's falling awful hard."

She nodded and trudged forward. I walked behind her, watching as she dragged that pathetic broken umbrella, using it as a walking stick.

I contemplated the word "self-centered." The rain pelted my already soaked clothes.

A chill ran through my body, but it wasn't from the cold. The journey had turned out to be much longer than I thought it would be, and we were still a long way from warmth.

Chapter Twelve

A ranger found us about an hour before dinner. Of course he knew Rachel, who had neglected to tell us the turnoff was the *second* road after the fishing access sign, thank you very much. Even though things between Mom and me were tense, I opted to go into town and spend the night at Mom's friend's house. I was sure Rachel didn't have a bathtub in the cabin where she was staying, let alone hot water.

As we sat in the cab of the ranger's truck, my body vibrated from shivering. An icy cold ran through my veins, and my head ached. My tennis shoes were gooshy with excess water. Every time I put any weight on them, it was like wringing out a sponge. My hair weighed an extra two pounds and lay flat against my head. Rain: nature's mousse. To top it all off, I sniffled when I talked. This was OK, because neither Mom nor I was talking much. Did she really think I was a self-centered slut? Was that the sum total of her opinion of me?

I glanced over at her once. She looked worse than I felt. She had black circles under her eyes from where the mascara had run. Her hair had escaped from the tight braids in erratic strands, some matted against her face, some standing straight up. Her jaw hung as though her face were too heavy for her bones, the sparkle was gone from her eyes, and her shoulders slumped forward.

She did a strange thing when she caught me looking at her. She reached over and patted my hand. Her touch was so light, I thought a butterfly had fluttered against the back of my hand.

I pulled away, cradling one hand in the other.

The ranger dropped us at the house and said he'd look into getting Mom's car pulled out.

Mom's friend Naomi lived in a square, plain house with an immaculate flower garden. Naomi was one of those women who looked like she was eighty but moved like she was twenty-five. She stood in the door, waiting for us, as the ranger drove away.

"Come inside, you two, you must be chilled to the bone." She gestured with the strength of a woman accustomed to manual labor, slicing the air with her muscular arms. She was a big, short woman with a bubble of white hair. She wore a floral-patterned dress and probably had twelve just like it—same style, different print pattern—in her closet.

Naomi pulled some dry clothes for us from her closet. I was right. All her dresses were the same basic cut, different print. The blue-and-yellow flowers on my dress were kind of pretty. I had room for an extra person in the clothes, and the hem hit me way above the knees, but I was glad to be dry.

Naomi called out from the kitchen, "Dinner is ready when you are."

Mismatched but beautiful china decorated the table.

"I picked up all the dishes at garage sales." She touched the delicate floral pattern on a plate. "Such a blessing."

The meal she'd laid out was fit for several very hungry kings. Garden-grown string beans, peas, and carrots were displayed in separate bowls, not to mention the meatloaf, rolls, gravy, and mashed potatoes. I ate without talking.

"Naomi was a missionary in Africa for twenty years." Mom directed the comment toward me. Dry clothes and a full belly had helped her perk up a bit.

"Oh," was all I could manage as I stuffed a hot buttered roll into my mouth. I wasn't sure how much I wanted to talk to my mother anyway. My behind still had a pump-shaped footprint on it. Was she just going to return to cheerful Christian-woman mode as though nothing had happened?

Naomi cleared the table. "How about some coffee and chocolate cake?" She picked up dishes so fast, I thought a whirlwind had blown across the table. Don't ask me how, but she managed to do dishes, cut cake, and pour coffee while Mom and I sat letting our food settle.

She was one of those women who never stopped bustling, never stopped cleaning. Even when she sat down to have her cake, she used a towel that she had slung over her shoulder to wipe some crumbs off the table. All that bustling should have made me nervous, but it had quite the opposite effect. I felt calm and taken care of.

Mom sliced a small piece of cake with her fork. "The Lord called Naomi to remain single while she was in Africa."

Again, "Oh" was all I could manage as I slathered my tongue with creamy white frosting. The sweetness made my taste buds tingle. I am always skeptical of Christians who say that God has told them not to get married. I suspect that no one has proposed to them and, instead of dealing with the rejection, they put it on God as some kind of higher calling. Besides, I wasn't all that anxious to chitchat with Mom. Her returned cheerfulness was making me angry.

For some time I had been staring out at the hot tub I'd noticed beyond Naomi's sliding-glass doors. An extravagance like a hot tub seemed out of place in Naomi's simple house. I mentioned the hot tub during our second cup of coffee.

"Oh yes, that. It was given to me by a couple in the church who were moving. Such a blessing. It's helped so much with my arthritis."

Naomi, the mind reader, asked, "Would you like to soak in the hot tub?" She rose to her feet. "I have a towel and a suit you can borrow."

While Naomi was gone, my mom reached across the table and grabbed my hand. "I'm sorry I kicked you and for saying that about you sleeping with those men." She looked me straight in the eye. "Please forgive me."

I noticed she didn't ask forgiveness for calling me self-centered. That's what really hurt. "The truth rises to the surface. You've had that thought about me before." I didn't want to forgive her. I was still mad. I glared at her, and she pulled her hand away.

Her face drooped. I saw lines around her eyes that I hadn't noticed before. "I love you, Ruby. No matter what," she pleaded. "I make mistakes. Sometimes my anger over my mistakes gets directed at you. I know I'm not perfect."

I pushed the chair back. I didn't know what to say. Actually, her anger was easier to deal with than the kindness she was showing me now. I knew how to react to an angry person—get angry back. But the kindness, the butterfly touch, it made me ashamed of my own anger.

I was grateful when Naomi returned holding a bright yellow towel and an orange swimming suit. I needed to get out of the room. This whole thing with Mom was confusing. Why would she say she loved me when I kept being mean to her?

The suit was a little loose on me, but I didn't care. With Naomi's towel in hand, I walked out onto the patio and hit the switch for the jets in the hot tub. I stepped in up to the first stair. My frozen anklebones and muscles began to warm up. I descended to the second stair and then plunged in up to my chin. The rush of heat was almost unbearable as the water pulsated around me. I lay back, resting my head on the rim of the hot tub.

The night sky twinkled with a billion stars. Lazy, gauze-like clouds floated by, and the moon stared at me like a huge discerning eyeball. I knew that God had made this sky, and I suppose I had always known that. But what did he have to do with me?

Naomi was one of those people who had Bibles lying everywhere in her house. There had been one on the counter in the bathroom and one on her living-room coffee table and one on the stairs leading up to the hot tub. I pictured the active senior citizen bustling from room to room, suddenly realizing that she'd forgotten to take her daily dose of verse, snatching up her Bible and frantically turning the pages like a diabetic in need of an insulin shot.

I picked up the Bible she had laid on the stairs and turned to John 4. Fortunately, it was a large-print edition, and if I angled it just right, I could read by the patio light. The story goes like this:

A woman comes to a well to get water. She is by herself. Jesus is sitting there resting, and he asks her for a drink. She points out that he shouldn't even be talking to her because he's Jewish and she is Samaritan. Jesus starts up on the spiel about living water. He tells her that if she had living water, she would never be thirsty. By the time he is done, the woman is foaming at the mouth for this living water. Jesus should have gone into advertising. And then he hits her with the news that he knows that the man she is living with is not her husband and that he knows that she has had four husbands. Her response is strange. She starts talking about how great Jesus is and how he must be a prophet.

Why does Wesley like this chapter so much? Two things struck me as interesting. First, even though Jesus knew all these dirty little secrets about this woman, it's not the first thing he talks to her about. Instead, he offers her something better than what she has, living water, and he makes her want it. Second, when he drops the dirt about her past, he just states the facts. He doesn't punctuate his assertion with any name calling, like, "You slut, you," or "No wonder nobody wants to come and get water with you." Mom couldn't help saying those things to me, but somehow I didn't think Jesus ever would. Mom was right, she wasn't perfect. But Jesus was.

I closed the Bible and set it back on the stairs. The warm water made me lethargic. I closed my eyes, breathing in the cool night air. When I was a child, Mom and Dad took Jimmy and me to church. Not because they had any deep conviction, but because it looked good to the community. I remembered one story where all these people are ready to stone this woman who had been fooling around on her husband. Jesus comes to her defense. He stands between the woman and the people who want to kill her. It didn't make a lot of sense to me when I was ten, but it does now. Both of these women were "bad girls," and Jesus cared about them.

A lump caught in my throat, and more than anything, I wanted to cry. Not just a little sniffling cry, but a good long weep as though the tears had been building up forever.

I've got a few sexual indiscretions in my life too. Would Jesus come to my defense? Would he stand between an angry, judgmental crowd and me?

My mother's words floated back into my head: "I love you. No matter what." Would Jesus say that to me? Whatever her short-comings, Mom was trying. She hadn't rejected me.

I stood up in the hot tub, and the cold air hit me before I could grab the towel. Despite the chill, I stood with the towel around me, staring through the glass patio doors. Mom and Naomi sat on the couch, sharing a magazine. Mom threw back her head and laughed. Like watching a movie with the sound turned down, I felt removed from them, completely alone.

I haven't told Mom everything about the fourteen years we were apart, especially the child I gave up for adoption. She didn't take the first bit of news about all the men that well. Would she still want me around if she knew I'd given away her grandchild?

I stood there, water dripping off my hair and forming puddles around my feet. I gazed in from the darkness into a lighted room, and I felt in my gut the emotion that was hanging on the fringes of my subconscious. I felt regret for the life that I had lived, the mistakes I'd made, the people I'd hurt, and it created in me an immense loneliness. Maybe I was self-centered. This feeling and these thoughts were so uncomfortable that I pushed open the door and rushed inside. These were not things I wanted to think about.

"Got any more of that cake, Naomi?" I've always adhered to the psychological school of thought that says chocolate is the best medicine.

I spent the rest of the night watching a movie with Mom and Naomi. Afterward, they excused themselves, and I was left to fall asleep on the couch. Naomi gave me a soft pillow and a pile of blankets (way more than I needed for a summer night). I fell immediately into a deep sleep.

At two in the morning, the pendulum swinging in Naomi's mantle clock woke me. I felt wide awake. That clock had to have been making that noise the whole time I was asleep. Why now had it suddenly become so pronounced as to wake me up?

I laid my head back down on the pillow but knew that sleep would be impossible. The three channels on Naomi's TV offered a great deal of amusement if you like to watch station IDs and snow. I looked around the room. There was a bag of knitting by the couch, some very old scratchy records on the shelf behind the couch, and some craft magazines Mom and Naomi had been looking through earlier. I leaned back on the couch and stared up at the ceiling, counting the bumps and indentations. What would I do without a textured ceiling? I quit counting at 157. When I sat up, my eye caught sight of the Bible on the coffee table.

I sighed deeply. "Oh God, if you are real and you care about me, show yourself."

I looked around, not sure if he would come through the window or the door. He was an omnipotent being; he could probably just come through the wall. Of course, I wasn't really expecting that. It just seemed like my first real prayer ought to be met with a little heavenly commotion.

My eyelids felt heavy. Now I could sleep. How strange.

The next morning, Naomi dropped me off at the Fish and Wildlife center in town. Mom's car was parked outside. A ranger who said his name was Rick (don't laugh) offered to drive me out to where Rachel was.

Rick looked like he was a few years younger than I was. He had the premature wrinkles and red cheeks of someone who spends lots of time outside. A smoothly tucked shirt revealed a lean, flat stomach, and his deltoid muscle made the fabric of his uniform tight across his shoulders. I noticed the wedding ring on his finger and wondered if his wife was equally into fitness or if she shuffled around their house eating quarts of ice cream and wearing those fuzzy slippers that made the flap-flap noise when she walked.

Rachel's ranger station wasn't a cabin at all. It was a camper, maybe ten feet in length, parked in a clearing. A four-wheel-drive truck was parked next to it. Rick waved good-bye and headed up the road. Rachel had left a note on the door, saying she was out doing observations and that I should make myself at home.

The musty confinement of the camper stood in sharp contrast to the clear, fresh outdoor air. I was tempted to wait for her outside. A miniature sink and stove took up one side of the camper. Cupboards above and below the sink provided storage. There was a floral-print sleeping bag, probably not ranger regulation, folded beside a matching pillow on a ledge with a foam pad on it.

A table with piles of papers, newspaper clippings, and an open laptop computer caught my eye. The papers were some kind of data sheets that made my eyes glaze over when I tried to understand them. One newspaper clipping looked like it was downloaded off a computer. It was an article, dated four years ago, about some activist who had injured a hunter while he was trying to shoot a buffalo, because it had wandered outside the park. The other clipping was original and more recent. It was about three men who had made sizable donations to the Rancher's Relief Fund. The money went to a private fund that was set up for ranchers who had suffered loss due to natural disaster or bad market prices. One of the names of the donors caught my eye: J. MacDonald. I wondered if he was any relation to the elusive Serena MacDonald.

Rachel opened the door and popped her head in. "You made it."

"A little late, but yes."

She stepped inside, holding a handful of wildflowers which she placed in a soda bottle by the sink. Only Rachel could make a ranger uniform look attractive. Her tanned skin harmonized with the light brown of her collar. Her long dark hair was fastened with a gold scrunchie. "Can I get you a cup of tea?" She pulled off the binoculars that were hung around her neck and set them on the table.

"That sounds good."

She filled the teakettle with water. "I see you found my notes and research." After setting the kettle on one of the two burners, she pulled two teacups out of the dish rack and flipped them upright. She sat opposite me while waiting for the kettle to boil.

"These data sheets don't make a whole lot of sense to me."

She pulled the computer toward her and typed. "Basically, all they say is that the buffalo counts are a little down. Which wouldn't be that alarming, except we can't find any carcasses and no evidence of disease in the buffalo we track. The carcass you and Wesley found was one of the few we did locate."

I've always been suspicious of counts on numbers of animals. It's not like the rangers can put a pencil in the critters' hooves and have them fill out a census form. "So obviously they are not booking flights to Hawaii. Where are they going?"

"That's what I'm working on. What would make buffalo vanish into thin air? Couple that with the carcass you found—an animal that apparently fell from a great height when the closest cliff is five miles away."

"Could somebody move buffalo with the helicopter Wesley and I saw? Wesley said they were Hueys, strong enough to haul an army Jeep."

"Possible, with some kind of harness device. The carcass you and Wesley found had abrasions across his belly consistent with a harness. We're talking about an animal that weighs two tons. That's some pretty heavy-duty lifting. They sure wouldn't carry him far that way. Someone would notice." The kettle whistled, and Rachel jumped up to stop it.

"I guess it's not like you can sling a buffalo over your shoulder." I picked up one of the newspaper articles. "So who's J. MacDonald?"

Rachel set Fig Newtons still in the package and the hot cups of tea on the table. She stood leaning against the counter, sipping her tea. "Jason MacDonald, inventor and entrepreneur. He came up with the high-powered trail mix a few years ago; before that, it was a special clip for the ropes rock climbers use. Anything to do with the outdoors, he either invented it or markets it." She gestured for me to follow her outside. "I get claustrophobic in here."

We sat on the bumper of her truck. The forest surrounded us with a quiet that was not silent. If you listened, you could hear the creaking of trees, twittering of birds. Far off in the distance, a river murmured.

"So what about the other article?" I asked.

"Well, Mr. MacDonald is pretty much a straight-arrow businessman, but his daughter is out there—radical environmentalist. She was involved in that incident with the hunter. The article doesn't name names, but I got a list of the people charged from the sheriff's department."

"Was Serena one of them?"

"You know her?"

"It's a long story. Tell me more of what you found." Setting my teacup on the hood of the truck, I reached up to the sky, stretching.

"Serena was the one who put the ski pole through the hunter's stomach, but she got the same sentence as the others. I suspect Daddy's money talked to the judge."

"So was Daddy's money talking again when he gave to the Rancher's Relief Fund?"

"Probably. I can't prove it because I don't know who got the money after it was laundered through the fund. Maybe a rancher who saw something or helped them."

"Helped in what way?" A sequence formed in my mind. I thought out loud. "Buffalo are pulled out by helicopter and then shipped somewhere—in what? A semi truck? Could they get them across state lines without being noticed?"

Rachel crouched on the ground, resting her buttocks on her heels. "Maybe the rancher supplies the trucks or the space. Or maybe he just saw something he wasn't supposed to see. Or maybe Jason MacDonald really was just helping a rancher who needed help."

Long-standing questions were beginning to be answered. But the puzzle I had to solve was a little different from the one Rachel was working on. "So what does Serena need with Brian?"

"Brian and Wesley know the area around the park like the backs of their hands. I suspect Serena and her party needed a guide." Rachel stood up, brushing invisible stuff from her clean pants.

A twinge of anger pinched my neck. "You've been camping with Wesley, have you?"

Rachel studied me for a moment before saying, "I've got to hike over the hill. Why don't you come with me?"

"OK." I was planning on attending the squirrel's performance of *Romeo and Juliet* later on, but I supposed I could squeeze her into my schedule.

Rachel strode to the camper, leaving the door hanging open while she stepped inside. In a moment she returned holding two pairs of binoculars and wearing a light backpack. "These are for you." She handed me the smaller pair of binoculars.

We hiked up the gradual incline, which quickly became a hill. Rachel stayed in step with me so she could talk to me. "Wesley and I aren't involved. We never have been. We just know each other from the singles group when I was living in Eagleton."

"I didn't mean to imply anything." Actually, I did mean to imply. I was attempting to be nonchalant. If I allowed myself to express any emotion about Wesley, my feelings would overwhelm my rationality. The only thing that was keeping me from falling completely apart was the physical distance Wesley and I had put between each other.

Rachel continued. "Wesley has a lot he still needs to work through. Sex and using women is still more important to him than the Lord."

"But he's admitted that." Why was I defending him? "And he's resisting temptation."

"I know, and with God's grace, someday he will be a wonderful man of God."

"What do you mean 'grace'?" Mom had used the same word.

Rachel stopped to tighten the strap on her backpack. "Well, I think of grace as the opposite of judgment. Judgment says, 'You've been bad. Go away from me because that is what you deserve.' But grace says, 'You've been bad. But I want better things for you, so fall into my arms.'" She shrugged her shoulders. "That's how I think of it anyway."

The phrase "fall into my arms" hung in my head. We walked to the top of the hill and sat down behind a rock that Rachel said would shield us from any buffalo that showed up. Rachel lay on the rock on her belly, scanning the hills with her binoculars. When I looked through my binoculars, all I saw was prairie grass swaying in the breeze.

"What exactly are we looking for?" I asked.

"There's a herd whose grazing habits bring them this way. I think the buffalo being taken are those that are right on the park border, because those are the ones who get shot. The funny thing is, they mostly wander out in the winter. The snowmobile trails provide a nice road for them, and food is usually scarcer in the park in winter. If they are being taken, I don't understand why they are being taken in the summer."

I offered a solution. "Can you imagine moving a buffalo in the winter?"

Rachel shrugged and put her binoculars up to her eyes. "That could be it."

"So you think you're going to catch them in the act?"

"Maybe—hard to say. There's miles and miles of park border. My boss says I can't spend much more time on this. I'm not officially a park investigator anyway. I'm a biologist. My theory could be totally wrong."

I leaned back against the rock. "If your theory is wrong, the only other possibility is that UFOs are picking up the buffalo and taking them to Jupiter."

Rachel laughed as she pulled a water bottle out of her pack. After a lengthy swig, she handed the bottle to me. The cool water traveled down my throat and splashed in my stomach. Naomi's huge breakfast must have been wearing off.

Rachel slid off the rock and sat by me. "I doubt that we're going to see anything today."

"So, do you need grace for anything?" I asked.

Rachel brushed an invisible wisp of hair off her cheek. I was sitting close enough to her to see that even without makeup, her olive skin was flawless. "Yes, I do." She hung her head and looked at her hands as though they held the secrets of the universe. "Sometimes I'm prideful about the way I look."

Wow! That was not the kind of honesty I had expected. I thought she was going to giggle and say sometimes she had evil thoughts about ignoring dosage recommendations on the Pepto Bismol bottle. "Well, you have reason to be prideful."

"It's my insides that need to be beautiful."

I stood up and looked out on the empty field. "So what's the big deal with buffalo wandering out of the park?"

"They don't want the buffalo to come in contact with the neighboring cattle. The buffalo can transmit a disease called brucellosis. It causes the cattle to spontaneously abort their calves."

All the info she'd just given me faded, and one word burned in my mind: abort. Abortion. The brain works in mysterious ways, connecting seemingly unrelated things. Now I knew why I could not find any record of Serena MacDonald having given birth. "Rachel, I have to get back to town. I need one more piece of information, and I think I'll know why Brian is somewhere in these hills."

"I thought we were going to hike in to the cabin."

"Yeah, but that will have to wait. I need to ask for a huge favor. Can you drive me to Eagleton—right now? It's really important."

I had a feeling the final piece of the puzzle was about to fall into place.

Chapter Thirteen

It was about suppertime when Rachel dropped me off in front of the Big Sky Women's Health and Reproductive Clinic. The clinic was in a building that also housed offices, a medical lab, and a pharmacy. This was the only place in town that openly advertised that they did abortions.

The sign posted on the door said they closed at five, which was in half an hour. Three women occupied the waiting room, flipping through magazines.

I didn't need a law degree to know that they weren't going to turn over medical records. The occasion called for a little drama. I entered the clinic and leaned on the counter. The nurse was perched behind the counter, filling out a form. She wore large plastic-frame glasses and had blond-from-a-bottle hair, and the flaps of skin on her triceps jiggled when she moved her pen across the form on her clipboard.

"Uh, I really need to see a doctor." I made my voice quiver.

She set the form aside and pushed her glasses up on her face. "There are no more appointments left today. Is this an emergency?"

She needn't assume I was here for an abortion. The sign said the clinic dealt with all aspects of "women's reproductive health," including birth control, STDs, and prenatal care. I glanced around nervously. "No, it's not a big emergency. Maybe I could just wait and see if somebody cancels or if the doctor has just a few minutes."

"That would be fine, honey. We got one little gal who hasn't shown up yet. Maybe we can work you in."

I sat down and picked up a magazine that said I could lose ten pounds in three days. The nurse rose from behind her desk and disappeared down the hall. The clinic was set up so that two hallways bordered either side of the nurses' station. I slipped down the hallway opposite from where the nurse had gone. I did a quick survey as I passed each door: exam room, exam room, bathroom, supply closet. No sign of a records room or doctor's office. I checked my watch. Ten minutes 'til closing.

I slipped into the bathroom and hid in one of the stalls. With any luck, the nurse would think I'd just gotten scared or impatient and left the clinic.

The bathroom door swung open. I pulled my legs up on the toilet lid and pressed my knees into my chest. I listened while a woman used the stall next to me, flushed, opened the door, washed and dried her hands, and sang the first two lines to "Oklahoma" over and over. She must have restyled her hair, because after the hand dryer turned off she stayed in the bathroom and continued to sing. I can only assume she stood in front of the mirror the whole time. By the time I heard her footsteps click across the floor, I was seconds away from screaming, "Learn the rest of the song, lady!"

As the door swung shut, I checked my watch—ten after five. The staff probably needed at least a half hour to close up after patients were out. My legs were cramping, so I stood and stretched, listening to the drip-drip sounds of the pipes.

What do you do for twenty minutes in a bathroom? I regretted not grabbing a magazine. What do you do? I stared at the ceiling, counted cracks in the floor tiles, and tried to remember the words to the Gettysburg Address. What do you do? Talk to God?

Hey God, I'm still waiting for you to show me that you are real.

I have extended the gauntlet. It is your turn to respond. I consider it a big step for me to even consider that you might be interested in me. My mom thinks I'm self-centered. Do you think I'm self-centered?

I waited for some magic something to happen. Nothing. I sighed deeply and picked the dirt out of my fingernails.

At 5:35, I finally ventured out of the bathroom. All the lights in the clinic were turned off. I hadn't noticed a keypad by the entrance or anywhere else. Far as I could tell, there was no security system other than the locked doors.

Crouching by the nurses' station, I peered through the big windows. A janitor swished his mop back and forth in the hallway that connected all the different businesses. I wondered if his contract included cleaning the clinic.

Outside on the street, a cop car drove by slowly. I pressed closer to the side of the counter. So that was their security system. He would probably go by two or three more times before the night was over.

I checked doors. The exam rooms were all open, but the supply closet was locked. Not surprisingly, no records of any kind were in the exam rooms. If Serena MacDonald had had an abortion, the records were at least eight years old. For all I knew, they could be in a basement somewhere.

Moving along the wall to avoid having the janitor see me, I made my way to the nurses' station. The file cabinets were all locked. There had to be a key around somewhere, providing the nurse didn't take it home with her. I hit pay dirt in the third drawer I checked: a little plastic container holding keys labeled "file no. 1," "file no. 2," and "supply closet."

Files number one and two were right behind me. I opened the top drawer, A thru F for the current year. The other drawers revealed that the records only went back two years. I glanced at the nurse's computer. I doubted that the computerized file went back even that far. No use wasting my time trying to figure out passwords.

I grabbed the supply closet key, glanced through the doors—no sign of the janitor—and headed down the hallway. I opened the door and located the switch for a single naked bulb that hung from the ceiling. Boxes labeled with medical terminology were stashed on shelves and scattered around the floor. A bucket with a mop rested in a corner. Four file cabinets lined the opposite wall. I tried the top drawer of the nearest cabinet. It opened. So much for patient privacy laws. The records were dated ten years ago and ran through the letter *F*. If each cabinet contained a year's worth of records, I should come up snake eyes on the far cabinet.

I was right. The *M*s were toward the back of the middle drawer. Hopefully, Serena had used her real name. She had. I found her file sandwiched between an Erin Mablim and a Candice Macduffy. Maybe she had just come in for an OB exam or birth control. Something in me did not want to learn that Serena had had an abortion.

I found what I was looking for on the second page of her file. Written in doctor's scrawl, it said "D and C, no complications." A thought pierced me to the marrow of my bones. It could have been me with "D and C" written on my medical chart. All those years ago, when I found out I was pregnant, I'd made the appointment and stood outside a clinic like this one for an hour, unable to go inside.

I leaned back against one of the boxes. Serena had lured Brian up into the mountains with the promise of seeing his young son. She'd shown him pictures that she probably borrowed from a friend. Brian had risked everything to see his ghost child, a child who had been aborted.

My hands shook, causing a paper from the file to float to the floor.

I bent over to pick it up, knocking over a box behind me in the process. A pile of medical instruments enclosed in sterile wrapping fell to the floor. Kneeling, I tossed them back in the box. The instruments were packaged; so one side was clear plastic and the other side contained instructions and warnings. I held one of the instruments up to the light. It was a knife with a loop-shaped blade. I knew exactly what it was used for. I remembered seeing it on the table of sterile instruments the nurse had brought in when I had brought a friend to a place like this and held her hand.

I know people like my mom want to think all doctors who do abortions are cruel, gruff men with dirty fingernails, men who take pleasure in hurting and misleading women. During my friend's abortion, the doctor spoke very kindly to her, saying things like, "You'll feel a little tug here," and "This will hurt a bit."

The nurse stroked her forehead, leaned close to her ear, and said very gently, "It won't be much longer now."

I held my friend's hand, and her grip turned my fingers white. To keep my mind off the intensity of her hold, I stared up into the bright light above me until I had dots in front of my eyes and my vision blurred. I remembered the loop-handled knife and the sound of the suction machine humming, like a low-caliber vacuum.

I remember the doctor saying, "I think we got everything."

I was seventeen at the time. I suppose the memory of my friend's sadness after her abortion discouraged me from getting one when I got pregnant.

All day long, I had been hating Serena for what I was sure she had done to Brian's child. I was no better than she was. I could have made the same sort of choice. No wonder God wasn't talking to me. For the first time since I'd been reunited with my mom, I was feeling something I'd managed to push out of my conscience—deep regret.

It had been so convenient to blame my parents for all my pain—to view myself as the victim. But now as I sat on the floor of the cold, confining room, the memory of the kindness of different people floated back to me. People did try to help me, tried to rescue me from my destructive choices. I remember a foster mom who stayed in touch with me after I turned eighteen. She was a Christian lady who brought me cookies and helped me buy pots and pans when I moved into student housing. She was the one who encouraged me to go to college. She helped me fill out the financial-aid forms.

I was mean to her, because I had met a guy and he moved in with me. I didn't want her to know. I quit returning her calls.

Isn't it funny how I'd blocked out the memory of that woman's kindness until now? I could list ten examples of Christians behaving badly at the drop of a hat, but all the kindnesses I'd been shown by Christians I had forgotten until now.

My stomach twisted. All these years later, I felt awful for what I had done to my foster mother. She'd saved my life in a way. Without her support, I would not have gone to college. College took care of me; it gave me something concrete to work on so I didn't fall apart. Who knows what kind of life I would have drifted into.

I think I'd rather live through food poisoning again than endure sincere remorse. The symptoms are the same: an overwhelming feeling of toxic matter in your gut and blood stream and the need to throw up. The only difference is with botulism, you get to vomit and sweat the poison out. I sat staring at Serena's file until the words blurred.

I could hear the janitor's vacuum cleaner running on the carpet in the clinic office. Part of me wanted to get caught. Would that be just punishment? The vacuum cleaner moved up the hallway. I stuffed Serena's file back in with the other *M*s. The vacuum cleaner stopped, and heavy feet treaded on the carpet outside, back and forth. Emptying garbage?

I did not relish having to wait until the janitor was gone. All my muscles were taut, and I wanted to get out of this confined space. A heavy, invisible weight pushed against my chest. I couldn't get a deep breath. I gazed at the ceiling and the row of file cabinets full of women's secrets. The closet felt claustrophobic with God, me, and every selfish thing I'd done in my life crammed in there. I waited until there was no more noise outside.

Cautiously, I opened the door. Still on my hands and knees, I stared down the dark hallway. One light illuminated the entrance outside the clinic. Beyond that, I could see a gray sky. The cop car went by on the street. My watch said it was close to nine. The glass doors were locked from the outside.

I pushed them open and stepped out into darkness. Cool evening air rippled over my skin.

Just as I stepped off the curb, a car turned the corner. A young woman hung her head out the back-seat window and screamed, "Whee!" I noticed four other heads in the back seat as the car roared past. Her voice was abrasive to my ears.

I crossed the street and started running. My feet hit the pavement hard as I rushed past the brick structure of the courthouse with its wide cement steps and ornate cornices. I willed one foot in front of the other until I came to a stoplight. I leaned over, gripping my knees and breathing hard. My chest was sore, and my legs shook.

The streets of downtown were empty, like an end-of-the-world scene out of a movie: dark shop windows, vacant sidewalks, and abundant parking. A single car sped by. With my heart pounding and a burning side ache, I crossed the street and headed for home. I concentrated on counting my exhalations, not wanting any other thought to enter my head.

By the time I turned the corner onto Mom's tree-lined street, I'd been reduced to walking fast. Not terribly concerned about theft, I kept the keys for my Valiant in the glove box. I snapped the box open, shoved the key in the ignition, and tore off down the street. I knew where I was going. Back to where I felt comfortable— the garbage dump.

This was my life. Always running away. But no matter where I went, I was always there. That was the problem. I wanted to be somebody else. Someone who hadn't given a child up for adoption, hadn't slept around, hadn't been so mean to her mother and other Christians, and didn't have to feel this kind of regret.

A semi passed me on the road, and I thought about turning the wheel of my car until I was crushed under the huge tires of the vehicle. Forget it. With my luck, I'd only be seriously injured and have to spend the rest of my life crippled up with pain.

My hands formed tight fists around the steering wheel, and I pressed the accelerator. A truck sped ahead of me and pulled back into the right lane. The taillights stared at me like bloodshot eyes.

I pulled onto the gravel road that led to the dump. I slowed down and listened to the crunch-crunch rhythm of the rocks beneath my tires. I brought the car to a stop outside a twelve-foot-high chain-link fence.

The smell of refuse wafted in through my open window. My mouth went dry in response to the bitter smell. I left the window rolled down as if I were punishing myself with the bad smell.

The last time I'd come here, I'd been running from Wesley's rejection. Who had rejected me this time? God? I was certainly unworthy of his favor. I had been mean to his people—mean to my mom. This hurt more than any rejection from a man.

I prayed a stupid prayer: God, please take me back in time so I can undo what I have done. At that moment it seemed like the only plausible solution. I thought about the child who had been in my womb. My little girl. Where was she now? I'd given away my mother's grandchild. Because of my foolish actions, two people would never meet each other. The thought was almost unbearable. Maybe she had said some cruel things, but my mom was right about one thing: I am self-centered.

I stared up at the dark sky and the searching eyeball of the full moon. All right, God, I'm in a pretty deep pit here. Time to pull me out. Hello?

"Jesus." I said the name in a whisper. Jesus, defender of sluts and adulteresses and prostitutes. I released the tight grip I had on the steering wheel and slumped back in my seat. This was pointless. What was I praying for anyway? I wanted to cry but couldn't. I wanted to scream but couldn't find the strength.

It was as though all the muck in my life had been lying on a river bottom, and now God and his standards had come along and stirred the river until the water turned brown. I thought conversions were supposed to be a positive experience. I didn't feel any happy, light, dipped-in-sugar feelings. I felt the heavy tentacles of remorse. I could not undo the past. This was not a dance through a spring meadow with butterflies flitting around. This was a walk through a muddy swamp.

Sleepiness filled my brain, and I nodded off, resting my head on the frame of the open window. I slept, woke with the acrid odor in my nostrils, and then fell asleep again.

While I slept, I dreamed. I stood naked at the edge of a body of water that looked crystal clear, but when I stepped in, watercress and other plant life made it almost impossible to move.

Slimy mud oozed around my bare feet and sucked me down. Something compelled me to move toward the opposite shore. I pulled my arms up out of the lukewarm water; they were covered in muck. Saliva formed in my mouth in response to the acidic smell. When I covered my nose and mouth, even my hand smelled bad. Debris floated by, and I realized I wasn't in a swamp at all; I was wading through raw sewage.

I could see the distant shore, some force compelling me to push toward it.

My legs felt heavy, like pushing through newly poured cement. I turned to measure the distance I had come so far. Would it be easier to turn back? I could see dark trees leaning toward the water, their leaves dangling in the sewage. My eyes watered from the smell. Still, something told me to go forward.

I reached the bank and dragged myself up out of the thick liquid, using the grass on the bank as a rope. I heard a voice and felt a hand on my forehead.

"Now drink." Another hand held a cup beneath my nose.

I looked down into the cup filled with the same stuff I had just crawled through. "When does it end?" I cried.

The rim of the cup touched my lips. Closing my eyes, I prepared for the bitter drink.

"It ends now," whispered the voice.

The liquid touched my lips, washed over my tongue. Instead of warm sewage, I tasted the cool purity of mountain water. The water rolled down my throat and made my whole body tingle.

Without knowing how I got there, I stood on the top of the bank. I looked out at the water; the river was crystal clear. I had the sensation of being held even though there were no arms around me.

I heard the voice again, only this time it resonated from inside my chest cavity. "There now. You are my child."

The dream ended, and I jerked awake. Two headlights glared at me through the windshield.

"Ma'am, are you all right?" I could just see the dark policeman's uniform around the glowing rim of the flashlight.

I shaded my eyes from the intense light. "Except for the fact that I'm now blind, I'm fine."

He didn't appreciate my sarcasm. "I'm going to have to ask you to step out of your vehicle, ma'am."

I fought my way through the fog of waking up. The images of

the dream slipped away, and I oriented myself. "There's so much light."

He clicked off the flashlight. I pushed open the door and set my feet on the gravel. I was still groggy. I wobbled as I stood up. I touched my face where the frame of the window had left a deep impression. "Honestly, I haven't been drinking. I come here to think . . . to pray." To pray? He probably thought I was really out of it.

"Most people pray in a church. Can you walk in a straight line for me, please."

Now I know God has a sense of humor. Moments after I decide to follow him, I get falsely arrested for drunk driving. Ha ha, God, very funny. "Well, I don't quite fit in at church. I like it here better. God's here in this garbage dump, you know."

I couldn't see his face clearly. He stood just outside the rim of light created by his headlights. But I could have sworn I saw the corners of his mouth turn up. "This is not the time for theological arguments, ma'am."

"Please quit calling me 'ma'am.' It makes me feel eighty years old." I stepped closer to him so I could see his eyes. I stared into an ocean of dark brown. "We're in the same club, aren't we? You know, the blood club, washed clean and all that."

He raised his dark eyebrow in amusement but maintained his official tone. "Step back into the car and go home, please."

After I got into my car and closed the door, he leaned in, resting his forearm on the windowsill. "You realize that your club dues have all been paid by the president himself?"

"I understand. Tell me, Officer . . ."—I glanced at his name tag—"Officer Cree. Is the garbage dump part of your regular route?"

"No. Something told me I ought to come out here tonight."

"I had a feeling," I said as I turned the key in the ignition. I backed away and watched Officer Cree walk back to his patrol car. Strange, very strange. Downright mysterious.

Chapter Fourteen

I wish I could say the next day had the same ethereal quality as my meeting with Officer Cree, but after that, my life slipped back into mundane ordinariness despite the change in me.

I woke up on the couch where I'd fallen asleep. The air was heavy with the smell of bacon. I could hear the sizzle and crack of the salty pork as it fried on the stove.

Maryanne poked her head around the corner. "Got some bacon and biscuits if you're interested."

Mom would not be home for at least another day. I wondered if Maryanne would notice anything different about me. I sat down to a steaming plate of scrambled eggs, biscuits, and bacon.

Maryanne picked up her fork. "You came back early."

I ran my fingers through my tangled hair. "It's a long story." It was a story I wanted to tell, but every time I tried to put words to what had happened the night before, it diminished the experience. If I was truly a transformed person, maybe I could show it by what I did. "Maryanne, I have something to tell you."

Maryanne spoke between bites of marmalade-slathered biscuit. "I have something to tell you too."

"You first."

She gulped orange juice, then cleared her throat. "I've decided to move here, to Eagleton. It's time I made some changes in my life and quit waiting for some man to make me happy."

"What are you going to do?"

She stood up and refilled my empty glass of orange juice. "Get an apartment. I spoke to Dad last night; he can loan me some start-up money. I might go back to school or get a new job, something totally different from being a bank teller."

Maryanne's news made me uncertain of how I should present my information. "What about Ed?"

"I still hate him." Maryanne plopped the pitcher down on the table so hard that the silverware vibrated. "We haven't found him yet. I drove by some more of those 'Smith' houses the other day. We could be looking forever. He's probably in another town swindling another woman."

If Maryanne was moving here, she was bound to run into Ed sooner or later. It would be best to take care of this while I still had some control. "Do you still have the .38?"

"It's in my makeup case. Why?" Maryanne hovered over me with her hands on her hips and her forehead wrinkled.

"Sit down, Maryanne."

"Why? What have you found out?"

"Sit down, Maryanne." I pointed to the chair closest to me.

Never taking her eyes off me, she lowered herself slowly into the chair. "Tell me."

"Promise me you'll stay calm." She nodded. "Promise me you will not take that gun out of the makeup case." She nodded. I took a deep breath. "I'm pretty sure the Gladys Smith I saw at the bowling alley owns the glass shop downtown."

Maryanne erupted out of her chair. "I'll kill him! I'll kill him!" She strutted down the hall toward the guest bedroom, shouting the whole time. "I'll kill her too!"

I realized then that any rationality that Maryanne had managed was predicated on the assumption that she was never going to see Ed Lawson again.

I raced after her. "Maryanne, calm down. We'll get the car back, and that's all." I could hear her throwing things around in her room. "But we aren't going anywhere until you calm down."

When I got to the room, her bag and her makeup case were flung wide open. Mascara, compacts, curlers, underwear, jeans, and blouses were strewn all over the room.

"I thought I put it in there. Now I can't find it." She looked at me, and her anger aged her ten years—eyes drawn into a squint, cheeks red with rage. She stopped to catch her breath, her chest heaving up and down. "Did you take it?"

I shook my head.

Maryanne plopped down on the bed and, with her fingertip, touched a tear that had formed in the corner of her eye. She turned her head toward the window. I placed my hand on her shoulder. This comforting other people was new to me.

"OK, we'll get the car back." Her whole body rocked back and forth.

I sat down on the bed beside her. "I'll go with you. And then we'll look into filing some theft charges against him for the money he took out of your bank account and the credit card bills he ran up."

"I don't want to do that." Maryanne sniffled. "I'm embarrassed that I let a man do this to me."

"I know a really nice police officer here in town. His name is Officer Cree."

Maryanne touched the back of her blond hair where it curled under. "We'll get the car back first. Then I'll think about filing charges."

I waved my finger at her. "But no guns. I don't want to be cleaning up dead people all over the place."

She slapped the palm of her hand on her forehead and shook her head. "Just when I think I'm over it, the anger comes back."

"I understand. I still feel angry at men who hurt me."

"Your mom keeps telling me about forgiveness, but right now it feels like I'll hate him forever."

I stood up, picked up one of Maryanne's blouses, and folded it. This was weird; it was the kind of thing Mom would do. "I don't think forgiveness is about feelings, and it's certainly not about pretending what he did to you was right."

Maryanne sighed resolutely. "I can clean up this mess."

"I have some other business I've got to take care of. I'll come back in a couple hours when the glass shop opens up. And we'll go down there together, right?" I gave her the best furrowed-brow, concerned-mom look I could manage on such short notice.

Maryanne nodded like an obedient child. "I'll stay right here."

My other business was going to be even more difficult than the news I'd had to give Maryanne. I still didn't know where Brian was, but I knew why he had left. As I drove the Valiant around town, I debated about telling Laura. I hadn't found Brian yet. Why did she need to know that Brian had kept such a significant thing from her?

I drove and thought and debated and drove some more. I was within a few blocks of Wesley's house. Maybe I'd try the news out on him first. Maybe he could help me deliver it to Laura. I parked in front of his house and headed up the sidewalk. The yard looked about the same in daylight as it had at night—smooth, newly flattened black dirt in desperate need of sod. I knocked on the big wooden door. The last time I'd been here, Wesley had given me the red light on any romantic embraces, long kisses, things like that. Why was I really coming back here?

The man next door was watering his irises with a hose. Fluffy white hair protruded from beneath a baseball cap. He popped up the dark lenses on his glasses and addressed me. "You looking for Wesley? He's on a job up on High Street. House number 480, my brother's house."

"Thanks."

"Nice boy, that Wesley," the man said to his irises.

I noticed Wesley's truck with the name of his roofing company painted on the side before I spotted Wesley. I parked my car and crossed the street. Piles of shredded shingles populated the flowerbeds and sidewalk. I could hear voices and the thundering of hammers. I shaded my eyes and stood on tiptoe. This side of the roof contained rows of neatly placed shingles and a tool belt. He must be around the other side.

The other side of the house featured a boy of about seventeen cutting the strip of plastic that held shingles together. He was shirtless, and his skin was tanned the deep chocolate of a kid who had spent the summer roofing. There were no pasty white roofers in this world.

"I'm looking for Wesley."

Though his hair was buzzed and he was leaner, the kid had the same clear, intense green eyes and arched eyebrows as Wesley. Before he could answer, I heard Wesley's voice.

"Incoming." A pile of shingles thundered to the ground.

"Hey, Wesley," the kid shouted.

Wesley peered over the side of the roof. "Hey, Ruby. Down in a minute." Wesley was attached to a rope at the waist. He rappelled once off the two-story brick building and planted his feet on the sidewalk. Unhooking himself from the rope, he walked over to us.

"Ruby, this is my nephew, Jason."

Jason nodded, said something about wire cutters, and disappeared around the side of the house.

Wesley unhooked his tool belt, opened up a cooler, and pulled out a bottled iced tea. "You want some?"

"No, thanks. I have something I need to talk to you about."

The iced tea was gone in three gulps. "I hope it's good news. I had all these jobs lined up before Brian disappeared. I hired my nephew to help. Feels weird replacing Brian." Wesley wiped sweat from his brow with his forearm. The early morning sun caught the highlights in his hair. He wore a sweat-drenched T-shirt and jeans. He was still the most handsome man I'd ever seen. My cheeks were getting warm, and it wasn't from the sun. Whatever else about me had changed when I found God, my biochemical responses to attractive men hadn't disappeared. I guess I'd just have to learn to control them. This Christianity stuff was going to be hard.

I debated whether I should tell Wesley about my dream and my encounter with Officer Cree. I wasn't sure how to phrase it. I was absolutely convinced that my dream had been more than a dream, that the position of my soul had shifted 180 degrees, yet I was having trouble verbalizing my faith. I was afraid that if I spoke of my new understanding, it would trivialize it. "I know why Brian left, but I still don't know where he is."

I filled Wesley in on everything. That Serena had aborted Brian's child, but that Brian had thought for all these years that she had given birth to his son. That he'd probably been lured into the woods with the promise of seeing his kid. I told him about Rachel's disappearing buffalo theory.

Wesley shook his head in disbelief. "Brian would have told me if he had gotten a girl pregnant."

"This all happened while you were in the marines. He was probably ashamed."

"I'm his best friend." He tossed the plastic bottle from the ice tea container. "He should have told me."

I sat down on the cooler, the warm sun bathing my skin. "How much do you think I should tell Laura?"

He picked up the plastic container and banged it against his leg. "I think we need to find Brian. You and me, Rachel, and maybe Laura. We need to comb that whole area around the park until we find him." Wesley paced up and down the sidewalk.

"I don't know how feasible that is. That's a big area for four of us to cover."

He leaned over close to my face and pointed at his chest. "This is my friend we're talking about here. I don't care if I have to crawl every inch of it on my hands and knees."

"OK." I reached up and touched his cheek with my fingertips. "I guess that's what we do." He held my gaze for a moment before turning away.

"You're right. We could be up there forever and not find him. What do you propose, inspector?"

I shook my head and shrugged. "Maybe the police can do something now with the information we have."

Wesley lay down on the grass and stared at the sky, crossing his legs at the ankles. "If this Serena is as unstable as Rachel says she is, she might just stab Brian with a ski pole when she doesn't need him anymore. We gotta do something."

I stood up. "You're right. But it's got to be rational, or we won't be helping Brian at all." I kicked the bottom of his workman's boot. "So pray about it, OK?"

Wesley sat up. "Pray about it? You?"

"Yeah, me." I leaned close to him. "I didn't have a change of heart so you would date me, so don't flatter yourself. This is about Jesus, not about you."

Wesley raised his eyebrows. "Oh, well, excuse me," he teased. I held out my hand and pulled him up. The heat from his hand rushed up my arm, and for a brief moment our eyes met. I looked away first. No matter what I did, I could not shut down my attraction for him.

"I'm happy for you," he whispered.

"Thanks."

I was almost around the corner of the house when I heard him shout. "Call me when you and Laura figure out a plan."

So it was up to me, huh? I'd hoped that he would at least volunteer to help me tell Laura the news. I had another confrontation to take care of before I called Laura.

When I got home, Maryanne was waiting for me. She sat on the couch, clutching her purse and wearing the same lemon yellow suit she had on the day I met her. Her elbows formed symmetrical Vs at her sides. Her feet were aligned so precisely on the floor, I wondered if she had measured before planting her pumps. A black vinyl purse rested in the center of her lap, her hands white knuckled from her grip on the strap.

I stood in the doorway, the screen door swinging shut behind me. I tried very hard not to speak to her like she was a child. "Maryanne, what do you have in the purse?"

"A pack of gum, my compact, and two dollars and forty-seven cents. No gun."

"Good. We're just going to get the car back, right?"

Maryanne nodded. "I thought about it. I don't want to file charges or do anything legal. I want him out of my life. I don't want to spend months in court looking at him."

"Come on, let's go."

As we drove toward downtown, doubt entered my mind. "I'm pretty sure the woman driving the Thunderbird at the bowling alley is the same one who owns the glass shop. How many Gladys Smiths can there be in this town, right?"

Maryanne twisted her purse strap. "Did you ever see anyone who looked like Ed there?"

I shook my head. Maybe we were driving into a dead end. I hoped not. For Maryanne's sanity, I wanted the Ed saga to be finished.

I couldn't find a parking space on Main Street, so I circled around to the back of the glass shop. The T-bird was parked by the "employees only" entrance. Maryanne was out of the car before I had come to a full stop.

She peered into the windows of the powder blue classic. "This is it. This is my Bird. My father did the upholstery on those seats." She ran her hand along the metal wing on the back of the car and tapped the round taillight. "Daddy put so many hours into this."

"Let's go inside."

The employee entrance led us through a storage room with a card table, folding chairs, and a coffee machine resting on a wooden box that had the word "fragile" on it upside-down. Maryanne walked three paces ahead of me. Her blond hair bounced as she strutted deliberately into the shop. I realized at that point I had lost whatever control I had over the situation.

I caught up with her. The shop was empty except for a woman

carrying a box so large, it covered her face. Her pants were of the stretch leggings variety with a very busy tropical pattern. There was a zebra on one leg and a giraffe in palm trees on the other, and I was pretty sure I saw a gorilla on her hip. The woman set the box on the counter by the cash register. She bore a vague resemblance to the Gladys I'd seen in the bowling alley. Her hair was now jet black and less bouffant, cut in a short, turned-under style.

She saw us immediately. "The shop isn't open yet, sweetie. How did you get in here?" She spoke with the gravelly voice of a woman who used cigarettes as a diet aid. Her noodle-like arms and skinny legs suggested that the diet was working.

Maryanne stepped forward before I had a chance to respond. "That's my car out there. I would like it back."

Gladys put her hands on her hips. "You must be mistaken, honey." She hustled around the counter and set an ashtray and a pack of cigarettes on the counter. "That car was given to me as a gift from my son."

"Is your son's name Ed Lawson?" There was a quiver in Maryanne's voice as she spoke each carefully enunciated word. She elongated the s in Lawson so that his name was almost hissed rather than spoken.

"Yes, Eddie is my son." She pulled a cigarette out and lit it. "And who are you?" She shook the match out and let it fall into the ashtray.

And all this time I had assumed Gladys was another conquest. Gladys must have had at least two marriages, since she and Ed didn't share the same last name.

Maryanne stomped toward Gladys, pointing through the walls at the car. "I am his wife, and that is my car. He stole it from me."

Gladys squared her shoulders. Her back straightened. "You must be Maryanne. Ed was afraid you might show up. I warned all my employees not to give out information." She took a long, slow drag on her cigarette. "Now honey, Ed bought that car fair and square from your father. I'm sorry if you feel like it wasn't a good deal."

"That's a . . . that's a lie." Maryanne shifted her weight from side to side. "We were married. I have the license right here." She yanked open her purse. A compact and a pack of gum fell to the floor before she pulled out a folded manila envelope.

Had she been carrying that around in her purse all this time? I pictured her taking it out of her purse periodically, reading it with a mixture of regret and rage. She hadn't said she had a marriage license in her purse. I hoped she hadn't lied about the gun being in there.

Maryanne set the envelope on the counter by Gladys and stepped away.

Gladys pulled a pair of reading glasses out of a big purse resting on the counter. I had become a spectator in a strange drama.

Gladys held the paper at arm's length. I watched her facial muscles slacken. She shook her head and then shook the paper in the air. "That little . . . He told me he wasn't going to do this anymore. That little . . ."

Maryanne said, "I can show you the title to the car, too."

I heard the back door open. Heavy footsteps pounded through the storage room. With timing that only occurs in the movies, a large man filled the doorway. He was over six-feet tall, wearing a plaid shirt that bulged at the belly. His dark hair was slicked back and glistened even in this dim light. This had to be Ed Lawson.

His eyes moved from his mother, to me, to Maryanne. His lips formed a big grin complete with yellowing teeth. "Annie, don't you look pretty."

"You!" Maryanne was on him before I had a chance to stop her. Her fists pummeled his chest and face. Using her elbow as a weapon, she jabbed him in the stomach.

The beating didn't seem to have much effect on him. He turned his head to the side to avoid the blows to his face, but his feet remained planted. The whole time, he spoke softly to her. "Now, now, it's all right." Like he was trying to calm an agitated dog. "It's all right. There, there." His huge hands hooked around her wrists like handcuffs.

She was running out of steam. Her shoulders heaved up and down. She turned her face toward him. "You!" she whispered, her jaw rigid.

I didn't believe what I was seeing. I thought I was going to puke.

With his hands still clamped around her wrists, he'd begun to sway with her. The whole time he continued to make soothing sounds. "It's all right, baby. It's all right."

Maryanne put her head against his chest. Every few seconds, she'd make a halfhearted effort at wrenching herself free. Each time, she fought less. This guy, who would never be a candidate for the cover of *GQ,* was the poster boy for romantic manipulation.

I cleared my throat. "Maryanne?" Now I regretted making her leave the gun at home.

Her head jerked off his chest, and she looked at me through tear-filled eyes. The whole universe sucked back a million miles, and there was just me and Maryanne and the choice she had to make. What was she willing to give up for the appearance of happiness?

I could guess at the debate that was going on in her head. Well, he's not perfect, but at least I'll have someone. Nobody else even wanted to marry me. I guess this is the best I can do.

Ed cooed, "I'm so sorry." He touched her hair with the palm of his hand. Her free hand went limp at her side. "I'm so sorry, baby."

She opened her mouth to speak.

A large brown object loomed behind Ed's head. It wasn't until it hit him that I realized it was Gladys's big old honking purse. "Didn't I teach you anything, you little no good—"

The purse hit him on the side of the face. His hand went protectively to his cheek.

Maryanne stepped away, but not before a poorly aimed shot struck her head.

"Sorry, honey." Gladys and her purse were all over her son. One, two, three blows. She hit him hard twice in the stomach and once in the face. Good old Gladys had had a self-defense class once or twice in her life.

Ed held his arms up trying to shield the softer parts of his body. "Ma, stop it. Ma!"

This was better than watching him fry in court. Eddie's getting a whipping from his mama. Na na na na na na.

Gladys stopped for a moment, yanked something out of her purse, and tossed it to Maryanne. "Take the Bird, honey. It's yours."

Maryanne and I were on our way out the back door just as Gladys pulled a bottle of pepper spray out of her purse. Spankings and time-outs just weren't going to work at this age.

We heard Ed's scream of pain just as we stepped outside. The blow to her head must have brought Maryanne to her senses. "Let's go for a ride, Ruby."

We took our victory lap with the windows rolled down and the radio blaring. Maryanne drove the T-bird down a winding two-lane highway. We laughed for quite some time with the music in our ears and the wind in our hair.

A quiet song came on the radio, and I reached over to turn it down. "I thought you were going to go back to him, Maryanne. Pretend like he hadn't done all those horrible things to you."

"I had a moment there. All kinds of thoughts were running through my head. I thought—well, he doesn't drink or do drugs, and he says he's sorry." She shook her head. "Thank God for Gladys's big purse." She laughed. "Are there any decent men left in this world?" she asked, her laughter fading.

"There have to be." I sighed. "We just got to raise our standards. Instead of just wanting a relationship, we gotta want a good relationship."

"It's better to be alone than be tormented and used. That's my new theory anyway."

Maryanne turned the Bird into a tight corner. For such an old boat, it handled rather nicely. The wheels turned smoothly and silently on the highway. I closed my eyes. I wanted to remember this moment and this feeling.

The leather upholstery felt soft against my back. The cool breeze touched my skin lightly. And the rhythm of the song palpated my eardrum. I had done something right. Maryanne was going to be OK, nobody was dead, Gladys had probably run Ed out of town, and my friend had her Bird back.

The emotional weight of the phone call I had to make to Laura still pressed on my mind, but I had at least done something right today.

And for that, I'd sleep soundly tonight—or at least that's what I thought.

Chapter Fifteen

The phone call came at two in the morning. I knew that because the glowing red letters of my clock were the first thing I saw when I sat bolt upright in my bed.

Trying to clear my head, I stumbled down the hallway to the phone. Who would be calling at this hour? Had something happened to Mom? As I picked up the receiver, I tried to wake up by opening and closing my eyes.

I stood in the dark hallway, leaning against the wall.

"Hello," I mumbled, pulling the receiver away slightly. My voice didn't even sound like my voice. I swallowed hard to clear the gravel out of my throat.

"Is this Ruby Taylor?" I went through the catalog of familiar voices but couldn't find a match. Certainly the telemarketers hadn't reduced themselves to calling at two in the morning.

"Yes, this is Ruby." Or at least I was when I went to bed. I shook my head to try and clear out any dream ghosts that remained.

"This is Meagan Struthers over in Sparkling Gulch. I got your name from Officer O'Reilly."

My head was beginning to clear. "Yes, I know who you are."

"I've been feeling guilty ever since you and your friend were here. Serena's doing something really wrong. She won't tell me, but tonight she showed up with blood on her clothes. But she didn't have a mark on her. She got really bent out of shape when I asked her what was going on. She waited for those three creepy guys to show up. The one with the ponytail scares me."

An image of blood-spattered clothes flashed through my mind. "Was Brian, the guy in the picture with you two, was he with them?"

"No, Brian's never been with them. Even after all these years, I know I'd recognize him."

I turned the corner into the kitchen and collapsed into a chair by the table. The light above the stove glowed in the darkness. "So did they say where they were going?" I yanked on the phone cord to eliminate the tautness.

"No, not directly to me. But one of the men kept yelling that they had to get up to the Lazy KN Bar by two."

I fumbled through the pen holder on the table, found a pen, and wrote the name down on the corner of a magazine. "Do you know what that is? Is it a bar, like a drinking bar?"

"No, it sounds like the name of a ranch, I think. I come from a long line of farm people and I've never heard of it, so it can't be from around this area."

"What time did they leave?"

"It was late; the kids were in bed, probably ten. Serena told me I should burn the bloody shirt. When I ran with her in high school and before I was married, we were always doing all kinds of dangerous stuff. She had Brian wrapped around her finger. He would do anything just to please her. She has that effect on people."

"So what did you do with the shirt?" What sort of arrogance leads you to believe your friends will help you destroy evidence? Serena must be the queen of the manipulators.

"I gave it to Officer O'Reilly."

"You did the right thing, Meagan."

"I don't know where that blood came from." Her voice broke. "I'm afraid she might have hurt someone."

"Me too." Visions of Brian bleeding to death in that cabin flashed through my mind.

I hung up and dialed Laura's number. It rang six times, and the message machine clicked on. I hung up and dialed again. Sooner or later, someone would become annoyed and pick up the phone.

Laura answered on the twenty-eighth ring. I told her to bring camping gear and her cell phone and meet me at my house.

"What's this about?" she asked through a yawn.

"This time Serena is not going to get away from us, and Brian might be in close proximity."

"I'll be right there."

I sat for a moment in the darkness, trying to formulate a clear plan. I needed all the help I could get, and I needed someone who knew the area around the park.

Wesley picked up on the first ring. I pictured him barefoot in T-shirt and jeans, sitting at his architect's table. I told him the same thing I'd told Laura. He didn't know where the Lazy KN Bar Ranch was either.

After I slipped into jeans and a sweater, I called Rachel's house but got no answer. She was probably still out at her camper. I grabbed the copies of the news clippings Rachel had given me and several Montana maps Mom kept in her kitchen drawer.

Then I crept into Maryanne's room. She lay on her side, the covers half pushed off, making her feet stick out. I pulled the makeup case out from under the vanity by the bed and slowly clicked it open.

Maryanne rolled over. "Ruby, what are you doing in here?" she said sleepily.

"Looking for your gun," I whispered.

"I thought we agreed not to shoot old Ed," she laughed, her voice fading. "His mom is taking care of him for us."

"I need it for protection from a different kind of bad guy—a bad girl."

"It wasn't in there when I looked for it. Check under the bed." She propped her cheek on her palm, resting her elbow on the bed. "This sounds serious. Do you need me to go with you?"

I palmed the area under her bed and around the vanity. I found it in a corner by the wall. "No, go back to sleep. You've been through enough today."

She smiled dreamily and laid her head back down on the pillow. "OK."

The gun felt heavy in my hand. My heart pounded a mile a minute. I touched Maryanne's shoulder. "If I'm . . . if I'm not back in a few days, tell my Mom I love her."

Maryanne's eyes popped open. She stared at me for a long moment. "Are you sure you don't need my help?"

"I'll be all right. Just tell Mom I forgive her."

Maryanne nodded as I rose from the floor.

In the light of the kitchen, I held the gun out at arm's length. Don't ask me what was going on in my father's head, but he had taught Jimmy and me how to shoot when we were in junior high school.

He hadn't taught us how to shoot hunting rifles, which would have made some sense, but he made sure we were both proficient with handguns. Perhaps my father's crimes had made him paranoid, and he had visions of his children protecting him. I will never know. But I was glad to have the skill now. I pushed the release and checked the cylinder of the revolver. It was full, six rounds.

Wesley and Laura showed up within half an hour. We loaded our gear into Laura's sports car. I noticed that Wesley had brought his hunting rifle. We were thinking the same thing. I hoped we were wrong.

"Which way?" Laura asked as she crawled into the driver's seat.

I answered from the back seat, where I already had a map of the park and surrounding area spread out. "Toward the park. I'll give you a clearer destination as soon as I figure it out."

I pulled out Rachel's clippings to see if the article about the donation to the Rancher's Relief Fund mentioned a town or area. It didn't. So much for this being easy.

I handed Wesley the cell phone. "Try Rachel every fifteen minutes, and start calling the sheriff departments of all the little towns around the park starting with Garden Spot. Ask them if there has been a shooting, and find out if they know where the Lazy KN Bar Ranch is."

I looked at the map. If Serena and gang had left at ten and had to be at the ranch by two, that would be about four hours of travel from Sparkling Gulch.

With the phone pressed against his ear, Wesley leaned over the seat. "There has got to be an easier way to figure out where this place is."

He was right, but my mind stalled. I sat watching the scenery going by. We were almost to the edge of town. I could see the yellow line on the highway as the streetlights came farther apart. We passed the feed store where I worked. My brain revved into high gear. "Stop!"

"What!" Laura pressed the brake and pulled over.

I dug my fingers into the back of the front seat. I realized that my heart had been pounding since I'd gotten off the phone with Meagan. "We have to go back. Back to the feed store where I work." I spoke so fast, my words ran together. I needed to calm down, or I would be totally useless.

While Laura turned the car around, I rummaged through my backpack for keys to the store.

"Why are we stopping here?" Wesley was still on the phone, enjoying the gentle rhythms of a busy signal.

"Georgia has a book that lists all the ranches in Montana. I'll be back in a minute." I pushed the car door open and stepped out into the early morning grayness. My feet crunched on the gravel of the parking lot.

Her Majesty, the Siamese, greeted me at the door with an indignant yowl when I came in. She rubbed up against my leg while I rifled through Georgia's desk. "Come on, be here. Be here. Dear God, please be here." Did that constitute a prayer? I looked around Georgia's tiny office. Where else would she keep it? By the phone on the counter?

I checked the counter, around the cash register, and the shelves underneath the counter. Nothing. My pulse throbbed in my neck. We were cutting it close as it was. If I didn't find that book, we could spend the rest of the night driving the perimeter of the park, checking every local phone book.

Her Majesty yowled again and jumped up on the windowsill. She continued to make gravelly moaning sounds. "Shut up, Princess, I'm trying to think here." I glanced over at her.

A streetlight shone through the window, rimming her silhouette in a soft glow. What was that she was sitting on? I bolted across the room and pushed her off the stack of books she was using as her throne. The hair on her arched back ruffled as she turned her head away from me.

The first book was the phone book and the second was *The Breeders Guide to Montana Ranches.* For the first time in ten minutes, I took a breath that filled my lungs and expanded my stomach. My heart slowed as I stared outside. I didn't know if that was an answered prayer or not, but I thanked God anyway.

I hopped into the back seat. "Drive like a bat out of you know where, Laura." I opened the book to the section that listed the ranches alphabetically. "I'll give you a more precise heading in a moment."

Wesley clicked off the phone. "That was the ranger station in Garden Spot. Rachel didn't come to work tonight. She was supposed to show up at ten for some kind of nighttime wildlife observation."

"Wasn't she staying at that camper?"

"Yesterday was the last day. The other ranger checked there just in case. Rachel is the most conscientious person I know. For her not to show up to work, something has to be seriously wrong."

Visions of a bloodstained shirt danced in my head. Had Rachel stumbled onto Serena and been injured? Or worse? "We better hurry and get up there." Perspiration trickled down my armpits as I flipped through the pages of the guide.

Even my feet felt sweaty. The book said the Lazy KN Bar was by a little town called Garnet. After some searching, aided by the flashlight Wesley held, I found Garnet on Mom's map. I added up the mileage. Garnet was about an hour west of Garden Spot. It was almost three now.

The soonest we could get there would be five, and that wasn't accounting for the time it would take to find the ranch. Serena was supposed to get to the ranch by two. I hoped that whatever they were doing took longer than three hours. Was I leading us on a wild goose chase?

Even though Laura had the gas pedal pressed to the floor, I felt like we were driving through pea soup. There was little traffic at this hour, and I was grateful for that. I checked my watch, studied the dark, thickening forest that bordered the highway, and checked my watch again.

It was a quarter to five when we pulled into Garnet. The welcome sign said the population was three hundred, but I seriously doubted that. The "town" of Garnet consisted of a bar, a post office that was also a convenience store, and about ten houses.

Laura slowed the car. "Now which way?"

I did a full 180 in the back seat, looking for signs of life in Garnet, Montana. "I was hoping some place would be open." Laura drove at a snail's pace. No early morning joggers. No lights on anywhere. "What I'd give for a donut shop or an all-night diner."

The town ended, and we continued down the two-lane. A truck driver had pulled over to a grassy spot with a picnic table on the outskirts of town. A man who I assumed was the driver lay on top of the picnic table, a jean jacket over his face.

"What would a truck driver be hauling to Garnet?" Wesley asked.

"Or hauling *out* of Garnet," I said as I swung open the door while Laura was still coming to a stop. I could hear the truck driver's snores as I circled around the trailer of the truck. I peered through the holes in the metal. It looked like the man was hauling a very large load of air.

Wesley and Laura stood by our car. I walked over to the sleeping man, debating what to do. The coat floated up and down with his breathing. His leathery, work-worn hands were interlaced over his belly. "Excuse me." The snoring stopped and the man pulled down a corner of his coat. "You wouldn't happen to know where the Lazy KN Bar Ranch is, would you?"

The man sat up, rubbed his face with both hands, and yawned. "As a matter of fact I do. I was supposed to pick up a load there early this morning." The truck driver's hair was black with streaks of gray. His bloodshot eyes and deep wrinkles suggested a man accustomed to long hours and lots of coffee.

"So where's the load?" I glanced over my shoulder at the semi.

"When I got there, they said there had been a delay. They said they'd pay me for my time and that I should come back around midday."

"What did they want you to haul?"

The truck driver swung around and planted his cowboy boots on the seat of the picnic table. He looked at me out of the corner of his eye. "You sure do ask a lot of questions."

I attempted casualness by sitting on the picnic table beside him. "My name's Ruby." I held out my hand. "What's yours?"

"Earl. Earl Malcovich."

"It's just that I have some friends up there, Earl, and I was kind of curious what they were up to." That had to be the worst lie I ever heard, but Earl bought it. It occurred to me at that moment that there were no great intellectuals in history with the first name of Earl.

"My specialty is hauling livestock. That's what my ad in the Yellow Pages says. So I reckon that's what I'm hauling."

"Which way is that ranch?"

The truck driver pointed west. "'Bout five miles down that dirt road."

"Thanks."

I trotted back to the car, and the truck driver yelled back at me, "I don't know what livestock I'll be hauling. That ranch hasn't been operational for years."

The three of us piled back into the car, leaving Earl to his nap. I clued Laura in on the directions. After about fifteen minutes on the dirt road, I could see the outbuildings and the ranch sign in the distance.

"Wait a minute, we can't just drive up there." Wesley held the phone, clenching and unclenching his hand around it. He must be as nervous as I was.

Laura slowed the car to a crawl. "Well, what *should* we do?"

"I don't know." Wesley swung the phone as he threw his arms up, and hit me square in the nose.

"Owww." I cupped my hand over my nose.

"Wesley, be careful." Laura pushed him on the shoulder.

Suddenly, I felt like we were in an episode of *Three Stooges Solve a Mystery.* My nose tingled with the pinpricks of a thousand little needles. I pulled my hand away and looked at it. No blood.

Wesley's forehead wrinkled with concern. "Are you OK?" He reached over the seat and touched my cheek.

"Well, there goes my modeling career." I found myself pulling away from his touch, not wanting to feel the intensity of emotion that it caused. I was OK as long as I kept emotional and physical distance between us.

Wesley reacted with a smile, not picking up on my coolness.

"Let's park the car over there behind that bunch of trees and hike in the rest of the way."

We parked the car. I pulled out the .38 and stuffed it in the waistband of my jeans.

Wesley's suggestion seemed like a good one until we were actually walking toward the house and outbuildings. We made our way through a wide stretch of field that didn't provide many places to hide. If anyone was watching from the upper story of the house, we were an easy target. As we neared the gate, we lay down in the tall grass, pulling ourselves along with bellies dragging like three soldiers ready to make a surprise attack.

I peered around the corner of the wooden fence that framed the property. There was a two-story house with a porch, a barn with an attached corral, and a smaller building that was either a chicken house or a cellar. Haying equipment, a tractor, baler, and a run-down truck were parked on the far side of the barn.

Scanning the doorways of the barn and the windows of the house, I saw no signs of life. A light shone in a window of the lower floor, but I couldn't detect any movement.

Wesley darted the forty yards to the barn. He leaned against the structure and peered around the corner before signaling for us to follow. Laura and I ran toward him. My cowboy boots pounded on the soft dirt, sending vibrations up my calves. Adrenaline made the blood course rapidly through my body. My leg muscles tightened, and my heartbeat increased twofold.

Before we reached the barn, I heard the distant crunch of tires on a dirt road. I turned to see a white vehicle, Serena's white SUV, stirring up a cloud of dirt and pulling a horse trailer.

I felt Wesley's hand grab the back of my collar and pull me into the barn. Laura was already inside, crouching on the floor. "Do you think she saw us?" she asked in a frantic whisper. Fear made Laura's voice sound like it was on fast forward.

Wesley glanced in the direction that the car was coming from. "I don't know." Obviously, he couldn't see anything through the walls. So why was he looking that way? Unless, of course, he was Superman and had failed to mention it to me. Mild-mannered roofer by day, dashing superhero by night. Mentally, I slapped myself back to reality. If fear made Laura talk fast, it made my imagination shift into overdrive. This was no time for escapist fantasy. Keep your faculties planted in reality, girl, because that's where they are needed right now.

We sat and listened, eyes darting from ceiling to floor, as the roar of the vehicle grew closer. My eyes adjusted to the dim light of the barn. A dirt bike rested against the opposite wall. The barn smelled of musty hay. Light sneaked in through cracks in the walls of the rundown building.

We heard the crunch of gravel in the driveway. The car engine stopped, and a door slammed. I held my breath. With my hands wrapped around my knees, I remained still, tuning my ears in the direction of the driveway. Had she seen us?

Footsteps echoed solidly on wood, and a male voice yelled, "What is that for?"

A female voice responded. "Horses. We can get the buffalo out with horses. Like they do with cattle."

More pounding footsteps. "Serena, this is nuts. Buffalo don't herd like cattle. We can't move this many buffalo out at once. It was OK when we were moving them one at a time. Using the helicopter and the harness to get them to a road was brilliant."

"Until the harness broke." Bitterness oozed in Serena's words.

"Accidents happen. And this is a bigger accident waiting to happen. I say we do what we *were* doing. One buffalo at a time in your trailer." The floorboards of the porch creaked as he stomped back and forth. "I don't think we should get that trucker involved. He might talk."

"We just tell the driver they are part of my privately owned herd." Serena's voice quivered. "John, the bison will die if we don't get them out. I can take better care of them on Daddy's ranch." I heard the shuffle of footsteps. "Please, help me, John, please."

His voice softened. "This is crazy, girl. This is plum crazy." I could only imagine what expression of helplessness Serena had worked up for John's benefit.

"Please, John."

"Oh, all right. But promise me we'll get some medical help for that friend of yours."

"Sure, no problem." A car door squeaked open, and the engine revved to life.

I peeked through a crack in the barn just in time to see the dust cloud that the white SUV left behind.

"Did you hear her?" Wesley darted across the barn and flipped the kickstand of the dirt bike back with his foot. "That guy said 'that friend of yours.' He had to be talking about Brian."

"I'm sure Serena has more than one friend," I reasoned.

Apparently no one had heard me, because Laura piped up, "That would mean that Brian's injured. We have to get up there."

Wesley held up a shiny silver object. "Ah, they always leave the key in the farm bike." He inserted the key and jumped down on the kickstarter. The bike roared to life on the second kick. Wesley signaled for me to get on the bike.

"Why me?" I screamed above the bike engine noise.

Laura pointed across the field. "I'll go back and get the car and search the house for Brian," she shouted above the roar of the bike engine.

Wesley jerked the bike forward until it was beside me. The engine hummed and rattled in my ear. I thought the barn would explode with the energy of the bike. He answered my question by leaning close to my ear and shouting, "Because you have the gun, and you know how to use it. Get on!"

I'm an argumentative gal. I'll fight with the best of them. But now didn't seem like a good time to quarrel about who went where. I hopped on the back of Wesley's sputtering machine and wrapped my arms around his waist. Wesley cranked his handgrip, and the engine yowled like two cats fighting.

The bike surged through the large open doors of the barn. Wesley turned so sharply that the back tire slid out and both of us tapped the ground with our feet. Out of the corner of my eye, I caught a glimpse of Laura running; she was already halfway across the field.

The only thing racing faster than the bike engine were my thoughts. If Brian was the injured "friend," we could not get up this road fast enough—unless they had him tied up in the house. The thought of actually having to use the gun I'd brought terrified me. A thousand bloody scenarios stampeded through my brain.

Please, dear God, don't let me have to use this gun.

The bike raced up the dirt road toward a grove of evergreens. I saw no sign of the white SUV or the horse trailer. This was the only road they could have gone down. Or had I missed something, not noticed a turnoff back at the ranch?

The engine faltered, and my hold on Wesley's waist tightened. I glanced at the darkening sky. Rain for sure. I knew it rained a lot in Montana this time of year, but it always seemed like I was outside when it started. The wind swirled around us, and I tucked my head against the back of Wesley's neck.

The back of his hair brushed my forehead, and his body warmed mine. *Why me?* I asked again. *Why not take Laura and have me run back for the car?* Wesley and I were both playing the same game—looking for excuses to be together, then putting up emotional barriers because we both saw the oncoming train in the distance. Neither one of us was good at having healthy relationships.

I enjoyed the sensation of his hard stomach pressing against my hands and arms. I rested my cheek against the back of his shoulder, not allowing myself to dream of or hope for more.

This is all you get, girlfriend.

As the bike entered the grove of trees, I peered over his shoulder. No sign of Serena's SUV. I was safe . . . for now.

Chapter Sixteen

I spotted the open doors of the trailer just as we came out on the other side of the trees and the road turned into a two-lane trail. The rocks grew bigger and the plant life more abundant. I showed Wesley what I saw by resting my arm on his shoulder so he could follow the direction of my pointed finger. To our right, a gradual slope led to a river bottom where the car and trailer were parked. On the other side of the level land, where the SUV was parked, a river rushed by, and beyond that was a thick, sloping forest.

Wesley turned and headed down the grassy hill toward the white SUV. The trail in front of us disappeared. The bike followed one of the lines of smashed-down grass where Serena must have driven.

Clumps of grass and stones used up whatever suspension was left on the bike tire. I felt every rock as we bumped down the hill. The view was jarring, like a camcorder held by a running child, and I didn't see any sign of Serena or her friend John. My vital organs floated up to my throat and back down to my toes repeatedly.

"Maybe I should get off and walk," I shouted in Wesley's ear. My voice vibrated from the hum and chugging of the bike engine. I sounded like Katherine Hepburn after a strong cup of coffee. Wesley answered my request by not stopping the bike. Oh well, I could probably tack my bones back in place with Mom's hot-glue gun.

We came to a stop by the open doors of the horse trailer, and Wesley turned off the ignition. I swung my leg off the bike. My bones still vibrated from the ride. My teeth ached from having clanged together so many times. I was going to feel this ride for many days in my legs and bottom.

I circled around the trailer and strode to the other side of the car, peering inside the windows. The photos of the nonexistent child were no longer sitting on the back seat. I wondered if Brian had figured out yet that the child he had given up so much for had never been born.

A flock of birds passed overhead, a hundred wings fluttering in the still air. An ominous gray cloud hung above us. The river gurgled softly as I surveyed the trees on the other side of the water. There was no obvious trail they could have taken.

Wesley kneeled, examining the ground. "We can't be that far behind them. There are a few hoof prints here." Still kneeling, Wesley touched the ground and studied the forest across the river to the north. The river bottom stretched to the east and west. It was flat enough that they could have continued in the truck and trailer once they'd navigated the bumpy hill we'd just come down. If they had abandoned the vehicle, they must have crossed the river.

A distant whinny and the brief chatter of voices caught my ear.

Wesley rose to his feet and ran toward the riverbank. I followed. The direction of the voices was hard to pinpoint. The forest rested in a valley that created an echo chamber. "They had to have forded the river and taken a trail on the other side," he said.

And me without my waders and rain gear. The sky thundered. Soaking wet was not my favorite fashion look. But this wasn't about me and my comfort. It was about Brian. If Jesus could be in agony for me on the cross, guess I could get a little wet for one of his children.

Wesley pushed the bike to the river's edge. What marvelous transportation idea did he have in mind?

"We're riding across," he proposed.

I responded with a gaping mouth and furrowed brow.

"It doesn't look that deep, Ruby. Where's your spunk?"

"I lost it on the way down that hill."

"We'll stay drier this way," he said.

My whining was drowned out by the roar of the motorcycle. I hopped on the back and shouted in his ear. "You sure know how to show a girl a good time."

I glanced back up the hill. Laura couldn't be that far behind us.

Wesley revved the accelerator so hard that my head jerked back. The water parted where the tire hit. At its deepest, the river covered most of our front tire. The bike wobbled but remained upright. Water splattered on my jeans and sprayed my arms. But I was a lot drier than I would have been if I'd waded across.

We parked the bike and searched the area along the river until we found hoof prints in soft dirt. Wesley moved like a man on fire. He pushed the bike so it could be seen from across the river. "We'll leave this here so Laura will know which way we went." He slapped the kickstand with his foot.

I gazed up the narrow, rocky trail. Wesley read my thoughts. "The bike can't make it up there. We'll go faster on foot. They can't be moving those horses very fast."

"That's probably for the best anyway—Serena won't hear us coming," I piped up. I didn't think my body could stand another bike ride.

Wesley bolted up the trail before I could finish my sentence. The trail was more of a trickle, a thread-width space between trees.

The trees were of the gnarled juniper variety, growing close together, and none of them was more than five-feet high.

Every so often, Wesley stopped to point out a faint hoof print on the hard-packed dirt. Twisting his feet sideways like a duck, he gained the traction he needed to push himself up the hill. I followed suit, a poorer, slower imitation. Occasionally, the clink of metal, a horse snort, or a short verbal exchange reached our ears. We were on the right trail. The sky thundered so intensely, my chest cavity vibrated.

A raindrop hit my forehead and another hit my nose as the trees thinned and we came out on a ridge that looked down into a clearing. Wesley and I dove to the ground at the same time.

Below us were about twenty buffalo, a helicopter, and a tent. Two men with large-caliber rifles knelt beside the helicopter. The tall grass tickled my neck, and I brushed hair out of my face. My heart pounded out a rhythm a rock-and-roll drummer would have been proud of.

Serena and her friend John had followed the ridge around into the clearing. Neither of them was riding the horses. Instead, they pulled their unwilling accomplices down the hill by the reins. The horses nodded their heads and danced sideways at the sight of the buffalo.

Laughter rose up from the two men sitting by the helicopter. "Oh, come on, Serena," said one of the men. He sauntered across the camp toward the horses. He had slick hair pulled back into a ponytail. When he walked, he led with his chest. Ponytail pointed at the horses. "You can't be serious."

Serena threw the reins in Ponytail's face. "You don't care. You just don't care what happens to them." She stomped off toward the tent.

Ponytail stalked after her, grabbed her arm, and yanked her around. "I do care what happens to these bison. I don't want to see them shot." He poked his finger in her chest. "We can't move this many at once! Will you listen to me? One or two at a time was OK. You've gotten out of control."

Serena responded by placing her hands on Ponytail's shoulders and pushing him back. "I'm tired of hearing about what we can't do."

Ponytail shouted at Serena as she jerked the tent flap open. "We need to get out of here, or we're all going to end up in jail."

Moments after Serena disappeared inside the tent, a man with a bandaged arm stepped out. He glanced at the two men with guns. Between his thick beard and baseball cap, his features were almost indiscernible. His tattered clothes hung on him like they belonged to a bigger man, a mountain man, a hermit.

"Brian," Wesley whispered.

I looked at the man again as he walked toward the horses. He held his injured hand out for the horse to sniff. Could it be? Under the beard and baseball cap, only the eyes were familiar. And they were hard to see at this distance. They had only stared at me from photographs. I'd have to take Wesley's word for it.

Brian removed his baseball cap and nuzzled against the horse's neck. John tethered the other horse on a cord that held the tent down. Brian murmured sweet nothings to the untied horse. The bandage, which was actually a T-shirt, was soaked in blood. His cheeks were sunken in. Only the blond hair, the same blond hair I'd seen in the photos, told me this was the man I'd been tracking for weeks.

The blood on the shirt Serena gave Meagan must have been

Brian's. Serena hadn't been treating her former boyfriend very well. I could only guess how she had inflicted the damage—with another ski pole or a knife. Maybe Brian had tried to escape.

I'm no psychologist, but I suspect she hated him because the sight of him reminded her of what she had done to their child. No one walks away from an abortion unscathed.

"Brian can ride." Serena stood at the door of the tent with her arms crossed over her chest. "He knows these hills better than anyone. John knows how to ride; he can take the other horse." She pointed to the flat land behind her. "We can take them back that way and double back to the ranch."

John, the man who had brought the horses in with Serena, shook his head when Serena made the suggestion. Bits of brown hair peeked out from underneath his cowboy hat. He was short, maybe a few inches over five feet, medium build.

Ponytail threw back his head and laughed. "Give it up, Serena. Let's get out of here."

Poor Serena; her mad world was falling in around her. She was losing support by the minute.

Ponytail approached Serena. "Let's just take the 'copter and go. Take a reality check. We are not going to get all these buffalo out of here." He leaned close to Serena. "We need to save our own skins. And you need to do something with Brian. Next time he tries to leave, you might not catch him."

Serena responded by slapping Ponytail in the face.

The helicopter was on the far side of the camp. The other armed man, young-looking and sandy haired, paced around the helicopter. He held his rifle across his body, the butt of it in his palm and the barrel across his shoulder. I squinted to see better. He glanced

241

around and continued to pace, nervousness punctuating each step. His shoulders slumped forward with the awkwardness that a quickly growing adolescent body causes.

Ponytail had left his gun resting against the helicopter. Ponytail and Serena continued to exchange words, and the occasional shove. John went inside the tent. Brian stood apart from the rest of the camp, stroking the horse's neck.

The teenage kid was the only one close to a weapon.

If we were going to do anything, now was the time.

Chapter Seventeen

Wesley signaled for me to stay put as he pulled himself through the grass. When he was about fifteen feet from Brian and the horse, he lifted his head above the grass. My breath caught in my throat. I glanced out at Serena and Ponytail, who were too involved in their fight to notice Brian.

Wesley whispered "Brian," and then held his finger over his lips.

Recognition spread across Brian's face, but he continued to murmur to the horse.

Ponytail raised his voice. "You got to do something with him, Serena. He's seen everything we've done."

Wesley scrambled back up the hill, and we both crawled to the safety of the tree line. I pressed my body flat against the earth, willing myself to be invisible. My heart pounded in my chest. The cool metal of the revolver pressed against my lower back.

Serena yelled at John, "Tie him up for now. We'll leave him in the tent until it's time to herd the buffalo out."

"What's to stop him from taking off on the horse, Serena?" Ponytail shouted.

"Oh shut up, Eric. Start packing up gear."

"We're going to have to kill him—or we end up in prison. We'll be charged with kidnapping. What were you thinking?"

"I thought . . ." Serena's shoulders slumped forward. She spoke so softly, I almost couldn't hear her. "I thought he would still love me. I thought he would come around to my point of view."

Ponytail shook his head. I could make out the sneer on his face.

Brian didn't resist as John grabbed him by the upper arm. He stumbled slightly and glanced back in our direction as he was yanked inside the tent.

Leaning close to Wesley's ear, I whispered, "We've lost our chance. Now what?"

Wesley made an arc in the dirt with his finger and then pointed to the tent. I understood. If we circled around the back, away from where the helicopter and buffalo were, maybe, just maybe, they wouldn't see us. In my peripheral vision, I caught sight of the teenager with the rifle, continuing to pace. And maybe we'd be riddled with bullets.

I stared back at the trailhead on the ridgeline. Where was Laura?

Wesley waved me forward. Crouching low to the ground, we used the trees for cover until the forest descended into the meadow. About twenty feet of grass, with no camouflage, lay between us and the back side of the tent. I could just see the tail end of the helicopter and hear the loud voices of Serena and Ponytail.

"Let's just leave him here to starve. Forget the buffalo. We need to get out of the country."

"I'm with Eric," said a younger male voice.

"Certainly your father can arrange for us to get out of the country."

"But what about the buffalo?" Serena's voice faltered. Her resolve about moving the buffalo must be weakening.

We darted across the grass to the back of the tent. Wesley pulled a pocket knife out of his jeans pocket. "Always carry one of these with you," he whispered.

Great time for a survival lesson.

He slit open the nylon fabric of the tent, and we stepped inside.

Brian, his hands secured behind him, looked up from where he sat cross-legged beside some packages of food.

"I was wondering when you were going to get here." His voice was faint, but he managed a weak smile.

Wesley wrapped his arms around his friend. "I didn't think—I was afraid I'd never see you again."

I pulled the pocketknife out of Wesley's hand. "I'll untie him so he can give you a hug back."

Brian furrowed his forehead and turned his head to stare at me. "Who is she?"

I sawed through the cords that bound Brian. "Hey, you're being rescued. I wouldn't complain about the company."

With his hands free, Brian hugged his friend. "Laura? Where is Laura? I tried to do the right thing. I didn't want my kid to grow up without a father like I did, but Serena lied to me." He swallowed hard.

"It's all right, Brian." I touched his shoulder lightly. "God knows you tried to do the right thing."

Eric Ponytail's voice grew closer. "The rest of the gear is in the tent."

My heart crawled up into my throat, and every muscle in my body turned to stone as the tent flap swung open.

"Well, what have we here." He offered us a grin with lots of teeth in it.

I glanced at Ponytail's hands, which held no rifle. Tossing the knife to Wesley, I pulled the gun out of my waistband. "I don't know. What *do* we have here?" The tough, growling voice that came out of my mouth did not match my vibrating knees and trembling hands. I tightened my grip on the pistol to hide the tremble.

Eric Ponytail backed out of the tent with his hands up. "I know you. You're the chick I took aim at in the forest. I'd recognize that red hair anywhere. Took you awhile to find us."

"Yeah, but I found you. Not bad for a chick, huh?" I resisted the urge to pull the trigger on him as I stepped out of the tent. How dare he refer to me as barnyard fowl. Keeping my eyes on Eric, I yelled at Wesley, "Get the other rifle." I nodded toward the helicopter, where the rifle was propped. I couldn't see the teenager or his gun anywhere.

By now, Serena and John saw what was going on. They stepped away from the sleeping bags they'd been packing up and held up their hands.

Wesley was within four feet of the other rifle when I felt a gun barrel press into my back and a very frightened voice said, "Drop it. And tell your friend to leave the gun alone or I'll shoot you."

"Wesley." My voice quivered. Wesley looked up, assessed the situation, and stepped away from the gun. I let my gun fall to the ground. Serena scrambled to pick it up.

"I guess three people are going to die here today instead of one." She pointed the gun at me. I saw her blue eyes from over the top of the gun barrel. Something told me she meant it. Whatever hesitation she had about killing Brian, she didn't have about me.

I couldn't feel my heartbeat. My hands and feet went numb. Serena pulled back the hammer on the revolver and the cylinder moved a quarter turn. All I saw was her blue eyes and the round end of the gun barrel.

So be it, Jesus. Guess I'll be in your arms. Her finger wrapped around the trigger.

"Brian! Brian!"

The voice snapped me back to the here and now. Where had it come from? My head shot up to the ridgeline where Laura stood.

"Brian!"

"Laura, no!"

With open arms, Laura ran down the hill toward Brian.

The teenager sighted his rifle on Laura. Ponytail picked up the other rifle and shoved Wesley. Serena did not take her eyes or the gun off of me.

Then I watched the most amazing thing. With only a sidelong glance at the men with guns and Serena, Brian swung up onto the back of the horse and kicked the animal's flanks. The horse galloped across the camp toward Laura, his hooves echoing on the hard ground. Brian leaned forward and tucked his head against the horse's mane. Any doubt I had about the sincerity of his love for Laura dissipated.

The hollow crack of a gunshot resounded in my ears. My eyes traveled to the kid, who had just fired the rifle at the galloping horse.

The kid seemed to lose his nerve. His rifle fell to his side.

Momentarily distracted by the stray shot, Serena lowered her gaze and loosened her grip on the gun. I focused all my energy on Serena and her potential for ending my life. Lowering my head so it functioned as a missile, I shot across the seven feet of ground that separated us and barreled into her so that my head hit her square in the stomach. The momentum of my push caused us both to fall to the ground.

The gun flew a few feet from her hand. I would have landed on top of her, but she rolled away at the last second.

The chop chop of helicopter blades broke through the

numbness of my ears. Like a knife slitting a bag full of water, all my senses kicked back into gear; I took in the whole picture around me. I saw Ponytail and the teenager race toward the helicopter, with Wesley after them. John was already in the pilot's seat. The buffalo, agitated by the noise of the helicopter, snorted and stomped the ground. I was not up for any sort of *Dances with Wolves* reenactment, thank you very much.

Brian reached Laura and pulled her up on the horse. Just below the ridgeline, they raced across an open field.

Ponytail smacked Wesley across the bridge of his nose with the butt of the gun. Wesley fell to the grass, hand on his nose. He tried to pull himself to his feet. Ponytail raised the gun and hit him again across the face. Wesley coiled into a ball.

I crawled across the dirt toward Serena as she pulled herself to her knees. My hand wrapped around her ankle. She flipped over on her bottom and shoved the boot of her free leg into my face. There was no need to memorize the waffle pattern of her hiking boot. I'm sure the police would get a clear ID by making a plaster cast of my face.

I drew my hands protectively to my face, losing my grip on her leg. My cheek stung. My whole face tingled. I looked through watery eyes as she bolted to her feet.

She lifted her foot to smack me in the chin. I made eye contact with her just as Ponytail wrapped his arms around her waist and dragged her toward the helicopter.

The whir of the blades made it impossible to hear anything. Serena shouted and pointed toward me, and then glanced at the restless buffalo. The helicopter was about three feet off the ground. Ponytail tossed Serena inside like she was a bag of potatoes and then pulled himself in.

Wesley raced toward me as the helicopter lifted off, and an incredible wind engulfed us. He grabbed my arm above the elbow and I saw him mouth, "Are you all right?" Blood dripped from his nose and his cheek was red. Both of us had had our faces altered—plastic surgery, Montana style.

Except for the fact that my brains were lying somewhere in the grass, I don't think anything was broken. I nodded to him.

Wesley bolted to the other horse, still tethered at the tent. The animal raised its head up and down, scraping and pounding the earth with a front hoof.

The wind from the helicopter died as it gained altitude. Laura and Brian moved across the open field, the helicopter in pursuit.

I heard the distant zing of a rifle shot as the dirt around Brian's horse exploded. So that was the new plan. Kill us all because of what we had seen. Well, I wasn't going to wait around to die. And I wasn't going let my friends die either.

I searched the grass for the gun. I found it just as Wesley rode up. Leaning over the side of the horse, he offered me an arm for leverage. I tucked the gun in my waistband and swung up on the horse behind the saddle.

"We've got to stop meeting like this," I yelled in his ear.

He nodded and patted my hand where it was wrapped around his waist. I pressed my head against his back and tried to move with the rhythm of the horse.

More shots zinged through the air, causing tiny explosions in the dirt. I peered around Wesley's head to see what was happening. Brian and Laura raced toward the cover of the trees, their horse's hooves kicking up dirt. Both riders leaned forward, wrapped tightly around the animal. The trees surrounded a large lake.

It was only a matter of time before we became a target too. Even if Brian and Laura made it to the trees, the new-growth forest was too thin, the trees too far apart, to provide much cover.

I assessed the situation. We were outgunned, outnumbered, and they had better technology. Helicopter stomps horses easily. I pressed against Wesley, smelling his sweat and sensing his fear—because it was my fear too.

Hey God, it's your turn. Miracle time, please.

The helicopter turned, angled slightly, arcing around as Brian's horse galloped toward the trees alongside the lake. The helicopter hovered over the lake. Through the open door of the helicopter, Ponytail lined up a shot on the horse and riders.

I had an idea.

Thank you, God. A helicopter, as big a machine as it is, has an Achilles heel. I hoped that stopping the blades from spinning would cause it to fall out of the sky and into the lake.

"Faster, Wesley."

We were close enough to see Ponytail looking through his gun sight. I heard the thunderclap of another shot. A circle of water on the lake's smooth surface splashed up. Brian's horse bucked.

We neared the edge of the lake where the helicopter hovered. I slid off the horse and raced toward the water's edge. Sweat dripped down my face and my hand trembled as I pulled the gun out of my waistband.

You and me, God. You and me.

Gripping the gun with both hands, I inhaled deeply, tilted the barrel, and lined up the sight. The double blades of the helicopter were a blur. My whole body shook, my knees wobbled. I took in another breath and held it. Removing one hand from the gun, I wiped my eyes clean of sweat. My heart beat in my ears, and I could feel the blood pulse through my neck.

Again I peered through the gun sight. Beyond the tiny red dot that told me where to shoot, I could see the helicopter blades. Persistence of vision caused the blades to look like a huge circle. I found the area that was darker than the blurred area around it and waited for it to come around again. My arm slackened. I couldn't hit those. The risk was too great. They were moving too fast. I only had six shots.

Locking my elbows, I aimed at the stabilizer fin on the tail of the 'copter. The fin provided an immobile, bigger target. I pulled back the hammer and shot twice. Ping. Ping. I hit something metal.

The helicopter faltered in the air but remained aloft.

Like some prehistoric beast, it swung around to attack its attacker. Ponytail kneeled in the open door, preparing for another game of laser tag—this one fatal. I was really looking forward to having that red dot on my chest again . . . not.

I had four bullets left and a man about to drop me like a deer in hunting season. *Jesus, your will be done. I'm not afraid to die if it means seeing you face to face.* I raised the gun in steady hands and shot four times. This time I aimed at the spinning tail rotor, thinking that might affect the balance of the machine.

The monster wobbled and spun. The blades slowed. The engine sputtered. Like a drunk about to fall down, the machine lost equilibrium, tilting to one side. A cloud of smoke surrounded it as it spiraled toward the water and hit with a splash. Upon impact, the fiberglass blades shattered into a thousand pieces.

Mist from the splash cleared, as what was left of the helicopter sank slowly.

I prayed for the lives of the people inside as it disappeared beneath the dark water.

I looked around for Wesley and the others. Apparently they'd gone for a corn beef on rye while I was doing all the hard work. The riderless horse stood behind me. I looked to the far shore, where Brian and Laura were. Wesley kicked off his shoes, took off his glasses, dove into the water, and swam toward where the helicopter had gone down.

The teenager's head was the first to bob to the surface. Wesley dove and came back up, treading water as gear and debris floated up. Brian jumped in as well. How long can someone survive underwater? My intent hadn't been to kill anybody.

I heard another helicopter whirring in the distance, and my first thought was, "I'm out of bullets." Then I saw the Forest Service insignia. The helicopter landed near the lake, and Rachel jumped out.

I watched as Wesley helped John up toward the shore. Ponytail bobbed up some distance from where the helicopter had gone in. Serena was the only one left.

I didn't want anybody to die here today, no matter what they had done.

Rachel ran up to me, out of breath. Two other rangers with holstered pistols jumped out of the Forest Service helicopter. "Ruby, are you all right? I pinpointed within a twenty-mile radius where Serena's base of operations was as it related to the cabin. We saw the buffalo herd from the air."

The two armed rangers moved toward the shore where Ponytail, John, and the teenager were dragging themselves out. Brian and Wesley continued to dive for Serena.

"Serena's still down there," I yelled as I ran closer to the water's edge. My swimming skills would be of very little help, but I could pray.

Busted helicopter parts and camping gear cluttered the lake. I saw what looked like a head bob to the surface but then disappear. My eyes were playing tricks on me.

Rachel patted my back. "Good work. I'm going to see if those guys need help." She ran toward the shore, where the rangers were handcuffing various assorted criminals and Laura stood watching while Wesley and Brian continued to swim around where the helicopter had gone down.

I surveyed the water for signs of Serena and felt a sudden heaviness in my chest. Was she pinned under the helicopter? More than ten minutes had gone by. The horse came up and butted his nose against my shoulder.

Then I saw it, on the far shore—opposite where everyone else was. Near the bank, a head appeared. The bank was steep with trees coming nearly to the water's edge. Using a hanging tree as a rope, arms reached up, and a body pulled itself out of the water.

I yelled to the party on the shore, "Hey!" I pointed. But the wind carried my voice away.

Serena lay flat on her stomach, almost camouflaged by the trees. I had only a few minutes before she caught her breath and took off running.

"Hey, you guys," I yelled again. Even Brian and Wesley were too far out in the water to hear me. I looked to the far shoreline where Serena had pulled herself out. I'd been chasing that woman too long to let her get away now. The horse lifted and lowered his head as if nodding in agreement with my thoughts.

"It's just you and me, Tex." Since we'd be working together, I figured he needed a name. Gripping the saddle horn and placing my foot in the stirrup, I swung up on the horse, kicked his flanks, and headed into the forest after Serena. "You and me and the Lord, Tex."

Chapter Eighteen

I kicked Tex's flanks even harder and shortened up the reins. We took off for the trees at a gallop. Hopefully, someone had seen me leave and figured out that I wasn't just exercising Tex. The animal slowed to a trot as we entered the trees.

I searched the forest for signs of Serena, a quivering branch, a footprint, anything. The woods had an ominous quiet to them. I kept expecting a fog to roll in and Frankenstein to emerge from the trees. All I heard was the clop, clop, clop of Tex's hooves on the soft dirt. He jerked his head, and the metal on his bridle tinkled. He snorted.

I patted his neck. "Shush, boy, quiet."

The forest was still—not so much as a squirrel racing up a tree. I surveyed each evergreen as I moved forward at a snail's pace. How far could she have gotten in such a short time? She had to be tired from the swim. I studied the thicker trees on the chance she might be hiding behind one.

Then I heard it, the faintest gurgle of a cry. When I slipped off Tex, the creaking of the saddle made me wince. Serena's crying continued undisturbed. She hadn't heard me.

Placing my feet carefully, so as not to step on branches or anything that would alert Serena to my presence, I plodded forward toward the crying sound.

Serena moaned in pain as I approached on tiptoe.

She sat in a small clearing on a fallen log, her back to me. Her long blond hair hung down her back in wet clumpy strands. I moved around so that I saw her from the side. She leaned forward, gripping her ankle. Her hand touched a gash that started at her ankle and ran up her calf. She wasn't gushing blood, but the cut was long and nasty-looking. She sat back up, moaning, her hands drawn up into tight fists.

I felt the gun in my waistband, where I'd shoved it after shooting the helicopter. It was empty, but Serena didn't know that. I jumped into the clearing with the gun drawn. Stepping sideways, I moved in a half circle until I could make eye contact with Serena.

"You found me," she said weakly.

"I've been looking for a long time." I nodded toward the lake. "Why don't we head back?"

She bit her lower lip, probably to quell a surge of pain. "I cared about those buffalo. I tried to do the right thing. The laws are stupid. What kind of a law allows an animal to be shot just because they are in the wrong place?"

I stared at her bent form. She pulled her shirt up at the shoulder, where it had torn, then touched a scratch on her forehead. Serena, my nemesis and my mirror. How ironic that she would fight so hard and so righteously for the buffalo, but she would destroy the baby in her own womb. What kind of a law allowed someone to destroy a child just 'cause she was in the wrong place, her mother's womb? But what did I know. The only difference between the two of us was forgiveness and a man on a cross.

"Come on, Serena, let's go."

Bracing herself by planting the palms of her hands on either side of the log, Serena pushed herself up. A trembling cry escaped her throat. She plopped back down on the log. "I don't think I can walk," she muttered. Matted strands of wet hair hung in her face. Her hands were shaking.

I stuffed the gun back in my waistband and leaned down toward her, offering my arm for support.

"Thank you," she whispered.

"The horse is just through these trees," I said. I wrapped my arm around her waist as she limped forward. She rested her weight against me by placing her hand on my back and gripping the opposite shoulder.

This was not the Serena I'd seen in the photograph. This wasn't the Serena I'd seen at a distance at the camp. This was the Serena who was a human being made by God . . . vulnerable. The love of Christ could change her just as it had changed me.

Her hand fell down to my waistband and she pulled the gun out, stepped back without limping, pointed the gun at me, and yelled, "Ha! Gotcha!"

Well, maybe the love of Christ wouldn't be reaching her today.

"Go ahead, Serena, shoot me."

My calmness caused her to take a step back. She pulled back the hammer and then squeezed the trigger. Her eyes grew wide as she stared at the gun. Again her thumb pressed on the hammer, and she clicked the trigger. The cylinder rotated.

Her eyes darted from the gun, back to me. "What the . . ."

My pulse throbbed in my neck, and I swallowed hard. Staring down the barrel of a pistol was scary, even knowing it held no bullets.

One more time, Serena leveled the gun at me and fired. She punctuated her action with a curse word. She grabbed the barrel and raised her hand to hit me with the butt of the gun. Like I was going to let her do that again. I already had her footprint on my face.

"I'm getting really tired of you." I grabbed her long hair and dragged her through the trees. She'd reduced me to hair pulling. I know, I fought like a girl.

Serena boxed the air, trying to get a shot at me. Her fingernails scratched my cheek. She fought like a girl too.

"Daddy will file assault charges," she screamed. Her face turned raspberry red. She clutched her hair at the roots to minimize the pain I inflicted. "You're hurting me," she wailed, adding a string of expletives and insults.

"Assault charges are nothing compared to what you're going to be charged with," I spat back at her. My cheek stung where she had dug in her fingernails.

Serena planted her feet. She grabbed my shirt, yanked me back, and knocked me down by kicking the backs of my knees. I fell forward onto my hands and knees, bracing my fall with open palms.

Before I could catch my breath, Serena wrapped her hand around a strand of my hair and pulled hard. "How does that feel, Carrot Top?" After a final stomp on my back with her hiking boot, Serena bolted through the trees toward the horse.

Nauseated from the blow to my back, I stumbled to my feet and waited for the scenery to stop spinning. The trees were still fuzzy and dancing as I staggered after her. Pain radiated from my lower back. I ran, my feet pounding the ground. I was tired; my leg muscles screamed with each stride. Serena was maybe ten feet in front of me. Her head bobbed up and down.

Hello, God, miracle time, please.

Well, it wasn't the parting of the Red Sea, but Serena's foot caught on something, causing her to stumble and nearly fall. The stumble gave me time to close the distance between us. I leaped through the air onto her back, clamping my hands on her shoulders and using my weight as my weapon. She fell on her face with me on top of her. Serena howled in protest, grunting as she hit the ground.

"You're not going anywhere," I screamed, seizing her shoulders and digging my fingernails into the flesh. No more sissy fighting. This was wearing me out.

She flipped over, preparing to knock me off and wiggle away. This time, I was ready for her. Struggling to stay on top of her, I jammed my knee into her stomach. I balled my hand into a fist and slammed it hard into her solar plexus. This is a move known only to actors in martial-art films and the people who watch them. Couch potatoes triumph again!

Serena gasped for air as her eyes grew round. It would be a minute before she could get a full breath.

I heard someone crashing through the trees, and looked up to see a very wet Wesley.

A surge of pain ran through my back. "Could you have gotten here five minutes earlier?"

"I tried. . . . We couldn't. . . ." He was out of breath. "It took us awhile to figure out. . . ."

I released my hold on Serena. Wesley grabbed her arm as she staggered to her feet. The rangers came into the clearing and dragged her back toward the lake.

Wesley helped me stand up. Water dripped off his honey brown hair, and his shirt stuck to his body. "I got here as fast as I could." He steadied me by holding my elbow. "I was worried about you."

I brushed the dirt off my pants. "I was worried about me too.

But God took care of me, and you missed a terrific girl fight—hair pulling, fingernail scratching, everything."

He smiled warmly at me and touched the side of my head. "None of that beautiful red hair, I hope."

I stepped back. "Just a little." His touch still made me want to melt.

We trudged back to the lake where the others were waiting. Wesley walked ahead of me, holding branches out of my way. He turned and looked at me, touching my cheek where Serena had scratched it. "I'm really proud of you." He hadn't put his glasses back on, which made his green eyes and thick lashes that much more intense.

He even looked good soaking wet. But I did not appreciate the hot and cold games he played. He said one thing and did another. Did he want to be with me or not? Could we even make a relationship work?

"We'd better get back with the others," I said trying not to reveal any of the strong attraction I felt.

We'd been through so much. Right now, the only thing I wanted more than Wesley was a hot bath and a solid relationship with the Lord. I had to figure out how to do that. The bath would be the only easy part of my needs list.

Chapter Nineteen

When I got home, Mom was waiting for me on the front porch. Even before Laura's car came to a full stop, I jumped out and raced up the sidewalk. Mom bolted down the three steps on the porch and held her arms out to me. I felt her hand on my hair as I rested my head against her shoulder and wept.

I don't recall ever telling Mom we now shared the same Savior. Somehow, she just knew.

I couldn't work up the nerve to go to church, not yet. I still felt out of place . . . awkward. I went almost every day to the garbage dump, sat on the hood of my car, and talked to my Lord.

One day, as I got into my Valiant to drive to the dump, I noticed a wrapped package on the passenger seat. Inside was a brand new Bible, no card or anything. The crisp pages had that wonderful new-paper aroma. She probably got tired of me stealing hers.

Brian and Laura were married a couple of Saturdays after we found him. Wesley stood up as Brian's best man. And I sat in the second pew with Mom and Maryanne. Deedee and Susan had new haircuts and pretty pink dresses for the occasion. Their eyes beamed with admiration as they watched their big brother get married.

Maryanne had found her own apartment and decided to go to beauty school. Her Pinto never did run again, but she had her T-bird back. She mentioned to me that she'd gone by the glass shop. Gladys had told her that Ed had left town.

The wedding reception was held outdoors by a river. I kept

feeling someone staring at me, only to look up and see the back of Wesley's head. With Brian found and Serena in jail, we were out of excuses for talking to each other.

He stood watching the river and holding a plastic cup full of pink punch. He wore a black tuxedo with a white shirt and burgundy cummerbund. I had on my repaired Cinderella prom dress. Who would have thought there would be two opportunities to wear it?

He glanced at me and then turned away. This was ridiculous. I walked up to him, dress swinging gracefully, and tapped him on the shoulder. "Is there something you want to say to me?"

He gazed down at me with those warm, beautiful eyes and stuttered. "I . . . um . . . well . . . I . . ." He glanced at the wedding party activities.

Laura and Brian danced to the strumming of an acoustic guitar. Her head rested tenderly on his shoulder. There was such a thing as perfect, pure love between a man and a woman, and they had achieved it. I wanted that too.

Wesley continued. "So I guess Brian's filing kidnapping charges against Serena."

"Yeah, I saw in the paper that she's up on charges for stealing park property, the buffalo. I had a little explaining to do to the police about shooting the helicopter. I don't think they will charge me with anything. Is that what you wanted to say to me?"

He touched my cheek lightly. His fingers brushed across my lips. "I miss you. I miss . . . talking to you."

I closed my eyes. The summer sun wasn't as warm on my face as his touch had been. "I miss you too," I whispered. I opened my eyes. I could have drowned in the ocean of intensity I saw in his face, his eyes crystal clear, focused on me like he saw the depths of my heart.

A roar from the wedding party distracted us. Laura stood on a log, preparing to throw the bouquet.

"You'd better get over there." Wesley's arm slipped around my waist.

I pulled away. "No, Wesley, what you said all those weeks ago was true. Being with you is just too tempting, sexually and otherwise." This was not easy to say. I pulled each word up from the base of my stomach and forced it out of my throat. "I . . . I have some growing to do, and I can't do that if I'm emotionally tangled up with you."

He looked at me with those eyes, his smile fading. "I do like you . . . care about you."

"Knowing our track records, do you honestly think if we got involved we'd be able to have a relationship we'd be proud to show God?" I'd had weeks to think about this, to pray about it at the garbage dump.

He shook his head. "Guess not. . . . Not yet." He squeezed my shoulder, kissed me lightly on the cheek, and walked away. I could feel him staring at me when I turned toward the river. This was not going to be easy. I touched my cheek where he had kissed it. It felt like a hole had been burned there. The river rushed past, murmuring and roaring. A soft breeze rustled the surrounding trees.

Oh well, so I turned down a potential romance with a really nice guy. I got something better.

I got the Savior of the universe as my best friend. And in the game show of life, that's a pretty good consolation prize.